# Hospital High

## Based on a True Story

# Hospital High

Based on a True Story

## Mimi Thebo

**LODESTONE BOOKS**

Winchester, UK
Washington, USA

First published by Lodestone Books, 2017
Lodestone Books is an imprint of John Hunt Publishing Ltd., Laurel House, Station Approach,
Alresford, Hants, SO24 9JH, UK
office1@jhpbooks.net
www.johnhuntpublishing.com

For distributor details and how to order please visit the 'Ordering' section on our website.

Text copyright: Mimi Thebo 2016

ISBN: 978 1 78535 187 7
978 1 78535 188 4 (ebook)
Library of Congress Control Number: 2016939768

A CIP catalogue record for this book is available from the British Library.

Design: Stuart Davies


Printed and bound by CPI Group (UK) Ltd, Croydon, CR0 4YY, UK

We operate a distinctive and ethical publishing philosophy in all
areas of our business, from our global network of authors to
production and worldwide distribution.

# Prologue

*I wake from a familiar nightmare. The tree is coming towards us. There's panic on Kim's face. Outside the car, a meadowlark swings on a barbed wire fence and the rough, grey bark of the cottonwood tree comes closer and closer. We're going to crash. We're going to crash.*

*My body is covered in a fine sheet of sweat and I have to claw the duvet away from my face to breathe. I feel better when I sit up, but I am shaking.*

*For fifteen years, we've lived in England, but I'm still American enough to pull on a sweatshirt instead of a dressing gown. In socks, I slip down the hall.*

*Before I go, I open every door. I pull up duvets, click off bedside lights, retrieve a naughty phone from under a pillow and smooth hair back out of eyes. Downstairs, the dog gets out of his basket, only to collapse again by the big chair in the back room. I follow him and shut the door.*

*The Bluetooth speaker hums when it's switched on. I'll search and play the old songs, one after another, just as I think of them, low enough not to wake anyone, but loud enough to hear.*

*It is a black night in the garden. In the light of my phone and the speaker, the windows reflect hints of the room; the polished wood shines, gold lettering on books twinkles. And I'm there, too. My face floats, as white and insubstantial as a ghost.*

*I can feel the weight of my family, sleeping above me. All around me, I can feel my life, as solid and real as the heavy furniture or the deep old shelves. I curl up in the big chair and press play.*

*It's the only time I let myself remember when I didn't want to live at all.*

# Chapter One

## Soundtrack: 'Nothing from Nothing' – Bobby Preston

Let's start with the tree.

It was a cottonwood, a wild tree, native to Kansas, not something imported, like a maple or an oak. It was older than the road, and it crowded the curve. But it wasn't dying yet. Cottonwoods die secretly, getting more dry and hollow inside...you usually only find out when they drop a limb on your head. This tree was still healthy.

We hit it at about twenty miles an hour.

Kim's face whacked the top of the big steering wheel and her breasts hit the bottom of it. She broke her nose in two places and hurt her neck and her back. Her breasts were hideously bruised and later went all bumpy, purple and green.

I seemed fine. Everyone says I seemed fine. Evidently, I talked to people and everything. I don't remember any of that.

I remember Kim had picked me up from ballet class in her mom's fancy new LTD. I remember stopping to get Icees from the 7 Up mini-mart. Icees are like Slush Puppies – tiny bits of ice suspended in sugary goo. I know it was 1974 and I know it was America, but even back then and back there, we knew *something* about nutrition. Having Icees before school was just plain naughty.

That means they were my idea.

I was buckling my shoes when Kim turned the corner. Her Icee started to slide. She was terrified of spilling Icee on her mom's fancy new velour upholstery. So she grabbed for the Icee and forgot to straighten the wheel...and, just for a moment, I looked up...

How can I explain how slowly we headed for the tree? I had time to notice everything, the rough grain of the grey bark, the look of fear on Kim's face. How the sun was beginning to warm the earth. A meadowlark swinging on a strand of barbed wire, its little throat puffed out with singing.

And then my memory goes black.

I remember one moment after the accident. I was crawling up to the road on my hands and knees. The LTD's engine was still running and the wheels were still turning and that Bobby Preston was still singing, 'Nothing from nothing leaves nothing', on the radio.

Then it all cuts abruptly to black again, like a badly-made film. Later, I found out that's what happens when you go into shock. You might still walk around and talk, but you aren't actually processing.

Evidently, we were weaving like drunks all over the road when Bobby drove by, headed to the same play rehearsal. Nobody else was driving around before seven-thirty in the morning, just high school kids like us, with before-school sports and clubs.

It was legal in Kansas for fourteen-year-olds to drive to school and to work and home again. Farm kids could drive around their own land at twelve. All this time later and half a world away, the idea of kids zooming around in tons of metal seems a bit odd. But it seemed normal to me then. So it was normal that Bobby rescued us in his very own snazzy white Monte Carlo with maroon vinyl upholstery.

I had known Bobby and his family forever. They were the local funeral directors – and he lived near the graveyard. He loaded us into his car, dropped us off at my house, and then continued on his way to the play rehearsal. He waited until after the rehearsal to tell people at school about our accident.

Bobby was calm and cool like that: He had always seemed a little cold inside to me, as if he climbed into a refrigerator every night and slept with the family clients.

I had kissed him once during a spin the-bottle game and absolutely nothing had happened except our lips pressed together briefly. He'd reacted with a kind of mild disgust. My feelings would have been hurt, if ten seconds later Jack Clary and I hadn't started investigating the deep mysteries of French kissing.

One of the things I remember about the accident was worrying about Bobby's car – he wouldn't let any of us eat or drink in it. As I helped him half-carry Kim into my house, I remember worrying about blood stains. I only relaxed because I suddenly thought that Bobby's undertaker family probably knew all about how to get rid of bloodstains.

In the next scene, I was sitting on the stairs to my mom and dad's bedroom in the old, higgledy-piggledy house we'd bought two years before. Parts of it were built in brick, parts of it were wood construction. It used to be made of turf...it was that old.

It had some funky features. The kitchen and the porch had been built before there was mains water, so there was an old well in the porch, which was now the dining room. It was still there, hidden under a square of carpet, and I used to freak out my friends on sleepovers by prying it up and telling them it had a ghost living in it.

I just said it was my mom and dad's bedroom. But that day, it was really only my mom's bedroom. A month before, Dad had dumped us. He'd done it to me and mom together. There was none of the mom and dad sitting on the sofa and explaining it lovingly to the child. There were full-blown rows and plates thrown and nasty things said and I was right in the middle of it, with words like 'unworthy' and 'ungrateful' and 'unsalvageable' being thrown at me.

There were tears and snot and holding onto his legs and begging him to stay while he wrenched himself away and ran to his car. It had been properly horrible.

He'd seen me twice since. Both times he'd wanted to see a proper young lady in tights and a smart dress and instead had seen me with my enormous frizz of nearly black curls and wearing jean shorts, flip-flops and band T-shirts. Both times, he'd carefully explained why I was sending the wrong messages. He talked to me about my mother's politics and why order and respect were so important. He said that 'freedom' was actually anarchy and that identifying with Vietnam protesters, women's libbers and black activists was dangerous and wouldn't get me anywhere in life.

Also, he said repeatedly and with a kind of weary patience, if I couldn't brush the curls and frizz out of my hair, I should keep it cut short.

On both outings, we'd ridden home in total silence.

So the day we hit the tree was *already* a bad time. The dining room carpet smelled funny, because mom didn't have time or energy to sprinkle the sprinkle stuff and vac it every other day like she used to. It smelled like old people. Kim was lying on it, with her head nearly at the kitchen and her feet on the cover for the well.

I sat on the stairs, watching two policemen try to stop Kim's nose bleeding. They'd seen the wreck, found my address in my handbag and had tracked me home, sure that the people who'd walked away had been injured. They were good cops – they'd done that even before they knew I was Major Eugene DuLac's daughter. Now that they knew, they were being even *more* careful.

I asked my mom for a bit of kitchen roll. They were using loads on Kim, but I just didn't feel up to getting some for myself.

She brushed by, rushing for something else they thought Kim needed, and said, 'Get it yourself, Coco. Kim is really hurt!'

But I had wanted some kitchen roll because I knew I was

about to cough. And I could tell, from my long experience with chronic bronchitis and regular pneumonias, that this was going to be a productive cough, a really productive cough, and I wanted something to spit in.

And then I couldn't hold it back any longer. I coughed. And parts of me came up onto my hand. A gush of blood seeped through my fingers and trickled onto the light blue carpet. I tried to stop it, but I couldn't.

Everyone then turned from Kim to me. For the first time in my life, I didn't actually want to be the centre of attention. I wanted to go back in time to just a few minutes before, when Kim had been the sick one and I'd been the well one who everyone ignored.

My mother thought very fast. She pulled the radio from the nearest patrolman's belt and said, 'Dispatch, this is Diane DuLac. Get me Eugene, quick. His daughter is dying.'

I heard my dad's voice inside two seconds. He sounded pissed off, so mom talked fast.

'We're waiting for the ambulance, but she's already having trouble breathing,' mom said. The latter part of this was news to me, and it made me feel concerned.

I could hear Dad start his siren. 'I'm on my way,' he said.

The patrol car was back at the tree, red lights blinking so that none of the rush hour traffic would hit Kim's mom's ruined new LTD. Before the two cops with us could decide if they should run back to get it, Dad had already arrived, bundled us into his car, and started racing to the hospital.

Kim came, too, I think. All I really remember is mom holding me and us tearing through Kansas City. Dad knew the way to everywhere, always the fastest way. It was one of his things. He'd get cross at mom if she took the long way anywhere, even if he hadn't been with her and had only heard about it.

Knowing Dad was taking me, I kind of relaxed. I knew I'd get to the best hospital as fast as humanly possible. I didn't have to worry about that side of things.

No one had to tell me by then that I was having trouble breathing. My larynx was too busy falling apart to do much of its work of carrying air from my mouth (I was gasping, so my nose wasn't really relevant right then) down into my lungs. By the time we got to the emergency ward, and my dad had left the car in the ambulance place and run in with me in his arms, little pockets of air had started to gather under my skin. I thought they looked like frogs or mice, hopping and crawling in lumps around my shoulders and chest.

The next thing I remember is sitting on a blue plastic chair in a hallway. There had been a gang knife war the night before and the operating rooms were dirty. They were hurrying to clean one for me. I was getting very, very weak. I got a rather familiar feeling about the problems my body was having. I didn't care anymore. I just let it go...

I had done this before. I had come this close to death when I was just a kid...

Three summers before I was dying on the plastic chair in Kansas University Medical Centre, I had invited Mari LaBeouf to come swimming at Sun and Surf Country Club.

'Country Club' was a bit of an overstatement. It was a suburban swimming club, with a bar and a grill and a nice big pool with a diving area and a kiddie pool. There was a putting green, I think, and they were putting in a driving range. Still the 'Country Club' part was about as accurate as the 'Surf' part, and we were 1200 miles from the nearest coastline.

Anyway, all my cousins were members, and half my friends, and my hair was never really dry from May until September. One of my cousins was on lifeguard duty the day Mari came to swim.

'Can you swim?' I asked her.

'Oh, yes,' she said.

Reassured on this point, I suggested we play a game. You

walked along the slope towards the deep end until you couldn't touch any more, and then you swam to the side. I was tall for my age and Mari was a shrimp. We walked side by side until she couldn't touch and then I carried her until *I* couldn't touch.

'Okay, swim!' I cried and dropped her.

She couldn't. She panicked. She held onto me and tried to climb to air as I went down.

I came up twice and screamed and waved to my cousin, who glared at me and avoided my eye.

It wasn't his fault. Nobody looks at eleven-year-old girls screaming and messing around in water.

And then I didn't come up any more. I gave Mari an almighty push to the side with the last of my strength. I didn't see why she should die, as well. I then started to drift, down, down, to the cool aqua quiet of the bottom. I was quite content. My resentment towards Mari had gone. It wasn't her fault that she'd lied about swimming. She'd just been trying to impress me. Or had been afraid I would go off and leave her if she'd confessed she couldn't swim a stroke. The sad thing was, I *would* have gone off and left her. Like a shot.

Everything seemed very clear to me, under the water. I understood all kinds of things.

And then my cousin finally figured it out and saved my life.

All of this I remembered in seconds, sitting on the royal blue plastic chair in the hospital corridor, while everyone rushed around to try and get me into an operating room. And because I'd remembered it, I knew what that feeling of remoteness meant – it meant I was about to die.

I stopped breathing.

'She's stopped breathing!' my mom immediately shouted.

There was a great deal of lifting and bundling.

I was suddenly looking up and moving so smoothly that I knew there had to be wheels involved.

They took me to a small room – I knew because the ceiling was a small rectangle. It was one of those drop ceilings on grids, with metal strips holding up squares of white Styrofoam.

After they put me down, all the hands and voices disappeared. I could hear people shouting out in the corridor and scurrying around, but I was left alone for a moment in the antiseptic little room. And in that moment, as I kept looking up at the ceiling, the corner square dissolved. And then more squares faded…

They just kind of went away, as if a projector had been switched off. Lying there, I had this immediate understanding that the entirety of the world I knew was an illusion. The world I had known wasn't really real: there was a 'realer' real behind it.

I got up and floated to the corner of the room to have a look.

There wasn't a particularly bright light or an angel with white feathery wings. But there was something, and the something felt like some*body*. And there was communication, but not in words.

As I passed the ceiling and saw there was space behind it, I was burning to explore. I was all like, 'Let's go, Dude.'

But the somebody thing let me know that was bad manners. I had to say goodbye to my body, evidently. My 'host.'

I can't tell you how depressing it was to discover that a) there was still going to be manners after death and b) I was still not going to be very good at them.

Reluctantly, I turned and looked at the lump of meat on the gurney.

I've always thought my body was rubbish. It has zero hand-eye coordination. It's ridiculously prone to illness. It was lanky, and at that adolescent stage, I looked a lot like a stick insect. And my hair. It was just…wrong. Even now, I usually try not to look at my hair.

I was just about to say, 'Right, done it, let's boogie,' to the somebody-thing when my attention was drawn back to the room.

It was an OR nurse, all scrubbed up and masked and everything. She was screaming a swear word and hitting herself on her forehead, with knuckles. She was crying, bawling with frustration. And it was all about me – because I was dying. Well, because I was dead, I corrected myself.

Silly old moo, I thought. I was *fine*. I was feeling better than I had in *ages*. Being dead was a whole lot nicer than being alive.

I went down to tell her. I put what felt to me like an arm around her and said, 'Hey, it's fine. I'm fine. Don't worry about it. It's not a problem.'

And that's when all the people ran in. They cut a hole in my neck below my larynx so that I could breathe and started my heart.

It happened so fast.

One moment, I was all blissed out and comforting the nurse.

The next thing I knew, some idiot had stuck a grappling hook in my ribs and slammed me back into the gross, bloody lump of meat on the table. The pain and the shock of it meant I wasn't conscious for long.

But that was long enough to register one thing – utter and consuming rage. I was so peed off, I can't tell you. For years, every time I thought about it, it made my heart beat faster, my hands shake and my body sweat with anger. I felt total, complete, and palpably radiant *fury*.

My life had been saved.

Lord, was I ticked off about it.

# Chapter Two

## Soundtrack: 'Carefree Highway' – Gordon Lightfoot

I woke up like you do when you're sick or were very, very tired. Like I do now if I've had too much wine the night before. In fact 'up' didn't really come into it. I woke down, like I was at the bottom of a deep well. Up was somewhere else, and I already knew getting there was going to be difficult.

I lay with my eyes open just a slit... It was too much effort to open them fully and it was too much effort to hold them closed. I hurt everywhere. Not just my neck, which felt bulky and uncomfortable, but everywhere. My feet hurt (I found out later I'd arrived at my house with just one shoe). My legs ached (they always did if I laid in one place for too long). I'd snapped a hip flexor at eleven, and if I didn't lie just right my hip really started to hurt. I wasn't lying right, and it was hurting. But I couldn't even think about moving to make it stop.

My back hurt. My mouth was so dry that my tongue felt cracked. I could see tubes in my hand and arms and they all hurt. I'd been wiped down, but I still felt sticky and dirty all over. There was yellowy orange antiseptic stuff all over my arms, and crusted blood from the punctures that were clotting on my arms and hands. I've always hated having dirty hands.

I mean, closing my mouth so that it didn't get dryer seemed impossible. Rolling over to ease my hip was something it felt like I'd have to build myself up to attempt...maybe for a few months. Getting up and finding soap and a flannel and some warm water was simply not an option.

I could only lie there and feel horrid. I couldn't do anything about it.

And then I heard something above the whirr and beeps of the various machines. I managed to move my eyes slightly and saw two nurses silhouetted against the light of the door.

They were talking. 'I know!' one sounded excited. 'Two laryngeal fractures in one day!'

'Amazing!' the other woman said. She wasn't really excited, though. Her 'amazing' was flat and dry. 'So, this is the car crash?'

That's me. I'm the car crash.

'Yeah,' the first voice seemed disappointed in me. 'The other girl is a rodeo rider, a barrel racer. She has the most beautiful hair.'

I felt myself stiffen. I tried to open an eye all the way, to see if hers was anything to write home about.

The second nurse flipped pieces of paper. 'Resuscitated?'

'No,' said the first nurse. '*Her* parents got her here in time. Her mother hasn't left her bedside and her father just sits in the hall. She keeps worrying about her horse.'

'I meant this one,' the second voice was losing her patience. I liked the second voice.

'Oh, the car crash was resuscitated. She was out quite a while. We've got *some* brain function, but…you know…we told the mom not to get her hopes up. She went off somewhere with the priest.'

To pray. She'd worried my mom so much that she'd gone off to pray for me. Mom was probably lighting candles and saying a whole rosary right now.

Was there something wrong with my brain? It didn't feel any different. Charles Dickens wrote *Great Expectations*. JFK was assassinated in Dallas, Texas. Water is two parts hydrogen and one part oxygen…or was it the other way around? I didn't think I really knew before…

'She's a bit of a mess. I'll clean her up.'

I tried to open my eyes. I tried to move. I tried, really hard, to say, 'Yes, please,' but nothing happened.

'I'd rather you didn't waste your time on that right now,' the first voice said. 'By the time you get her clean, they'll be wheeling her to the morgue.'

Immediately that huge anger flared up in my chest again. *That's what you think, bitch*, I said to myself. But the effort of pumping all that adrenaline out of my brain left me too tired to use it. I was just about to say something, or at least I thought I was, when I fell back down the well into unconsciousness.

I had one last thought as I went down.

Where was Kim?

Kim was my best friend. I always needed Kim…and now that I was feeling so…bad…I needed her even more. Kim would have found a way to mention that I hated having dirty hands. She would have said just a little something, nothing that the grownups would think was pushy or pert, but something – and that something would have made them clean me up and change my gown.

I didn't know much that day, laying in the Intensive Care Unit. But I knew that I needed Kim.

I'd met her in the playground of Oak Grove Elementary School. Kim confidently explained to me, almost immediately, why her sister in kindergarten had a different last name.

I hadn't even known she had a sister, and could barely understand what she was talking about. It had been one of the rare moments when I understood that someone *else* was experiencing an emotion. I could tell Kim was anxious, and that something about her sister's name bothered her. I was very impressed with myself for noticing all this.

So I felt sorry for Kim straightaway, though she was clearly sick of people pitying her. A sensible girl would see that this was not a good start for a relationship. I found the whole thing fascinating.

Kim was reassuringly solid. She was tall (but not as tall as I was). Her hair was bright golden brown. She wore short bangs that curled on her forehead like a strip of paint. Beneath them, her slightly piggy eyes shone with unexpected intelligence. Full lips and a determined little dimpled chin made up for an upturned, slightly piggy nose.

I thought she was beautiful. But even as a kid, I knew her mother dressed her wrong. She should have worn plain browns, reds and golds. Her hair and face would have shone out of a brown corduroy pinafore like a Rembrandt portrait shines out of its dark background. But little girls weren't supposed to be beautiful, back then. We were supposed to be pretty. And efforts were made to make her so.

Kim got pushed into every extreme fashion of our 'sixties childhood. Her chubby bottom was squeezed into neon flip skirts. Her round little legs were zipped (and the skin often caught) into white knee-high 'GoGo' boots. Turtleneck sweaters made her meaty shoulders look like they led straight to her ears. Bright pastels and primary colours clashed with her fuzzy golden halo and made it look dull. Almost every piece of clothing Kim owned was wrong for her – too short, too tight, made for a darker brunette. I always thought her mom's choices were like a printed sign saying, 'I don't think this child is good enough.'

But forget the way she looked. What I noticed and liked about Kim when I was eight years old was what everybody else liked her whole life – she was a walking sense of ethics. She was the fairest person I've ever met, before or since. And Kim befriending me, a skinny girl, was a good example.

It wasn't that Kim's mother approved of me – we had a tiny house at the time that was in the wrong neighbourhood. I often looked scruffy. My parents were odd and my manners were dire. Also, I seemed pointlessly clever and far too pert with it... But her mother liked how little there was of me.

In my hearing, and every time she saw me, she pointed out to Kim how lovely and thin I was. Even at eight, Kim was bright enough to see this coming. And she *became my friend anyway.*

It was a day or so after we'd met in the playground, in first week at Oak Grove Elementary. The class was sitting around and chatting aimlessly (this would never have happened at Sacred Heart, and I was thrilled and surprised). I remember I was sitting on a desk and talking. I had seen some of the other children sit on the desks and the teacher had not hit any of them – which came as a huge surprise. I felt deliciously naughty when the back of my thighs touched the cool Formica of the table top. I was breaking Sacred Heart rules on three fronts – speaking without specifically being asked to do so by a teacher, wearing a skirt shorter than my knees and sitting on a desk. Sister Mary Wallberg would have literally murdered me...or at least come as close as she could within the law. And here I was, doing it...it was bliss.

I was wearing a pink and white mini-dress with pompoms down the front: yellow, blue, and green. Kim came closer and used her clever eyes on me nervously, like she thought I might send her away.

She was wearing a purple skirt and a purple cardigan, both swirled with orange, green and pink paisleys. They were hideous.

I had been describing the uniform we'd had to wear at Sacred Heart to six or seven of my thrilled and horrified new classmates. Kim anxiously chewed a nail until at last she shouldered forward to interrupt, asking, 'Do you like that?' and nodded towards my pink ensemble with pompoms.

'Yes,' I said, and then, 'Do you like yours?'

She shook her head. 'No. I hate it.'

We looked into each other's eyes and recognised a mutual depth of suffering, swimming under the reflection of the strip lighting. It only took a moment. Then Kim took me to see the goldfish, all alone, just the two of us, my hand safe in her recently chewed paw.

By lunchtime, after we'd discussed our reading habits, favourite colours and the fact that we both preferred the Monkees to the Beatles, I would have died for Kim.

But though Kim made the first move towards friendship, she never really let herself go into the animal intimacy of little girl best friends. From the very beginning, I felt Kim was holding back.

At eight, I was already Heathcliff – romantic, demanding and passionate. Kim was more measured – more Cathy. She didn't trust my sudden passions for people and things and she felt, straightaway, that I was too possessive, too excitable, too easily depressed and that I laughed too hard. *All* my emotions were too extravagant for Kim.

We loved each other, but we were never really sure of each other. All our lives together, I carried a small but constant pain of wanting more than Kim could give. To be fair, it must have been tiring for Kim, too, constantly pushing me away. We spent our childhoods shielding each other from loneliness, but we did it in a kind of uneasy truce.

Still, when I was pulled back down into unconsciousness, Kim was the one I wanted.

But the next time I woke up, my mother was there.

'How's Kim?' I asked, or I thought I asked. Mom's face crumpled, and I thought it was because of my question. She didn't answer me, just stroked my hair back off my face.

You get to have a pretty good idea of what your parents are thinking and I knew that mom knew something she didn't want to tell me. I was afraid the something was that Kim had died – that she hadn't made it back from the dissolved ceiling thing, that she'd gone with the somebody in the other reality.

I could feel myself being pulled back under by tiredness so deep and total I couldn't resist it.

'Where's Kim?' I insisted.

My mother finally seemed to understand what I was asking. 'Kim?' she said. 'You want to know about Kim?'

I tried to nod, but nothing would move. My eyes were pulling closed.

'Kim is fine, honey,' my mother said. 'She's home. She'll be back at school tomorrow.'

No! I thought. How *could* she?

The panic woke me up for a moment.

Kim should be *here* at the hospital. She should be with *me*. She shouldn't have left the hospital without me. How *could* she do that to me?

Kim *at school*? Kim at school *without me*? People *liked* Kim. Without me around, she'd make new friends. *I would lose her.*

I had a flickering sense that I was being a little unfair. That it wasn't very nice of me, wanting Kim to be sick and unpopular, too.

But then I was gone again.

# Chapter Three

## Soundtrack: 'Tell Me Something Good' – Rufus with Chaka Khan

The next thing I knew, someone was jingling something. The sound of metal on metal used to set my nerves on edge. I couldn't stand keys jangling…even jingle bells made me feel tense. So when the jingling woke me up, I woke up feeling tense.

'Well, look who's awake!' a friendly voice said.

It was a nurse. Not one of the two I'd heard before.

I rolled over. It was easy. I stretched out my hip flexor and pointed my toes, easing the tightness in my calves and pressing my back into the mattress. It felt amazing. I was really grateful to be able to move.

I looked at the nurse and tried to ask for water. My dry mouth could hardly form the words. I pushed the air up my lungs and made the shapes with my mouth, but all that happened was a whistling noise from my neck.

Confusion hit me like something heavy on the back of my head. I suddenly felt tired again. It seemed a huge effort to remember what they'd been doing to my body. A hole in my neck?

My hand stole up my body. The nurse gulped a little and turned away to push back more curtains, as if she couldn't stand to watch. There was a large plastic tube coming out of my neck. When I put my hand over it, I couldn't breathe.

'It's a tracheotomy,' she said. 'Your larynx wasn't working to move air, so they made an opening further down for you to breathe through.'

'But I can't TALK!' I said, or tried to say. Again the air just whistled in my tube. It was hardly an elegant solution to the problem, was it? Just cut a hole in someone's neck? They needed

18

to come up with something better than *that*.

'I can't understand what you're trying to say,' the nurse said.

'I'm trying to say you people are complete savages,' I tried to say. I don't know why I bothered. It was the whistle again. I swore.

'I understood that word!' The nurse giggled. I smiled for a moment, but then it just fell off my face. I was too tired to smile for anyone.

How was I going to get a drink of water? I couldn't move much. I had tubes coming out all over me. They'd put more in while I'd been out of it. One was now taped to the inside of my thigh. There were machines everywhere, doing that beep, beep thing that they do, and there were little circles and wires on my chest.

'I know,' she said, and she went away for a moment. It was an effort to keep awake until she came back. It would have been so easy just to slide back down the well of unconsciousness. It was still there, pulling at me all the time. I pictured myself perched on the rim of it on my elbows, while the black depths sucked at my legs. Whenever I imagined that image, I realised I was so, so tired.

I tried to take an interest in my surroundings. I'd thought I was alone, but there were people all around me…or what used to be people. They were broken. Their skin looked grey and they were all lying completely flat.

The nurse came back with a pen and paper, and we both turned our attention to my right hand.

It was covered in white tape. One tube went in and another thing that looked like a hose connector, only plastic, also went in. It was sore, and on my right arm and hand were a series of little plasters with cotton wool underneath, which went some way to explain why it hurt so much when I tried to pick up the pen.

It was nearly impossible to grip it. My 'water' was all over the page, but the nurse could read it.

'I'll just see about that,' she said. She stroked my hair back off my face and left.

I looked at my skin...what I could see of it around the blankets, the tape and the orange goo stains. I still had a bit of a tan from the summer. I didn't look grey...at least I didn't think I looked grey.

The machines were beeping and whirring and squelching and dripping. Everybody around me was hooked up to the things. I wanted, immediately, to rip all the tubes out of my body and get off them, but I also felt like they were really precious and worried that they would go wrong. It was strange to feel both at the same time.

The nurse came back with two other people – and some water in a cup with a straw.

I tried to sit up, which was stupid. I tensed my stomach muscles and tried to heave myself upright and nothing really happened at all, except I started to pant and nearly passed out again from the effort.

'Whoa, girl,' the other nurse said. 'Let's just take one thing at a time, shall we?'

The nice nurse and the other one raised the head of the bed up between them. My eyes never strayed too far from the paper cup of water. I wanted it so badly I could have screamed, except of course that I couldn't.

'It's really extraordinary,' the doctor said, looking around at the machines. 'I mean, I knew that children were resilient, but...' He tapped one of my machines proprietarily with a pen. 'You'd think we'd have profound brain damage.'

I hated him straight away. It must have showed in my face because the nice nurse said. 'That's Doctor Kular. He saved your life.'

So *that* was the idiot, I thought. I should have known. He had a busy, interfering air about him.

My eyes locked back on the water.

'Now I want you to try and take a tiny, tiny sip,' one of the other nurses said. The doctor turned around and looked at me for the first time, not as if I was a human being, but as if I was something interesting to watch, like a television or an animal in the zoo.

I'd no idea how much air I usually used to drink. It was a bit tricky without it. But the water felt amazingly good rolling over my tongue, easing the friction of my gums against the insides of my cheeks, bathing my poor old throat. I managed. I swallowed.

The nurse started to move the cup away and I pounced on the straw and took a huge gulp, swirling it around my mouth and swallowing it bit by bit.

'Hey, tiger,' she said. 'I said a tiny sip.'

I grinned.

The nice nurse said, 'This one's gonna be trouble.'

I could tell the three people were getting ready to go. They were talking to the nice nurse. I could hear bits of what they said, instructing her on what I was allowed and not allowed to do.

I fumbled for the pen and wrote on my pad. They had started to walk away.

'Wait!' I tried to say, but only the whistle came out. With all my strength, I banged the metal binding of the pad on the bed guard. It rang through Intensive Care, and they all spun around. I waved to them and pointed to the pad, and they all walked back.

Doctor Kular took the pad himself. He said, 'Your handwriting is even worse than mine. You ought to become a doctor.'

And then he read, 'Please move these tubes to my left hand.'

I held up my right one and mimed writing, making exaggerated faces of pain and frustration.

'Okay,' he said, rolling back his sleeves, 'Nurse, get me an IV kit and a stent.'

Back then, only doctors could insert or change IV lines. The nurse made a big deal of how nice he was to do it during rounds. It didn't seem that nice, when I saw the size of the needle.

He must have felt me tense up, because he tried to chat with me. He wasn't very good at it. 'We're feeding you through this tube. You get some nourishment and lots of liquids. If you keep on drinking like that and you don't vomit, we might be able to take this out. We'll try you on a little bit of food tomorrow if you don't vomit, and see how you do with that.'

He paused and looked at me, like I should add something to the conversation. But even if I could have talked I don't know what I could have said.

So he went on. He didn't seem to mind the sound of his own voice. 'I think your stomach might be rather full of blood right now. You see, you lost quite a bit and we had to give you some more. And a lot of that went down your oesophagus and into the old tum. We expect you to poo that out sometime in the next few hours. Then if you haven't vomited up your liquids, we'll start from scratch with a nice clean bowel. Maybe with some Jello.'

Oh, yum. He sure knew how to start up someone's appetite. I hadn't felt sick at all before, but I suddenly came over a bit queasy. My whole digestive system was currently full of my own blood. I nearly hurled all over him, and I would have, but I wanted more water in my mouth pretty soon, and I knew if I *did* hurl all over his white coat, I wouldn't get any.

'Yes, well,' the nice nurse said, with steel needles in her voice. 'That's really interesting, *doctor*.'

He might have lacked bedside manner, but he knew his stuff. My right hand was free in no time. It was swollen and bruised yellow, blue and black. It was covered in the orange goo stains that were still the basis of my look. But I could move it.

Grudgingly, I picked up the pen and wrote, 'Thanks.' I showed it to Kular, who was talking *again*. One of the nurses had to nudge him to look at the paper.

'You've still got appalling handwriting,' he said. And then he walked away.

The nice nurse had to go but said she'd be right back. If I hadn't been propped up, I would have gone back to sleep. My mind kept making circles of thoughts and one of the thoughts was, *I am so tired.* I decided to try to write down the others.

*I want to be clean.*
*Where is my mom?*
*When can I sing again?*

All my family could sing. There wasn't one of my fifty-two cousins who couldn't carry a decent tune. Some refused to sing in choir at church or school, and some agreed to sing in choir at church or school, but every single one of us was *always* asked.

And we all *did* sing, all the time. You'd be at the supermarket with your aunt and she'd say to your uncle, 'I'll get the sugar, you get the tea,' and then he'd strike a pose and hold out his hand and start singing.

'When I take my sugar to tea,' he'd sing. Loudly. Proudly. Then your auntie would put her hand into his, roll up into his arm and sing with him.

They'd sketch a quick little dance move and sing the third line together.

If their kids were little enough, and knew the song, they'd join in. Aunt and Uncle might improvise a little dance routine using the trolley.

Did the other shoppers find this odd? You know, I can't even remember. I can remember loads of times when members of my family burst into song and dance, but I can't ever seem to see the faces of the other people on the street, in the laundromat, poolside, etcetera, etcetera, etcetera. I don't think I noticed what anyone thought. I don't think any of us cared, once a song took us. Until we got to about thirteen and became hideously embarrassed. But then, we were hideously embarrassed because our parents were breathing, too.

I've met lots of people through the years that hate musical theatre. 'It's so artificial,' they say. 'I just can't believe it when they all start to sing the same song and dance about.'

It always seemed like perfectly normal behaviour to me.

Our mothers sang while they did the washing up and cooked. Our houses were always full of music – radios and stereos and people playing instruments and singing to themselves. My father once stopped the car so that he and my mother could get out and jive to one of the songs they'd loved in high school. On the side of the road. In a suburban street.

Party invites would have 'Bring Your Instruments' down at the bottom and people would arrive with cases for their guitars, banjos, saxophones, accordions, violins.

I had been unable to learn an instrument. My hands were too clumsy for fingering. But I could read music, and I could sing in parts. I seemed instinctively to understand harmony and I can still hear music well, distinguishing individual instruments, and so on.

Now I've got thirty million songs on demand, but I hardly ever demand any. I know most of the music I love so well that I can just switch it on in my head. Once I've heard a song five or six times, I remember every guitar lick, every drum beat, every bass line. It goes in, and it stays in, until my internal DJ pulls up the track and plays it or I want to hear it. Then, it just plays – no speaker or headphones required. Although sometimes, I want to hear it outside myself, too.

So, music was in my blood, and my voice was my instrument. I was quite a good singer. And this was more important to me because it was the only thing, really, that I was any good at. I was a good actress as well, but it was really in singing that I had the potential to be excellent.

I wasn't always excellent. Sometimes I deliberately distorted notes…because I was angry or because I actually wanted to disappoint the people who'd asked me to sing. Sometimes I actually messed up. Sometimes I just couldn't bear being good. But usually, when I wanted to, I could make something happen with my voice.

Lying there, waiting for the nurse to come back, I remembered being at the lake with friends. We were in a boat, but we were just lazing in the middle and drifting, and we'd been singing something or other. Then my friends fell silent and I sang. I can't even remember what I sang. I loved the singer-songwriters: James Taylor, Carol King, even John Denver. I loved country rock: the Eagles, Charley Daniels, Lynyrd Skynyrd. I still loved the Monkees – I do even now – but I also loved the Beatles by then, as well. We might have been singing the Beatles together, we often did, because everyone knew all the songs.

So maybe I was singing, 'Imagine'. I could hold a note unfeasibly long, and so that would be a good one for me to show off with, that 'freeeeeeeeeeeeeee,' that I'd hold for an extra five beats before 'whoo-hoo-hoo-oo-oo. You can sayayay I'm a dreamer...'

What I really remember is the way the water and the light shone together.

I remember Kim and the rest of my friends being still and enjoying the moment. I remember the feeling of making a sound so beautiful, so right, that it had a life of its own. It left me, and became part of the wonder of the moment, part of the tone of the light and the water and the great beauty of the planet. I remember that, just for a moment, it felt like I was helping to make the world a better place. And although I knew that I wouldn't always sing that well or be that good of a person, I knew that moment would keep me going for a long, long time.

In my mind, I had a photo album of moments when I sang that well. Whenever I felt really low, I'd take out the photo album in my mind and remember those moments when life had been all right – when I'd sung with the planet and made things better.

When I had opened my throat and my heart and had actually belonged in the world.

I *really* needed to know when I could sing again.

# Chapter Four

## Soundtrack: 'Wishing You Were Here' – Chicago

The nurse wouldn't answer all my questions. My mother had gone home to get some rest and have a shower. It was the first time she'd left the hospital since the accident. My father was coming in that morning to be with me for a while, instead.

I wanted my dad. But I didn't want him like he was now.

I was twelve years old when my father stopped loving me. It happened just like that, like a light that was suddenly turned off, and never switched back on again.

Dad and I had been mates. We did stuff together. We went for pancakes on Saturday morning. We watched wrestling. We rode horses, swam and messed about in boats. We were fearless.

Even at twelve, I knew I owed my mother a great deal. I got my cleverness in reading from mom and she always told me things about the world that other kids in my school didn't know.

But if my mother *told* me about the world, my father *gave* it to me.

I've climbed mountains and jumped out of white-water rafts into the spring run-off (stupid, don't do it), and camped high in the Chiapas where the howler monkeys cough their weird cry in the night, and canoed through mangrove swamps, and snorkelled in the Red Sea; all because of my dad and the confidence he gave me. Through Dad I learned that I was an animal, and that the whole earth was mine to play in.

I adored him and he adored me. When I climbed onto his lap, he always held me as if he had been waiting for that moment a long, long time. I know it sounds kind of gross, but we liked to smell each other, nestled together that way. I tucked my nose in the folds of his neck. He rested his on my hair. Again, we were animals together, happy in our bodies.

But then, one day, when I was twelve, all that ended.

From then on, when I sat on his lap, he examined my grooming for faults and sent me off to correct whatever he had identified.

'You haven't washed your neck in a while.' 'You've got a booger in your left nostril.' 'Go clean your ears.'

He didn't sniff my hair any more. And I had to smell him on the sly, rubbing my face into his pillow. I stole cuddles in front of other people, when he couldn't push me away. But it wasn't the same.

I remember lying there that day. It was only weeks since he'd left us, but I was already used to waiting for my father. He was always late.

While I waited, I brooded on Kim's desertion. How dare she leave the hospital and go back to school, without me?

It reminded me of when we'd gone on a class trip to Chicago. Kim sat with Laurie Clarke on the long train ride, leaving me alone in the seat behind them, leaning forward, and trying to pretend I was included.

Laurie was a lovely, bubbly girl. She was as clever as we were and even funnier. When Mari LaBeouf left our school, Kim was quick to acquire Laurie as the next third person for our friendship. Laurie was easy to be with, and both our mothers found her charming. Of course, I was consumed by jealousy, but I didn't really mind having Laurie around…you just couldn't mind having Laurie around.

But on the Chicago trip, I wished either Kim or Laurie wanted me around. They didn't.

Everyone else had brought pyjamas and a change of clothes. My mother had sewn me a stretchy cat suit/jumpsuit, instead, and I had worn it for forty-eight hours. It smelled and was stained by the time we got to Chicago and I couldn't really blame

Kim and Laurie for not wanting to be seen with me.

I lay there, with the news that my best friend was well enough to go home and that my father was coming to see me, and swirled with grievances and resentments. I replayed a mental video of the whole Chicago trip and remembered every slight, every stain. I remembered the night my father left. Over and over I remembered falling to the floor and holding onto his leg, begging him not to leave us.

I was full of pain medication and other drugs. My anger and shame pumped adrenaline through my veins. My hands shook. My heart raced.

I tried to pray, but I knew what I wanted was unreasonable – I wanted Kim to be sick on the bed beside me and my father to be…somebody else.

I wasn't exactly a religious girl, but no concept of any God I'd ever heard would have listened to that kind of nonsense.

I stopped trying to pray, and became intensely ashamed of myself. A hot feeling of wretchedness slumped me back against the pillows.

I despaired. I looked around at the grey people. Were any of them horrible, like I was? Did any of them feel wretched because they were such nasty human beings?

If they did, it wasn't bothering them right now. I tried to relax into unconsciousness again, but I couldn't find the opening to the deep well. Just when I really wanted oblivion, oblivion wouldn't come. I just had to lie there and suffer.

Something about that word, 'suffer', made me feel better. I thought about it carefully.

Even as a teenager, I was addicted to the fiction the Victorians wrote for their children. I'd already read Francis Hodgson Burnett's *The Little Princess* about a hundred times and Louisa May Alcott's *Little Women* two hundred. In Victorian children's novels, suffering *always* makes the suffer grow – in a spiritual sense.

In the depths of despair, waiting for Dad to visit me in Intensive Care, I made this connection.

I mean, I knew I was moral pond slime. But I was about to become saintly. Because in my favourite books, children-who-suffer *always* became saintly.

I couldn't wait. I wouldn't have bad manners any more. I wouldn't be selfish. My soul would magically cleanse itself and become lily white. I would become (as they'd always told us in Girl Scouts was possible) a force for good in my family, my school, my city and the whole of the United States of America.

I lay there, thinking of the consequences of when I became saintly. It was going to be fantastic. I was going to be really, really good at being saintly.

America would withdraw her troops from Vietnam. The rich first world would feed the starving children of Africa. My parents would get back together.

I lay there for a moment, counting my sufferings, and presenting it all to God, like deposits in a savings account. I thought I'd already put in quite a bit of suffering and so should be able to withdraw the same amount of saintliness.

Perhaps, I thought, I was *already* saintly, but hadn't been aware of it. Thinking about it, listening to all the machines beep and whirr and click, I *felt* pretty saintly. I felt like a much better person that I had been, just five minutes before.

I even forgave Kim for not being injured enough. I graciously smiled down on Kim's return to Burner High. I hope it all goes well for her, I thought to myself. I hope she doesn't feel scared today. I hope she is happy and that people crowd around her and take care of her.

I really very nearly meant it, too.

By the time Dad arrived, I had even forgiven *him*. I forgave him for being late. I forgave him for leaving us. I forgave him for not loving me any more. He always said he had a lot on his mind, and, for the first time, I thought that being a Major in the police probably was a bit stressful. He probably *did* have a lot on his mind. I knew that mom's politics and my hair and our general way of looking at the world bothered him and worried him, but that was only because he loved me, and wanted me to be safe.

I let myself feel the love I had for him as he bustled in importantly and immediately put everything in Intensive Care out of scale. Dad never looked too big. He always just made everything else look too small...

He was wearing one of the suits mom had bought for his promotion and a beige shirt with a big collar. He'd finally realised that everybody under the age of fifty wore wide ties and that it wasn't a liberal politics thing, so his tie was one of the ones I'd picked out for Father's Day – brown with wide diagonal stripes of green and gold that matched the glints in his hazel eyes.

He'd had a big, black, curly moustache and a little, black, curly beard when he'd been undercover as a narcotics officer. Now he was clean-shaven. His gun bulged under his arm. His balding head was as brown as a penny.

He leaned over and kissed me on my cheek and I could smell Old Spice deodorant, gun oil and leather. I wanted to kiss him back, but he was too quick.

He looked at me and I turned my new saintly smile onto him at full beam.

I was ready. I had suffered and become saintly, so I could forgive my father for being a total jerk. Now was the moment that Dad, because he'd nearly lost me, would realise how much he loved me.

Dad took my hand and bowed over it as he sat in the chair. I could tell he was deeply moved.

He said, 'You know, life's so short.'

I squeezed his fingers and nodded, an 'I agree with you' nod but also a 'get on with it' nod.

I was waiting for his love to come back, to pour all over me. It was hard to keep my face still. A triumphant grin was lurking inside me. I sternly reminded myself that my newly found saintliness wasn't about my own personal triumph. It was about bringing us all closer to God, about doing the right thing, about doing *good*.

With his other hand, Dad reached into his pocket and took out a photograph.

I could only see the back, but I knew it had to be a picture of us together…maybe the one he used to keep in his wallet, of four-year-old me in a fluffy Easter dress and bonnet, sitting on his knee. He'd been wearing a sharp navy suit and a porkpie hat, like a Blues Brother. Or maybe it was that one when I was seven; the two of us by a canoe, with a string of trout, my big smile showing all my missing front teeth. Or, I thought, it could be that one of us when I was twelve, riding impossibly tall horses in a pine forest, leaning to hold onto each other's shoulders.

He looked at it fondly, and squeezed my hand again. I squeezed back again. When he turned it around, I couldn't wait to see the image.

And then I did.

It was an ugly woman. An old, ugly woman with a big nose and flat black hair. She smirked at the camera.

'This is Nina,' my dad said. 'She's waiting outside. I'd really like you to meet her.'

My utter dismay must have shown because he said, 'It would mean a lot to me.'

My father looked up at me from the visitor's chair in Intensive Care. He had this expression of total innocence that he pulled sometimes – his eyes would open wide and his shoulders would come up…he'd spread his empty hands. He did this now.

'What's the problem?' he asked me.

Of course, I *couldn't answer* and he knew that, but still he asked. He liked to ask 'what's the problem?' whenever the problem was too complex to boil down to four or five words. When mom, or me, or anyone else dumb enough would try and actually explain the problem, he'd just wave his hands after the first sentence and say, 'I don't understand.' If you kept going, he'd say, 'I'm not getting this. Are you sure you're making sense?'

When Dad did all this, he wasn't really trying to understand or communicate with the other person. He was just dominating the conversation, so that he could get his own way.

It made me absolutely furious. Mainly, I think, because it was such a cheap, unworthy trick. I'd seen my mother trying hard to communicate something terribly important, just to have Dad do that whole routine. He'd ended by shaking his head and saying, 'I know you're talking, but I can't really hear what you're trying to say,' and left her weeping with frustration.

And, because he wanted to bring Nina into Intensive Care to see me...and I had no idea why...he was pulling the whole 'what's the problem' routine with me. His fourteen-year-old daughter, who had just died in a car accident.

I even had an EKG hooked up to me, for heaven's sake, going beep, beep, beep, she's barely alive-live-live. Not to mention the IV and the catheter and the big plastic tube in my neck.

I mean, I didn't really want to meet the new woman in his life at all, especially not *now,* with a bunch of orange stains all over me and the hole in my neck and my hair doing God knows what.

But I was still saintly enough to give him a chance.

I looked at him, as if he might be able to see what I was feeling, as if he'd suddenly become an actual dad again and say, 'Sorry, sweetheart, I'm just a bit upset. How are you? Let me give you a hug.'

But Dad didn't say anything. He just looked at me impatiently, waiting for me to get with the programme.

I gave up on the whole saintliness project.

I banged my pad on the rail. Chring, chring, chring. The nurse in charge of keeping me alive hurried over. I scribbled on the pad and showed it to her.

She said, 'I'm sorry, Major DuLac, but we've got to let your daughter rest, now.'

'Oh, all right,' Dad said tetchily. He frowned at me the same way he had when I had swept the grass from the patio too lethargically or painted the barn against the grain. He stood over me for a moment, shook his head and sighed before turning and going out the door. In every line of his body, you could tell he was disappointed.

That's when I did what none of it had made me do before. I carefully put my pad down where I could reach it, with the words 'Get Him Out Of Here' still scrawled on the top page in big letters. I put my pen back through the rings, so I wouldn't lose it. I got some tissues ready from the nightstand, because I'd already learned that I couldn't sniff. I couldn't pull any air through my nose.

I wasn't any kind of saint. I didn't have any power to change anything. I was just suffering. And it sucked.

So I went ahead and cried. And then I found the opening of the well, and slept again.

Someone was crying. Once I was conscious, it still took me time to get back up the dark well and move my body around. At first I couldn't open my eyes to see who it was.

'I'm so sorry,' I heard the nice nurse say.

'But *why*?' the nasty nurse wailed, and then, as if she could tell she was being too loud, said with quiet intensity, 'She wasn't nearly as badly injured as this one.'

'I know,' the nice nurse said, 'but sometimes—'

'She was so *pretty* and so *nice*.'

And then I understood. The other laryngeal fracture had died. The barrel racer with the intact family and the nice hair.

The nasty nurse was still talking. '…it doesn't make any *sense*,' she moaned. 'This one's been resussed, and *why* they resussed her I don't know…it's a miracle she's not a vegetable…and her dad brought his lady friend right into the waiting room and her mom is one taco short of a combination platter, and…'

The nice nurse said something about me being conscious and about professionalism, and they went away.

I lay there for a moment. It didn't make sense. It didn't make any sense at all. I was still alive, and I didn't even want to be. I was still alive, and even a nurse who'd only known me for about five minutes could tell I had nothing to live for.

It didn't make any sense at all. So, I let myself sleep again.

# Chapter Five

## Soundtrack: 'Jazzman' – Carole King

They were always waking me up. They wanted blood, blood pressure readings. They wanted to get me to try to drink some more water. They wanted to give me medication. I started to get a bit ticked off with it all, especially when they woke me up in the night just to give me a sleeping pill. I was so cross about that one that I couldn't get back to sleep, even with the drug.

So the next morning, when someone started shaking me awake *again*, I clamped my eyes shut and tried to look unconscious.

'Honey,' my mother's voice said, 'the police need to ask you something.'

That makes a change, I thought, and pulled myself up on my pillows.

My mother was looking extra concerned. 'Was Bethany with you?' she asked. 'Was Bethany with you in the car?'

I was still sleepy. I shook my head, no, as if she was crazy to ask. And then I remembered...I had meant to be running away with Bethany...

Bethany was that rare thing at our school – even more of a freak than I was. She was a gifted pianist, fiercely intelligent, stolid and dark and chock-full of resentment. She knew how unhappy I was at home, knew all about being unhappy at home. We'd had to do something together at some point, her playing and me singing and she thought we might be able to do a lounge act in New York. She suggested we run away and had picked the morning of the accident for our escape.

I went along with this as a fantasy, talking about how much money I could lay my hands on (none) and what car to steal (one of her relative's vehicles). I was supposed to drive the 1300 miles to New York City.

For me, this was a pleasant dream. I once bragged to the rest of our nerdy gang about it and got told off for this by Bethany. Even at fourteen, I knew vaguely what would happen to two broke adolescents on the streets of New York, and my problems at home didn't come close to the problems I could imagine there.

But Bethany grew increasingly intense about it. She shook me by my shoulders, hard, at one point, trying to make me more serious. So I pretended and then, finally, told her I wasn't coming. At least I think I told her. I might have just stood her up.

I know my behaviour in this whole episode was not exactly covered with shining glory, but I didn't know what else to do. Telling parents or a teacher would have been an unforgivable betrayal. Actually going would have been stupid. And I couldn't talk her out of it. She *needed* the idea of New York. It got her through her days at Burner High. But I had my own troubles. Sometimes when Bethany came up to me in the hall and whispered, 'Do you have a large Thermos?' or 'Take a sleeping bag,' it took me a minute to know what the hell she was talking about. For me, it was a little game I played with Bethany. But she was playing all the time.

In those years, life seemed full of these complex layers of alternative realities. In the summer, you could become close to someone who would not acknowledge your existence once school started. A group of you, who had perhaps gotten access to some alcohol or marijuana, could do something – start a fire, steal a car, have sex – and never talk about it again...perhaps never talk to each other again. Someone could tell you they loved you the night before their friend was sent to your lunch table to tell you it was all over. The churchgoing cheerleader, squeakily blonde, could strip down to her panties on the roof of her car at the lake and no one who was there would mention it, not even when she stood up in assembly and spoke on the subject of 'modesty'.

I can't remember if Bethany had failed Drivers Ed or if her controlling parents wouldn't let her take it. But Bethany couldn't drive. So when I'd let her down, I'd assumed that, though she might hate me forever, she'd abandon her crazy scheme. I thought she'd shrug off that reality and go back to the one we all shared with our parents and teachers, the one that was always waiting for our acceptance.

Now, with the kind of blinding clarity you only get when it's too late, I realised that things for Bethany must be much worse than things for me. Even in the bed with the tubes, even with wanting to die. Because she'd gone anyway. She'd completely lost track of what was real and what wasn't and had stolen her relative's car, even though she couldn't drive and was all alone.

On the morning when Kim and I were only concerned with getting to play practice and scoring sugary drinks, Bethany had done what I'd promised to do with her. She'd run away from home to go to New York City, 1300 miles away.

It took me forever to write it all out on my pad and my mother just couldn't believe it. 'You were thinking about running away?' she asked, over and over. Like what part of Dad weird and gone and her depressed and no food and no housework done and dirt everywhere and crappy clothes and a bad haircut and a crap school where everyone hated me and no warm coat had she missed? I mean nearly *every* teenager thinks about running away. Of *course* I had.

But that would have taken too long to write down.

The police left and I got my first meal. Jello, wobbly red squares on a small paper tray with a plastic spoon. I had no desire to put this in my mouth, to feel the squares turn to liquidy mush against my teeth and slime down my throat.

The nice nurse observed my reaction and leaned over, pretending to adjust the bed. 'You get out of ICU two ways,' she hissed in my ear. 'You eat and you pee. If you want to get rid of your IV and your catheter, eat your freaking Jello.'

'Nurse,' my mother said, already treating them like staff. 'I don't think she wants this.' I grabbed the little tray as mom pushed it away and took a giant spoonful, glaring at the nurse as I chewed and swallowed the sickly mess. She gave me the thumbs up sign behind mom's back, and the fake perky smile that accompanied it nearly made me smile.

'That's it,' she said, signing something on my chart. 'You are outa here.'

I didn't realise how much the catheter was hurting until they took it out. I guess with all the pain relief, that particular pain had gone more or less unnoticed. By now I was getting a reputation for courage, but I nearly ruined my teenage stoic act when they pulled the tubing out and out and out, while the tender skin around my urethra rubbed and pulled and burned.

The IV was a whole different thing. I was so happy to see the damn thing come out of my hand that the impossibly long needle didn't faze me. I would have pulled it out myself with my teeth. My entire arm sighed with relief once the intrusion was over. The bruise it left was as big as my fist.

Not many people walk out of their Intensive Care ward. But with another hospital gown on backwards to cover my bottom, and my mother and the nice nurse on either side of me, I did. A porter hovered behind us with a wheelchair, just in case, but I wasn't going to need it. I was a bit stiff and my right foot still hurt, but I felt fine.

Doctor Kular had come in after my Jello. He had stopped looking at me like an animal in a zoo. He'd now started looking at me very suspiciously, as if I was an unexploded bomb. He checked my chart while the nice nurse was talking about releasing me from Intensive Care, and then checked my machines, and then checked the chart again, as if he thought I'd pulled a fast one.

He kept running a pen across his weasely moustache. He

kept saying, 'Hmm.'

Mom was off getting coffee, and that made me nervous. I didn't have anybody there to represent me. I was going to have to try to speak for myself.

The nice nurse had said something about a bed being open in the children's ward. Kular had said, 'Hmm,' again and looked at me again with that weird suspicious attitude. And then he'd said, 'That's too far away. What about ENT?'

He was looking at me, but talking to the nice nurse. He would have explained things if my mother had been there. But since it was just me, he talked about me like I wasn't there.

I wrote, 'I'm right here, you know,' on my pad and showed it to him.

He frowned. 'I know you are here, Miss DuLac. But you clearly cannot remain here, which is what I am discussing with the nurse.'

Jerk, I thought.

'They have room in ENT,' she said. 'But she's only fourteen and it's kind of...'

'It's the best place for her,' Kular said. 'Whether or not it's a bit...uncomfortable.'

He looked at me again, for the first time as if I was a real person. He said, 'I'm going to see you tomorrow in clinic. I'll be monitoring your stats today.'

I wrote, 'Be still, my beating heart,' on my pad.

He looked at my pad and then at my special 'sweet' face that I'd pulled. 'Your beating heart,' he said, 'is obviously not going to be still, which is why we have the problem of what to do with you.'

And then he walked away.

As we walked around the corner to the Ear, Nose and Throat ward, I remembered all of this. I remembered it because of the way the nice nurse had said it was 'kind of...'

I saw what she meant pretty much right away. There was a long leatherette sofa along the wall and an older man was sitting on it. A piece of cream-coloured tubing came out of his nose and he sucked something dark red from a cup up through it. He smiled at me, but I was too busy trying not to vomit to smile back.

Just then a round little nurse in a brightly-coloured checked top and white trousers and clogs came rushing by with an IV stand. 'Whoops!' she said, 'Gangway!'

Two middle-aged women in dressing gowns, with curlers in their hair, leaned against a wall talking to each other. They had weird machines pressed to their throats. Now I know that they sounded just like Daleks, but nobody in 1970s America knew anything about Doctor Who.

I felt my mother's arm stiffen and snuck a look at her horrified face.

'Are you sure there's no room in the children's ward?' she asked the nurse, after swallowing hard.

The nice nurse lied smoothly. 'No, I'm afraid not. But we can try and move her tomorrow.'

I kind of wanted to cry. I could hear myself whistling with little squeaks of utter terror, so I knew what I was feeling was fear. It was fear making my armpits sweat and my stomach knot.

Kular had said it was the best place for me. I hated Doctor Kular, but I also completely believed he knew what he was doing.

So, when the nurse and my mom looked at me to see how I was taking all of this, I gave my best insolent teenaged shrug. A 'whatever' shrug, as if the whole thing bored me. I don't think I fooled either of them, but we kept walking and got to my new room.

I saw an actual shower in the tiny bathroom as we went to my bed and my whole body ached with a deep longing to be clean.

But before I could write anything about taking a shower, we

were suddenly surrounded by people.

They took my chart from the nice nurse and took x-rays out of a folder and hung them on the wall by my bed on a special little holder. (When had I been down to X-ray? I didn't remember leaving Intensive Care...) They were talking to mom, talking, talking, loads of information coming at us. It was so noisy. There was so much going on. There was colour – I'd kind of forgotten about colour.

My mother was unpacking a bag. (Where had the bag come from? I didn't remember a bag...) The nice nurse backed off and then turned away. I reached out for her and someone slapped a blood pressure cuff on my arm and started taking my pulse. She looked back and I wanted to say, 'Thank you,' but all that came out was the whistle. And then she was gone, back to her cool, shadowy world in between life and death, without me.

I wanted to write something about her to my mother. They'd finished with my blood pressure, so I got my pad and was working the pen out of the rings when someone snatched it away from my hand.

'Oh, no,' she said. 'Have this.'

'This' was a cheap write on-wipe off toy – a Magic Slate. It was made of cardboard and had a plastic sheet over a sticky ink square. You wrote on them with a little plastic stylus, attached to the cardboard with a string and then lifted the plastic to erase it so you could write something else. This one was decorated with various images of Donald Duck, printed badly with the yellow, blue and red dots not lined up properly. It was the crappiest Magic Slate I'd ever seen and I wanted nothing to do with it.

I lunged for my pad, but she held it away.

'Use Donald,' she said. She was plump and smiling, wearing a bright blue tunic, white trousers and clogs. Her hair was improbably black and sprayed high.

'Give me my pad and pen,' I wrote.

'Those are much better – less wasteful,' the pad Nazi said to my mother. 'You can get replacements downstairs. They last a couple of weeks, depending on how chatty she is.'

But I wanted all my words. I wanted, 'Where's Kim?' I wanted, 'Be still my beating heart.' It wasn't just paper. It was my memory, it was the bit of me that I still had and a record of my time in the hospital, too. I lunged for the pad again and got it.

'I'll use Donald,' I wrote and then had to wipe it off to continue, 'But I need the pad for me.' She looked at me doubtfully and I underlined the last two words.

'Okay,' she said. She patted my cheek with her soft, pink hand. 'But you're going to have to let us help you. We know what we're doing.'

Then, in a whirl of colour and noise, they left us alone.

My mother and I looked at each other. I wondered if I looked as tired as she did. Then she started getting shampoo and conditioner and soap out of the bag and ferrying it into the bathroom. Toothpaste, a toothbrush. There were towels in there already, she said.

When I closed the door behind me, I felt the biggest sense of relief. I didn't have to be strong for anyone anymore. I stripped off my smelly hospital gown and dropped it on the floor. I sat down on the toilet just because the relief of being alone had made my legs shake, but once I was there, I was glad to find out that everything still worked. I carefully didn't look behind me. I certainly hoped I was flushing away the last of my own blood.

Getting water into a trachea tube is a bit of a shock, but I managed the shower without killing myself. I wrapped myself up in the towels without bothering to dry off too much. I was starting to get a bit breathless with the exertion.

I brushed my teeth over and over but my mouth still didn't taste clean. I wondered what had happened to me that my mouth was that disgustingly dirty. They'd put tubes in there. I vaguely remembered having one pulled out of my mouth, some kind of mask thing... And then I hadn't had any water for a long time. I thought maybe that was it.

When I pushed back up from bending over the sink, I nearly passed out. The world went briefly black and I wavered around on my feet like one of those punchable blow-up clown toys.

In hospital bathrooms now, they have those orange alarm cords. They didn't have them then, or I would have pulled it.

It took me five hundred years to shuffle to the door. Several times I had to stop because I thought I was going to faint. Then the blasted thing opened inwards, so I lost about half my progress, having to shuffle back again. I sobbed with frustration, but I just whistled. I cried out for my mother and whistled again.

I was panting and sweating with the exertion of standing up. Inching forward again seemed as impossible as climbing Everest.

I'd never felt so small and sad in my entire life. Everything was waaaaaay too difficult. Life – just inhabiting my body – was horribly stressful and hard. I wished I could have just gone through the ceiling and got it over with. If it hadn't been for nasty, interfering Doctor Kular, I wouldn't be stuck in a hospital bathroom, where I was clearly about to die again, anyway.

Suddenly my mother was there. She led me to a grab rail and towelled me off. She pulled a lovely blue nightgown over my head, silky and soft, that came all the way down to my ankles. She brushed through my hair and then led me to the bed, walking backwards, and holding me up in her strong arms.

The beds in Intensive Care had been hard, cold slabs. My new bed felt like a cloud.

I sank into it. Just before I was asleep, I grabbed my Donald and wrote, 'Do not wake me up...for ANYTHING.'

I was asleep before mom finished drawing up the blankets. I had walked several hundred metres and had a shower. It had nearly killed me.

# Chapter Six

## Soundtrack: 'After the Gold Rush' – Neil Young

The pain was incredible.

They had taken my notice seriously and really hadn't woken me up for anything. My throat was on fire – a horrible pulsing flame of pain. My head had an intense pounding thing going on and hurt like the blazes whenever I looked at the light. My mouth felt dry and sticky at the same time.

It was my first hangover.

A nurse I didn't recognise came into the room. She took one look at my face and said, 'Need your pain meds?'

I nodded and that made my throat hurt so badly that the world went black for a moment, clearing slowly, like a black curtain with holes gradually being burnt through it. Once it cleared, the brightness of the room stabbed my head.

Yet another nurse came into the room with a small paper cup full of various tablets and a larger paper cup full of water. I tossed all the pills to the back of my throat in one practiced movement and swilled them all down with the water, gulping the whole cup down in one.

'Wow,' she said.

But swallowing had made my throat flame again. I held onto the piping on the edge of the mattress through the sheet and through the bed pad. I squeezed and squeezed with my fingers. If I sat really, really still, and squeezed really, really hard, the pain in my throat wasn't as bad. I closed my eyes and started to count.

I got to five thousand, three hundred and forty-five before I could let go of the mattress. I opened my eyes and my head didn't stab with the light. The first nurse was back, with a blood pressure machine.

'Goodness,' she said. 'That looked pretty uncomfortable.'

I just looked at her, with a don't-expect-me-to-participate-in-your-stupidity look.

She waggled the blood pressure cuff. 'Ready?'

While she was taking my pressure, somebody else came in. 'Breakfast!' she said, and put a tray on my bedside table. Then she raised the bedside table and turned it so that it was like a desk over my legs.

Cool, I thought. Then I looked at the food.

There's a breakfast dish in the States called 'biscuits and gravy'. It's plain savoury scones in a kind of béchamel sauce with sausage bits in. I was never a huge fan, and even less so right then, when the sauce had a distinctly greenish tinge from the strip light and gently congealed around the scones.

I pushed it away.

'Did you like your IV?' the first nurse asked. 'Because if you don't eat your breakfast, you get it back.'

I cut listlessly into the gloop and put a bit into my mouth. It was completely tasteless. I mean, *completely* tasteless, as if I was chewing a sponge. Every once in a while I got a faint tang of black pepper. I chewed and swallowed with some effort, washing it down with some orange juice. That didn't even taste like oranges, but just burnt my mouth with acid.

The nurse was leaning on the blood pressure machine stand and watching me.

'I know,' she said. 'It's no fun eating when you can't taste.'

I looked at her, an interested, attentive look. An I-am-listening-don't-stop-now kind of look.

She sniffed theatrically. 'No smell, no taste,' she said. 'You've got no air coming in through your nose, so you've got no taste in your mouth.'

I cut another piece, a bigger piece, and chewed it. She was right. I couldn't taste a thing, except for some of the black pepper in the sausage. And that was why, I suddenly realised, I had brushed my teeth to the point of exhaustion last night. My mouth didn't feel clean because I couldn't taste the mint in my toothpaste.

I ate half my breakfast, and drank the oddly painful orange juice and the nurse left me alone.

I went to the bathroom, washed my face and brushed my teeth.

I messed with my hair a bit and put on some makeup, carefully avoiding looking at the bandages around my neck and the big blue plastic tube sticking out of it.

Back in my room, I discovered a matching dressing gown and slippers. I tried them on and went to look out the window. It had a lovely view of another wall. You couldn't even see through the opposite windows. I tried to look up at the sky, but I couldn't get my head close enough to the glass. Same with looking down at the ground.

Still, it looked like an okay day. It wasn't raining or anything.

I made my bed and sat on it. I played with it a bit, adjusting the back so it was more comfortable to sit up. This bed was all electric and I could do it myself. Then I had to adjust the table. I liked it over me like a desk. I arranged things on it. My pad and pen. A fashion magazine my mother had brought in for me. She'd also brought in my bedside clock and I took that from the chest of drawers behind me and put that on my table.

It was six forty-five.

I looked through the drawers. There were some more nightgowns. Some panties.

I got back on the bed and read the magazine until I was bored. It was seven.

I got Donald and went out to the hall. There were loads of nurses at a big round desk just down from my room.

'Wow,' the nurse who'd brought my pain meds said. 'Look who's up and about!'

Everyone stopped what they were doing and smiled at me. I

felt a bit embarrassed.

I got Donald and wrote, 'When can I go home?'

Everyone else suddenly got more interested in their work, so I knew, right away, that whatever the nurse answered, it wasn't going to be something I wanted to hear.

She cleared her throat. 'Well,' she said. 'You're going to see Doctor Kular this morning.'

I just looked at her. A come-on-and-tell-me-whatever-it-is kind of look.

She had a length of cream-coloured tubing in her hands and she twisted it around and around. 'Well,' she said, 'I know you're going to have some surgery.'

Yes, I thought to myself, that makes sense. They have to repair my airway so that I can use my voice again.

The man with the nose thing came up beside me and she passed him the cream-coloured tubing without really taking her eyes off me. He nodded at us both politely and went off, to stick the new tube up his nose, I presumed.

'Soooooo,' she said, 'with one thing and another, I think you're going to be with us for a while.'

I let this sink in, looking at her. She was about my mother's age. She wore browny-pink lipstick and had her light brown hair tied back in a ponytail, soft and unsprayed under a stiff white cap. Her soft brown eyes watched how I took all the news and she must have liked what she saw, because she suddenly reached out and patted me on the arm. She said, 'You're a good girl.'

And I knew that was because I hadn't cried or complained. I had just listened and tried to understand. Where I'm from, we put a lot of value on not complaining and just getting on with things. We use cowboy and pioneer terms for it, as if the strength and determination of the first settlers had come through the generations to us. When something is difficult, we're meant to 'pony up' and get on with it.

I got my pat and my 'good girl' because I had ponied up.

She said, 'You can move down to the children's ward if you want.'

Did I want to leave ENT? I looked around. The hall was nearly empty early in the morning. The nose guy had gone to his favourite sofa. This time his cup was full of something brown and he was patiently sucking it up with his fresh cream-coloured tube.

I had been to the children's ward before. I'd sung there, lots of times, for Easter and Christmas with my school choir, my church choir, and, one time, my cousins' band. In Girl Scouts, I'd helped to collect dolls and teddies old ladies had made and donated. I'd even danced for the sick kids in tap shoes which had echoed gratifyingly off the hard floors – routines from *Bye Bye Birdie*.

The walls in the children's ward were painted with circus motifs. People were always coming around to cheer the patients up. I presumed I would need to act grateful when somebody gave me a crappy teddy bear or tap-danced for me...I didn't think I could manage that.

I looked back at Nose Guy, who smiled at me. I smiled back.

'No,' I wrote on Donald. 'I'll stay in ENT.' I wiped it away, with the lift-off plastic thingy. 'If that's okay with you guys.'

'What do you think, team?' the nurse asked, and everyone stopped pretending they weren't listening. Some of them smiled, some of them looked sad and one or two seemed like they were seriously considering whether or not to let me stay.

'God, don't I have enough teenagers at home?' It was the plump one with black hair. She winked as she said it, though. Everyone laughed, then, and one said, 'Welcome aboard.' Lots of the staff stuck out their hands, to shake mine, or pat me.

I went back to my room and got back into bed feeling kind of weird. I got my pad.

'Staying in for surgery,' I wrote. And then I crossed out the 'in'. It looked nicer without it.

I was still trying to read the magazine when a whole bunch of other people walked into my room. They didn't knock or anything. I was glad I hadn't been picking my nose or adjusting my panties or anything.

A squat, powerful-looking man wearing scrubs was leading them and they all shuffled after him like baby ducks after Mama Duck.

Mama Duck was talking as he came in and he smiled briefly at me and took my wrist, still talking. I couldn't make any sense out of what he was saying. Doctor Kular detached himself from the rest of the baby ducks and got my chart, doing that smoothing-moustache thing with his pen. Mama Duck asked questions and Kular responded. Then Mama Duck asked if I'd had a BM, which I knew meant he wanted to know if I'd pooed.

Must we? I thought, sitting there with my Glamour Magazine still open on the table to, 'Houndstooth Check: Dos and Don'ts'. Must we really discuss my poo habits in front of everyone?

'Yes,' Kular answered, beaming at me. I was a good girl. I had pooed. Everyone murmured approval. I wanted the bed to open up and drop me into the core of the earth.

Mama Duck finished taking my pulse and smiled at me. 'I'm Doctor Morris,' he said, 'Chief Surgeon of the ENT Department.'

Then he turned back to the baby ducks and started talking. About me, evidently. He showed them my fingernails and started talking about lip colour. Then he looked at me closely.

'Are you wearing lipstick?' he asked.

I got Donald. 'No.' For comic timing, I erased Donald then and used a clean sheet to write, 'Lip gloss.'

Doctor Morris chuckled. His glasses were as clean as air and his eyes crinkled when he smiled.

'Well,' he said. 'You've got a hot date with Doctor Kular later.'

All the other baby ducks laughed and Kular blushed. I could suddenly see how utterly nerdy all the baby ducks were. Kular had another pair of polyester trousers with factory creases down the front and a cheap yellow shirt with a big collar that flopped over his white coat's lapels. He looked dreadful, but he wasn't the worst. In fact, compared to the others, he looked okay. The girls wore shapeless skirts and those horrible tights that look orange indoors. Their shoes must have been especially designed to make their ankles look thick and puffy.

I remembered back in high school when the guidance counsellor had given an assembly about avoiding tribalism. She'd been trying to explain us nerds to the cool jocks and gorgeous cheerleaders and groovy hoods. She said that when you care about your grades, you sometimes don't worry so much about your appearance. I had taken it rather personally at the time, mainly because I was growing out my hair and it hadn't yet reached the stage where I could slam it into a ponytail. Whenever it rained, my hair became a total afro. I cared about my grades, sure, but I was *desperately* worried about my hair.

The baby ducks had all obviously been caring about their grades a looooooong time. Really, they all should have just had G-E-E-K tattooed on their foreheads and been done with it. The word 'date' made them all shuffle and giggle like ten-year-olds.

I rolled my eyes, but they were already gone.

Suddenly my mother was there. 'I missed rounds?' she asked. 'Again?'

I nodded.

'Hell.' My mother rarely cursed. She was clearly really upset and dumped her bag down on the floor. 'Stupid trash truck,' she said. 'It blocked me at Merriam and I had to drive all the way around.'

When she said that, I realised she had stopped turning left. Again.

In America, of course, you drive on the right side of the road, so the left hand turn is the tricky one that goes across traffic. Whenever my mother felt sad or worried, she lost the confidence to turn left.

She had all these strategies to get everywhere in town by only turning right.

It used to drive my father crazy. He'd find out that she'd been late or hadn't done something because she couldn't turn left and he'd shout and shout and shout at her. And that would make her even more nervous and then she wouldn't be able to turn left for weeks.

I hated it when mom couldn't turn left. I sighed and my throat whistled.

'How did your stats look?' Mom asked.

She already spoke the lingo. She knew about blood pressure. She'd learned to read EKG printouts. All the doctors and nurses (except for the nasty Intensive Care nurse who didn't like either of us) already thought she was great.

In *her* high school, my mother had been in the top crowd, with all the rich and popular people. She'd been president of her senior class. She'd married the football captain – Dad, of course. And here she was, getting popular here in hospital, too.

I wrote, 'Good…I think.'

My mother looked at it. 'I think you should write in full sentences,' she said. 'Otherwise, you look stupid.'

I looked at her, a 'really?' kind of look, but she just shrugged, as if to say, 'go ahead and look stupid if you want.'

I erased Donald. 'They seemed to think my stats looked good,' I wrote instead. I showed it to mom and she nodded.

I erased it and was in the middle of writing, 'They got pretty excited because I pooed,' when my mother said, 'I'll bet they were pretty impressed that you did a poo.' I showed her Donald and she laughed.

'Jinx, you owe me a coke,' she said, because we'd 'said' the same thing at the same time.

I laughed, but my throat whistled and that made the smiles fall off our faces. Her eyes filled with tears and she held my hand tightly.

'Look,' she said. She took a deep breath. 'You do know what's wrong with you, don't you? Do you want me to explain or do you already know?'

I shrugged. I wrote, 'I have a laryngeal fracture,' on Donald.

'Yes,' she said. 'But do you know...'

I wrote, 'I have to have surgery,' and wiped it off. 'I'll be here a long time.' Mom looked up at the ceiling and blinked, which is what she always did when she felt like crying and didn't want to mess up her eye makeup.

'You're so brave,' she said. Her chin wobbled and did that peach-pit thing it always did before she lost it completely.

I really can't deal with this, I thought. I can't deal with mom falling apart on me right now.

Then the nurse that took my blood pressure and watched me eat breakfast came in with a little map. 'Right,' she said. 'The ENT clinic isn't in this building. It's here.' She made a little x on the page and started discussing with mom about how to get there and whether or not we wanted a wheelchair.

I really wanted a walk. I felt like if I didn't move soon, I'd explode. I wrote, 'I would like to walk, please,' on Donald, and we set off for my hot date with Doctor Kular.

# Chapter Seven

## Soundtrack: 'Second Avenue' – Art Garfunkel

We set off about ten.

My blue nightgown and robe were terribly glamorous and I liked the way the material swished around my ankles as I walked. It wasn't the right material for slippers, however, and my feet kept slipping right off them. It happened when we went into the first lift and I had to try hard not to think about all the nasty things that could have been on a hospital elevator floor.

There were about a hundred elevators at KU Med and not all of them took you to all floors. The hospital was as higgledy-piggledy as our house, and nobody seemed to be in charge of making the new bits match up to the old bits, or even to each other.

We got lost almost immediately, and my mother left me standing near a join between an older bit and a newer bit of the hospital. It was an awkward, lumpy, unsuccessful join. And it bothered me.

Until that moment, I had thought there was a responsible adult in charge of each of the world's details. I knew my parents could be pretty useless, but I thought that was just *them*. In this moment, on my way to my first ENT clinic, I suddenly discovered that I was wrong and *all* adults were more or less incompetent.

The higgledy-piggledyness of the hospital made it obvious. Buildings were large, substantial structures. It was easy to see a seven-story building. Even with my poor math skills, I could guess how you'd go about measuring to make sure that the floors in one bit matched up to the floors in another bit. And I could not help but wonder if the people at KU Med couldn't manage that, how they were going to fix something as delicate as my throat.

Mom came back, and we started walking, but I had stopped noticing where we were going. I was replaying my memory of all the treatment I'd had so far, wondering about the competence of the medical staff, considering if it was too late to run away…

And that was a mistake. Because it left the entire burden of navigating to the clinic on my mother's fragile shoulders. I didn't really notice how lost we were until we stopped walking completely.

Mom was trying not to cry, hunched over the map and taking terrified glances at her watch. I was getting ready to comfort her when she looked at me and said, 'God. You're getting tired.' For a moment, I thought she was going to totally fall apart, but then she stood up straight, as if she had shaken the wrinkles out of herself.

She took a deep breath and said, 'Come *on*, Dianne.' Her head snapped to look at a sign on the wall and back to the map.

'Right,' she said, showing me the map. 'If we go down one floor, we can get through *here* and go back up on *that* elevator. What do you think?'

I nodded a 'good plan' kind of nod and we walked off again.

One floor down was different. The floor was nicer and the walls were clean and painted a nice dull green. The door to the 'here' we had to get through was a big square of red-brown wood with glass panels and a brass pull handle. Mom opened it and we went into another world.

It was quiet in there. There was carpet on the floor and paper on the walls. A dado railing ran around the room and stretched towards a hall with more nice wooden doors. At the far end, a very pretty woman in a very nice suit murmured to a big, blinking telephone on a large mahogany desk.

More suited people were sitting in leather bucket chairs along the wall, reading thick, glossy magazines. They looked up when we walked in. Their eyes gravitated to my neck and widened in horror. Disgust flickered onto their faces, before they pretended to smile and dropped their eyes to their magazines. The lady at the mahogany desk started to get up, but mom walked quickly to the far door and opened it for me. This made the lady look relieved.

In ICU, I'd been the well one. In ENT, I'd been one of the less freaky ones. But in the real world, I was clearly a horror. Back in another elevator, I looked in the mirror at my neck, at the large turquoise tube whistling my air in and out. It was a horrible hole that shouldn't have been there.

My mother took my hand. She always knew what I was thinking when I looked in the mirror and always knew the right thing to say. When I first got my glasses, she'd said, 'It's more important that you see the world than the world sees you...and we'll find some blue ones next pay check.' When my legs shot away from me and I looked ridiculously thin, she'd said, 'You'll grow into them.' When I'd had spots she'd said, 'You don't have many, and they'll go away.'

She always seemed to connect me to a future me; a me with lovely blue plastic framed glasses, a me with long, shapely legs, a me with clear skin. And standing by her and looking in the mirror, I would be able to see that future me, too.

Today, she looked at the hole in my neck and said, 'It's temporary.'

But I couldn't see the future me without it. I couldn't imagine being better. So, I just stopped looking.

Doctor Kular's clinic had a line of chairs in the hall, too. But his chairs were plastic and the ENT clinic hall didn't have carpet – it had scuffed linoleum and puke pink walls. We were on time, after all, so we had to wait. They were always running late.

By now I was kind of used to trach tubes and missing bits in my fellow patients, but mom was still finding it difficult. She flinched when she saw one person walking along with an IV and a bag of pink fluid pinned to their chest. And then she got cross at herself for flinching.

The expensive clinic had bothered mom. She was imagining all the cutting things she could have said to the pretty receptionist. I caught her muttering some of them under her breath.

The receptionist at our clinic wasn't young and pretty, but she seemed to seriously know her stuff. She knew all the patients by name and she even got my nickname right. 'Coco and Mrs DuLac?' she said. 'You can go in now.'

It felt odd being alone in a room with just mom and Doctor Kular. He was frowning at my charts when we walked in but he flicked his eyes up at us to acknowledge our presence and told us to sit down on the chairs by his desk.

I'd never been to a doctor's office and been asked to sit in a chair. It had always been straight onto the table with me before.

Nothing in his examination room matched. My chair was dark brown wood and looked like part of a Victorian dining set. My mom's was a bright green vinyl office chair with chipped chrome accents from the fifties. Kular himself perched on a black metal screw up, screw down stool on wheels. This made him look like an insect, especially when he frowned again and, without warning, scuttled on his stool ten feet over to a counter to retrieve a pink card and then scuttled back, so at home on the thing you'd think he'd been born on it.

'Right,' he finally said, turning his desk lamp to shine in my face. 'I'm going to ask you to stick out your tongue and then I'm going to look down your throat with this.' He held up a dental mirror that I didn't remember him having. He must have grabbed it while I was blinded by the desk lamp.

What could I say, 'No, thank you?' I just looked at him.

'Right,' he said again. 'Stick out your tongue.'

I stuck my tongue out at him and he grabbed it with a cotton pad. 'Great,' he said, pulling. 'Now open your mouth really wide.' And down went the dental mirror.

Of course I gagged and my mother made sounds of distress.

Kular said, 'Oh, you'll get used to it. You won't gag nearly as much.'

He twisted the mirror this way and that. I noticed for the first time that he was wearing one of those headbands with the mirrored circle on it to reflect the light down my throat.

'Yep,' he said. 'It's horrible down there.' He removed the mirror and peeled the cotton off my tongue, dropping it into the bin in one practiced move. He scribbled a bit on a pad on his desk, looked up and then looked at both of us, as if uncertain.

He finally decided to address me.

'Your larynx is completely trashed,' he said. 'But the good news is that most of it is still there and the tissue you lost is from areas with good rates of healing.'

He paused. I didn't really have anything to add, so he kept going.

'Now the bad news is that the larynx is a stupid thing. We can go back in and reattach the vocal chords, etcetera, but it will just heal itself shut after surgery.' He made a tube with his hand and collapsed it into a fist. 'You can't breathe through that,' he said, referring to his fist.

I nodded. I wasn't really taking any of this in. I was still dealing with the 'horrible' and 'completely trashed.' Nobody had told me that before.

'So what we have to do is put a bit of silicone in there while it's healing. Then we'll go in and take it out and you should have a working larynx, or at least one that will carry air.'

All I really got was that all this was going to take time.

Last year, I'd sang a solo on Santa Lucia at Christmas with the school choir. We'd gone to the shopping mall and the hospital and several churches. The moment of my solo was one of my best photo album moments.

My top note had been so pure and sweet that I had made people cry. In the middle of a busy shopping mall, in the middle of the Christmas rush, people had stood with their shopping bags, tears running down their cheeks. Old farmers, suburban housewives, burly men, blue-haired grandmas. I can still remember how a little boy who had been scooting his toy dump truck across the floor stopped and stood and looked at me with wonder and delight as the next perfect note and the next and the next dropped lightly in the huge hall, bouncing off the walls and the shiny black floor.

The year I was sitting on Doctor Kular's mis-matched chair, our high school choir had a chance to be on television and I had sung my Santa Lucia for the television director. She wanted my solo to be the highlight of the entire programme.

It was my my big break. Out of all the hundreds of schools and thousands of teenagers that were singing on the programme, I was going to be the big star. Who knew where it might lead? At the very least, my uncle had said, it would be a hell of an audition tape.

I knew I'd need a few weeks of intensive practice time, so this whole surgery thing would have to be wrapped up by mid-November. That gave us six weeks.

I reached for my pad and wrote, 'How long will it be before I can sing again?'

Kular looked at it, reading the words out loud. He shook his head and lifted up the magic slate plastic, making the words go away.

Then he looked at mom. He looked at her for such a long time, that I turned and looked at her, too. She was smoothing the map of the hospital out on the leg of her jeans. She must have felt us watching her, but she wouldn't look up.

She was shaking.

In that moment, I knew that something horrible was about to happen. I looked back at Doctor Kular, and his face was...it was shut down even tighter than usual. He said, 'Listen,' and it slapped out of him flat and hard.

'Listen,' he said again. 'You've got to forget all about singing.

What we're working on right now is breathing. You'll be really, really lucky if you have any kind of voice at all.' He considered for a moment. 'In fact, with the way your voice box looks, if you were in almost any other hospital you could forget about breathing, too. But Doctor Morris has done some amazing things, and I think you've got a good chance of having something like a normal life.'

He scooted away to get a folder and then mom finally looked up and they started signing forms together.

And then he came back to talk to me.

My head felt...broken. There was a huge pressure, somewhere. Doctor Kular was trying to talk to me about anaes-thetics, and through the pressure and the pain and the...kind of deadness... I somehow gathered that it was all going to start happening in the morning and that I couldn't eat anything more today.

I understood that, but I don't know how. Because my whole head was full of understanding something else. Something I hadn't understood before. Something that was vitally important, but I just hadn't got. It was this:

Your larynx is your *voice box*.

Your larynx is your *voice box*.

Your larynx is your **VOICE**.

And mine had been completely trashed.

'You've got to forget all about singing.'

My photo album began to flash its pages through my head. Performances, messing around in basements with my cousins on guitars, and that moment the note rolled out, pure and clear, over the lake in the twilight.

Then I remembered a time in church – at a wedding? – and then back to the lake and then back to the wedding and then back to the lake and away to the little boy in the shopping mall and then back, back, back to that moment on the lake and the song on the water. And I wanted to swim after it now, dive into the lake and swim deep to the bottom to find my perfect note and keep it forever.

My face felt wet, and I realised my eyes were leaking tears.

That well of unconsciousness opened right under me. I was looking at Doctor Kular, who was *still* talking, but I was fighting sliding down into it, until I couldn't fight anymore. I just gave up, and then I started sliding and he finally noticed and reached out and...

...I fainted right into Doctor Kular's arms.

The next thing I knew, I was facing up again, on another gurney ride through KU Med Center. I could hear Doctor Kular and my mother arguing over my legs, so I knew a porter must have been pushing me.

'You said she understood!' Kular whispered.

'I thought she did,' my mother's whisper was interspersed with sniffs.

We rolled along. 'And anyway,' my mother hissed, 'is "completely trashed" a medical term? You were so insensitive.'

'Stop,' Kular said, and we all stopped. I didn't want to open my eyes. I didn't want to be there at all. I didn't want to *be* at all.

Kular put something on my legs. 'Here's the consent form. Sign, so I can leave you to it.'

'Gladly,' my mother said. 'I hope you're not performing surgery.'

'I am assisting,' Kular said. 'The Chief Surgeon will be performing the procedure.'

Somewhere in my misery, I thought, 'Mama Duck.'

I felt a slight pressure on my legs and heard the sound of my mother signing.

'I will sue you if it goes wrong,' she said. 'It doesn't matter what I'm signing here. I'll find a way.'

'We'll do our best,' Doctor Kular argued. 'Threatening the OR staff won't help Coco.'

There was a silence and I got the feeling they were looking at me. Maybe I should have opened my eyes at that point, but it was too embarrassing to admit that I'd been eavesdropping, so I had to keep on dropping.

'You should have prepared her,' Kular said. We *asked* you to prepare her. You *said* you would prepare her.'

'And just how do you prepare somebody for news like that?' My mother had stopped whispering. She said, 'You go to school to learn how to do this stuff. I'm just an ordinary mother.' I heard her voice catch and heard her sob. 'I'm not even very good at that.'

Whatever was on my legs got moved.

'Try to keep calm,' Doctor Kular said, in the kindest voice I'd ever heard him use. 'Coco wants to live. I've never seen anyone fight so hard for life before. I don't think she'll leave us now.'

No I don't, I thought. I don't want to live. I really, really don't. In the whole pain and mess of it, I forgot I was meant to be unconscious and forgot I couldn't talk and tried to say, 'No, I don't.' All that came out was the whistle.

'Doctor,' the porter said, with a heavy black Southern accent, 'I think the young lady is in pain.'

'Oh, God,' my mother said. 'Let's go. Can't we just *go*?'

When we got to the ward, I felt, rather than saw, a bunch of people cluster around me again. Then they rolled me onto my side and I felt a prick on my bottom and the world went away.

When I woke up, I tried to go back to sleep. All I wanted to be was unconscious. I lay there and fought to find the opening of that well. I looked and looked for it, in that strange, in-between region of consciousness.

'I'll see if she's awake,' someone said outside my door, and I heard the odd noise that meant nurse footsteps. They wore shoes with big foam wedges and you could more feel the percussion of their steps than hear them.

I left my eyes open and looked up at the plump nurse with black hair.

She pushed my button and sat me up.

That's when I realised I still had tears trickling out of my eyes. They'd been going into the hair on my temples when I was lying down. When I sat up, they slid down my face.

'There's someone here to see you.'

It was the detectives who had come to see me about Bethany.

'We found your friend,' one of them said. 'She'd stolen that car and was driving it without a licence.'

He looked at me and looked outside. 'You probably don't know that there's been snow back East. She was driving in the snow, following an eighteen wheeler with New York plates, stopping when he stopped.' He paused. 'Smart girl,' he said.

The second detective said, 'The truck driver noticed her on his tail. He's got kids himself. He got on his CB radio and called it in.'

The first detective eased his belt where it rubbed his belly and nodded. 'We had the APB out,' he said. 'Bingo.'

'That little girl is safe at home tonight,' the second one said. 'Because of you. Well done.'

He reached over and waggled my big toe through the blanket.

I was still crying a little. And I wondered exactly how safe Bethany's home was, if she'd been that desperate to get away from it. But I dragged Donald over and wrote, 'Thanks for telling me.'

They turned to go, but the second one turned back. 'I heard you sing,' he said. 'I heard you about a year ago, at a wedding.'

My cousin's band. I'd sang, 'Crazy', the Patsy Cline song. I'd sang 'Waterloo Sunset' by the Kinks.

'I was sitting with my wife and her brothers.' The second one put his hand on his heart. 'Swear to God, I turned to my wife and said you were going to be a big star one day, that one day we'd remember hearing you sing in a church hall and nobody would believe us.'

When you have a big wound, you can't bear anybody to touch it. If there had been any way I could have shut him up, I would have done.

It was like I had a hole inside me and he'd poured something into it that burned.

The first detective had left my room. I reached for Donald, thinking I could write something that would make him stop. The liquid was dropping faster out of my eyes...it didn't feel like proper crying, just...leaking.

He said, 'I'm not shitting you. My wife's brother, he said the same thing. You were terrific – just this little skinny thing and what a voice...' he trailed off and looked at me. Detectives' eyes are used to seeing pain. He didn't look away from my face. He said, 'It's a hell of a thing, honey. It's a rough break.'

Then he waggled my toe again and left. I lay down on my side again, so that the tears soaked into the pillow, instead of running down under the dressing on my neck, making it itch.

Mom's bag was by her chair, but she must have gone to get a diet coke or something. One of her soap operas was on television.

'He's got to have...' the actress playing the mother said, and the camera zoomed up close to her tearful eyes, '...an operation.' The man's face creased with a father's worry and, as he seized the actress playing the mother in his arms, minor chords crashed in an escalating scale.

Seriously? I thought. It seemed like everybody just wanted to mess with my emotions.

# Chapter Eight

## Soundtrack: 'I Shot the Sheriff' – Eric Clapton

It was about five thirty when they woke me up again. I didn't have any choice about it. They pulled back the bed curtains, and opened the blinds and curtains at the window.

'Breakfast!' one of the nurses trilled. I remembered my nurse in ICU fondly. She'd only talked like that when she was being sarcastic.

You don't just wake up after a long, drugged sleep and remember everything at once. First I remembered that I wasn't in ICU any more.

I could smell something – bacon. I opened my eyes.

I said, 'Breakfast smells good.' Or I thought I did, but all the came out was a whistling sound at my neck.

And then it all came back to me, the trach tube. The ENT ward. Nose guy. Surgery. My feet sliding off the slimy blue slippers. My voice box being completely trashed…

'Whoops!' the nurse said. 'No breakfast for you! I nearly forgot – you're in surgery this morning!'

*You've got to forget all about singing.* Kular's voice echoed in my head. *You've got to forget all about singing. You've got to forget all about singing. You've got to…*

The everlasting blood pressure cuff went on my unresisting arm. I closed my eyes, but I couldn't find the well of unconsciousness. It was too bright and busy, I had slept too long and I was too…healthy.

But being awake was too much to bear. It wasn't just the pain in my neck – the pain was inconvenient, not unbearable. The unbearable pain was in my chest, radiating out from that word, *singing*. Thinking the word 'singing' like that, to myself, on purpose, hurt worse than anything I had ever felt before in my entire life. I gasped and curled into a ball. Tears began leaking down my face.

'Hey!' the nurse said. 'You need your pain meds?' She scurried off, leaving the cuff still attached.

It came in waves, pure emotional pain. No wonder I hadn't let myself feel it yesterday, I thought. I held onto the bed as another wave came. I held onto the mattress piping, like I had when my throat had hurt so badly. I squeezed it as tightly as I could.

Each wave made me clench my face as much as my hands. The waves of total agony kept breaking out from my chest. You know how people say that their heart is breaking? This was it, this was my heart breaking. I'd never felt anything like it. Wave after wave of pain. My abs kept trying to fold me. They were kind of cramping, pulling my knees up and my head down.

The bouncy, redheaded nurse came back in with someone in green. 'I don't know what's wrong,' she said. 'She slept twelve hours and when she woke up she seemed okay. But now…'

Another wave hit and I contracted again. I couldn't stop my knees folding up to my chest. When I contracted, I couldn't keep hold of the mattress piping, so I clutched at two handfuls of sheets, instead. It was like my whole body was clenching into a fist.

The man in green leaned over to look in my face. 'Are you in pain?' he asked.

The wave eased. I shook my head, 'no', but then had a moment to feel my neck and grab my slate. I'd just written 'a little' when another wave hit.

No singing. Forever. It was so huge it was just unbearable.

I couldn't even get my head around it.

Again I folded up in a small ball, and would have sobbed if I could. As it was, I gurgled a little.

'Hey,' the guy in green said. 'Hey.' He sat down on the bed and kind of scooped me up and held me in his arms like a big, awkward egg. I was still clutching onto the bottom sheet, so it came with me. The nurse handed me a tissue, and I let go of the sheet with one hand to wipe my nose and face. She tried to hand me another one but another wave hit and I clutched another handful of sheet and curled up small in the man in green's arms.

This wave seemed a bit smaller and easier. The man stroked my hair and said, 'There, there.' I'd never heard anyone actually say, 'There, there,' before. I thought that only happened in movies.

'I'm your anaesthesiologist,' the man in green said, in a calm, friendly voice, as if teenaged girls curling up in a ball and clutching sheets on his lap was something that happened to him all the time. Anaesthesiologists are the people who put you to sleep during operations and keep you alive while you're having them.

Another wave hit, but this time, I didn't have to curl up. I just hurt and the tears spurted out again. He leaned over with me still on his lap and got the box of tissues and I actually managed to let go of my sheets to use one.

'Coco,' the nurse said. 'Can you tell us what's wrong?'

She held my slate for me and I wrote. 'I will never sing again.' Something about seeing the words there stopped the waves. Now the pain sat like a huge stone on my chest. I could hardly breathe.

'Were you a singer?' the anaesthesiologist asked.

To my surprise, the nurse answered. 'Yes,' she said. 'Her mom says she had quite a future planned. She was just about to sing her first solo on television. She's sung professionally already.'

Yeah, I thought to myself. That's all really true. No wonder it hurts so bad.

The anaesthesiologist put me back on the bed – somehow, while the nurse was talking to me, holding my slate and handing me tissues, she had somehow also smoothed the sheet back down, tucked it in, and made the bedding reasonable. Even right then, feeling so terrible, I couldn't help notice how impressive that was.

'Get her some pain meds,' he said. 'You'll have to inject them. I'll be right back.' He looked at me. 'I'm coming right back,' he said. 'Hold on.'

Everyone disappeared for a moment. There was a little sound on my table, and it was my breakfast tray. I touched the plate with one finger. It was still warm. Everything, I thought, changes so fast.

The nurse came back with a bottle and a syringe. She said, 'This really stings, but you'll feel better. In your neck, I mean.' She smiled. 'Roll over and show me your butt.'

She was right about the stinging, but it wasn't bad. She was right about the feeling better, too. Suddenly, I felt like I could control myself again. I took a deep breath and wrote, 'I'm sorry to cry like that.'

For some reason, this made *her* cry. 'Oh, honey,' she said, 'for goodness sakes, you go ahead and cry.'

Typically, once I'd been given permission, I didn't want to do it anymore.

Just then, the anaesthesiologist came back, with another guy in green.

'Doctor Morris!' the nurse said. 'Aren't you supposed to be in surgery?'

'It's okay,' he said. 'It's only that abnormal tonsillectomy. Kular's got it covered.' He sat down on my bed and took my hand. His was soft and white. He said, 'Do you want to talk about your voice?'

I got my slate. 'Dr G said to forget about singing,' I wrote. Without any warning, another wave broke out of my heart. I grimaced, trying to hold it in, but my eyes spilled over.

He looked at the magic slate for a while, nodding. 'We're going to do our best to give you some kind of a voice,' he said softly. He put down my slate and took my shoulder in his hand. 'But it won't be the same voice.' The wave hit and he helped me keep upright, as if he knew I was fighting curling up. At first, I thought it was an accident, but then he pushed my shoulder hard into the pillow with his hand.

He knew exactly what he was doing and what my abs and legs wanted to do. He had felt it himself? Seen it before?

And suddenly, I knew. Vietnam. Doctor Morris and Bob, the anaesthesiologist, too. It was something about the way they stood in their surgical scrubs, the way they acted together, the way they...understood what someone was going through who had just lost part of their body – part of their life.

They were the right age. It would have been a free medical education. And it would have been...horrible.

I don't know how much of my thoughts showed in my face. But behind his clean-as-air glasses, Doctor Morris' eyes softened and darkened, as if he had stopped hiding their depths from me. He said, 'Your voice box was almost completely destroyed,' in a clear, factual tone. 'I wish we knew how to make it just like it was before, but we don't.' He looked at me again, and I looked back. Shit happens, his face was saying. So much shit just happens, and we have to deal with it.

He said, 'We're in this together, though, okay? My job is to give you the best life I can. Your job will be to figure out what to do with it.'

These words seemed to go directly into the broken place in my chest. They didn't heal the break, not in any way. But they put a little fence around it, a little boundary, that let me know exactly how much of myself was lost forever. A lot. But maybe not everything.

'Okay?' he asked, as though we were making a deal. I looked again through his clean glasses to his eyes and the dark places behind them. I didn't want to give this man any more pain to carry. So, I nodded to Doctor Morris, and decided I would carry my pain myself.

He took his hand away from my shoulder and asked for a

handshake on our deal. And then he was gone. For someone so stocky, he could move really quickly.

'And no more crying,' Bob, the anaesthesiologist said. 'Or we'll have swelling right where we don't want it.' He started to explain the surgery to me as the nurse got my blood pressure reading, took my breakfast tray away and went to wake up her other patients.

Getting ready for surgery took the whole morning. Lord knows what time they woke up the poor abnormal tonsillectomy. He might have had to just stay up all night.

I had a shower because there was no way I was going to meet a bunch of new people un-groomed. And then I had to take off all my makeup again, because it was against the rules to wear makeup. Bob, my anaesthesiologist, might think I looked rosy and oxygenated because of my blusher and lip-gloss, while I really could be dying.

I was supposed to take out my earrings, but I'd just had my ears pierced and was worried that the holes would close up so, after a few phone calls, we compromised on taping over them. We then did the same with the ring Dad had given me for my thirteenth birthday, too.

Then they wanted me to take off my toenail polish, but I explained that my toenails looked totally grody without polish, all yellow and thick and they let me keep it on. I hadn't varnished my fingernails, so that was all right. I got an awful cap to wear and had to take off my new nightgown and put on a hospital gown again, but my feet were freezing, so they let me wear socks.

I was fully aware that I was getting away with quite a lot.

Bob came back and said he was going to give me a shot of something that would make me sleepy.

I felt a prick and then something cold in my buttock. Then all my emotional pain was gone...not just reserved, but wiped out completely. Life was suddenly utter bliss.

The porter laughed. 'She likes that,' he said.

Oh, I did like that, whatever it was. We took off for OR in a candyfloss world of warmth and happiness.

And then my mother was flying down the hall on her platform boots, her beige trench coat flapping open. Her red wig was the only thing not moving, the fringe unnaturally stiff. She had shopping bags.

'Where are you going?' she asked me. 'It's only seven-fifteen!'

The porter answered. He said, 'They take 'em down early, ma'am.'

I liked the porter. He was lovely. He answered for me when I couldn't. Everyone was so *nice* in the hospital, I thought. Lovely, lovely hospital.

My mother looked so worried that I thought it was a little funny. I giggled, making my trach whistle and that made me giggle more.

'I got you stuff,' my mother said, as she trotted along beside the gurney. 'I got books, and Coke and Pringles and Onion Dip.' She held up the familiar red tube of crisps.

The porter said, 'I'm afraid you can't come any further with us.'

I motioned to the Pringles and pointed to my stomach. '*My* Pringles,' I mouthed.

'I won't eat any,' my mother promised.

I waved. Bye bye, Mommy. I'm going now... Mommy's worried face went away and we went down some long halls. I was glad I had my socks. It was cold, just like I'd remembered.

I was in a hallway on my own for a moment, but I played with my hands. They seemed to go away when I held them under my chin, but they were really there, all along. I found this terribly amusing.

It was a small, bright room. Lots of faces came to bend over the gurney. Doctor Kular, Doctor Morris, Bob the anaesthesiologist. The OR nurse introduced herself. I waved weakly.

I was awake enough to protest getting another IV but I couldn't get out of that one.

'Okay,' Bob said. 'You're going to feel something cold going into your hand.'

And I did. It was cold but it also burned slightly.

'Now,' he said. 'I want you to count from one to ten out loud...just make the shapes with your mouth.'

Okay, I thought. One...um...Two. This was actually pretty hard to do. Uh...what was the next one? Three. And... ummmmm. Foooooouuuuuuurrrrr.

And then everything hurt. Someone had hit my head to wake me up. Maybe the same person who put all the broken glass in my throat. And God, I wanted water. I pushed as hard as I could to open my eyes but the effort was too much. I slid back down into unconsciousness.

It was later. I could tell it was later, and when I opened my eyes and again, everything hurt. Hurt, hurt, hurt. So, so bad. Ow. It was all I could think. Ow, ow, ow.

A face appeared over me. 'Take it slow,' she said. 'You can go back to sleep for a while if you want. The operation is over and you're in recovery.'

Sleep? No way...everything hurt so, so bad. Way too bad to sleep.

'Have you got any pain?' she asked.

I nodded energetically and nearly passed out from the pain this caused in my neck. It hurt so bad that I tried to scream. Two things happened from this; my trach tube whistled and I hurt a bit more. Hurt *more*. Ow, ow, ow. Ow, ow, ow.

'Oh, you really are hurting, aren't you,' she said. 'I'll be right back.'

Four hundred and fifty years later she arrived. 'This might burn a little,' she said. My arm became briefly on fire. And down I went again.

The third time I woke up, Doctor Morris was shaking me.

'Hey, lazybones,' he said. 'We need recovery for sick people. You can't stay here all day.'

This time I was kind of ready for the pain, but the depth and spread of it still came as a shock.

'Let's get her sitting up a bit,' he said and he and the nurse ratcheted up the end of my gurney. My head immediately felt a bit better and now I could see Doctor Kular was with us.

'Doctor Kular did a wonderful job,' Doctor Morris said. 'But we won't know how much articulacy you'll have for a while. You have the silicone stent inside your larynx, and to keep it in place, we've run wires through your neck. There are buttons on the ends of the wires. That's going to be a bit sore for a while. Around Valentine's Day, we'll take it all out again and see what we've got.'

Through all of this, Doctor Kular stood on one foot and then the other. He looked at my face once or twice, but when I made eye contact with him, he looked away. Rather absent-mindedly, he rested his hand on my foot. The blankets were too little for tall people, they were always coming undone, and my feet were freezing. In fact, *I* was freezing. I just hadn't realised it before with all the other stuff going on.

Kular frowned, touched my foot again and rooted around in the gurney between my legs to find my socks, which he put on my feet. Then he flipped the blanket back down.

It all only took a second or two. But something about it bothered me.

I looked at Doctor Morris and nodded my head a tiny bit. I got it. I understood what he had said. He patted my hand and they went over to somebody else, on the other side of the room, somebody rather deaf because they had to shout.

Kular hadn't asked if I wanted my socks on. He hadn't asked permission to feel between my knees. He was just casually in charge of my body, and looking after it was something he thought he should do.

And I didn't know how I felt about that, except that my feet were warming up and they'd been cold before.

# Chapter Nine

**Soundtrack: 'You Ain't Seen Nothin' Yet' – Bachman Turner Overdrive**

I vomited.

Everything.

For days.

I wouldn't even try to get up. I wet the bed and lay in it all night.

Mom was horrified by my attitude. When she tried to lecture me, I gathered the strength to write, 'Get lost,' on my magic slate. Well.

From the way everyone reacted, it was like I'd punched her. Mom started to shake, cry and totally melt down. And all the hospital people came and cuddled her, looking at the horrible thing I'd written and shooting me evil looks.

One of the nurses said, 'It's the drugs,' as if I wasn't right there. 'It makes some of them really grumpy.'

'She's not just grumpy,' Mom said. 'She's possessed.'

One older nurse was in the middle of mopping up more vomit from my chest, and took my part. 'Well, she *is* a teenager, Mrs DuLac. And she's dealing with quite a lot.'

'She hurt my feelings. On *purpose*.'

Mom would never shut up about this, I knew. She would whine about it *forever*. I wrote, 'I. Am. Sorry.' on my magic slate and prepared to have my dressing changed again, because it was soaked in gastric juices and that was not good for the wound.

Ages went by like this. And then, one morning, I was all right again. I mean, my neck still really hurt and I now had not only the lovely turquoise tube but a huge crusty ladder-shaped wound and four turquoise buttons coming out of my neck on wires, and I *really* needed a shower and still had an IV because I couldn't face any more hospital food, which was even worse coming up than it had been going down, and my mom and dad were still split up and we were still broke and everything.

But I felt...okay.

Dad had come by with Nina, who wasn't nearly as ugly as she'd looked in the photograph. My grandparents had been in, both sets. I vaguely remembered it all.

It was...dawn, or close to it, and my bed was a tangled mess. I got up and wheeled my IV stand into the bathroom. I had a wee and washed myself all over with a flannel.

Then I came back, turned on the light and tidied up my bed. The sheets were dry, thank God, just rumpled. There were literally hundreds of cards behind my bed. There were flowers and teddy bears. There was a huge homemade poster from the drama club at school that my mother had taped to the wall. I looked inside a few of the smaller cards. Kim was sending one every day.

The card I looked at said, 'This is Thursday's card. I hear the surgery went really well and that you are being very brave!!!' Three hearts and a smiley followed the forest of exclamation marks.

I peeked inside another few to find Wednesday and Tuesday's card. Tuesday's card said, 'You're out of ICU and I can send you cards!!!!!!!!!!!!'

I wandered down to the bottom of my bed and checked my chart. This was Friday morning. Kim and I had been on our way to a Monday morning play rehearsal.

I flipped back, back through all the blood pressure readings and temperatures. No, that was right. I'd only been in here for five days.

Five days?

ICU, the nice nurse, moving to ENT, my surgery, all the vomiting...my dad's visits...the police and all that stuff about

Bethany...it had only been *five days*?

I sank down onto my visitor's chair and immediately jumped back up because I'd forgotten I was still wearing a hospital gown and my bare bottom had touched the vinyl. Eurgh.

Honestly. It felt more like a month. Five *days*? I couldn't get my head around it. Then some of the times I thought I'd slept all night had just been a few hours...or maybe even minutes... *Five days?*

Kim had gone back to school the next day. Her nose and her chest would have been really sore and she would have looked all... For the first time, I wondered how she'd been, walking around the halls like that.

Vulnerable. You really didn't want to be vulnerable in the halls of Burner High. Kim *hated* to stand out too much. That was one of the problems she had with me. On the other hand, I kind of refused to be vulnerable...

On my first day at Burner, I was in the line for lunch, snaking drearily through the halls. You could hear the roar of teenagers from the lunch hall, punctuated regularly by a weedy adult voice asking everyone to 'settle down.' Right at the door was a big cooler for milk, and we were all supposed to get a carton on our way to the lunch counter. Just as I came level with the milk cooler, the whole place became deathly silent.

I looked up, and everyone was looking at me.

Every single kid in the whole, huge lunchroom was staring at me. I looked at Kim, and Kim, terrified, gave a tiny shrug that let me know she couldn't see anything wrong with me without letting everyone else know that she was with me.

Then the oinking started. Very softly at first, and building to a crescendo. Everyone was making pig noises at me.

And that was thanks, of course, to Dad. The summer before I started high school, in the middle of the 1970s, my father had taken over Juvenile Narcotics. I hadn't really needed help to be desperately unpopular, but Dad had provided it anyway. Thanks so much, Dad.

The weedy voice told everyone to 'settle down' again, I got my lunch and we all hoped they'd forget about it.

But it happened again the next day. Deathly silence. Staring. Pig noises.

Kim had started leaving a significant gap between us as we came in the door, and really, who could blame her? She still sat with me, though. All the theatre kids thought it was 'really unfair' and that 'I couldn't help what my dad did.' So, I didn't have to sit on my own, or anything, I just had to face the whole school on my own, every lunchtime.

The vice-principal took me to one side that afternoon. 'We think they'll get tired of doing it,' he said. 'If we make a big deal about it, it could get worse for you.' So, only two days into my secondary education, I knew the staff at Burner were totally ineffectual.

But that night, in bed, I woke up with an idea.

My third lunchtime at Burner High, I walked gingerly down the corridor in the lunch line and Kim begged me not to do whatever it was I was planning. She wasn't stupid, she knew I was wearing tap shoes, and she knew *me*.

I didn't really listen, because I was concentrating. I had to time this perfectly. There was a window for my plan to work, and I had to hit that window hard.

And I did. Just as the entire cafeteria fell silent, I spread open my arms, stepped forward with a broad grin and sang the first few lines of 'Tea for Two' before breaking into a nifty little tap shuffle change. I kept dancing through the entire verse and then did a very loud, very perky tappy-tappy-ticky-ticky spin-spin-spin move.

Their mouths were hanging open and one poor boy's spaghetti dripped off the tray in his sagging hand.

I sang the chorus and tapped *even louder* for the ending.

Tickedy, tickedy, tickedy, tickedy tap-tap-tap – big finish. Jazz hands. Aaaaand bow.

There was a smattering of involuntary applause and then, collectively, the population of Burner High decided to ignore me. I never had anyone stare at me entering the lunch hall again. In fact, usually, if anyone's eyes rested on me for a moment, they looked hurriedly away, for fear I'd burst into song again.

Kim had been utterly horrified and grudgingly admiring, at the same time. The vice-principal, when he saw me in the hall, raised his eyebrows and gave me a rueful smile.

But Kim wasn't tough in the same kind of way. When the jerks asked her if she'd been trying to kill me or what kind of car her mother drove or if her boobs needed any massaging to get better, she'd just try and shrink into herself and disappear.

What, I wondered for the five hundredth time, was wrong with people, anyway? Why couldn't they just put their energy into doing the best they could with their lives? Why did they have to mess with other people all the time, trying to bring them down? Wasn't there enough shit in the world without people making it worse?

I didn't get it. I just didn't get it.

On one of my first days at Burner, an older boy, on the football team, had come up to me and pointed out another boy. He'd said, 'Can you ask him how his mom is? She's been sick…but if I ask, I'll look like a wuss.'

I wasn't stupid – I had lots of boy cousins and could kind of smell a setup, but the football player had said, 'He's my neighbour,' and…he'd convinced me.

I had gone over to the other boy and asked. I'd said, 'He wants to know how your mom is doing,' and nodded at the football player.

The boy's face had crumpled with pain and anger. 'She's dead. He knows she died. He does this to me every day.' He'd pushed me aside and run into the boy's restroom and I...

...I looked at the football player laughing with his mates and I just did not get it. I did not see how it could be funny, to hurt someone like that and to make someone like me feel the pain of doing it. I just did not get it.

Kim would have been dealing with this kind of crap all week. No wonder she had so many exclamation marks...

There was a stack of books. I pulled *Little Women* off the top and then I saw the can of Pringles behind it.

Pringles used to come with metal top that opened with a ring pull like a premium brand of beans. I had to clamp the canister between my thighs to pull the metal open, because I was so weak. I nearly cut my finger. But I managed. I put a stack on my table.

I looked at them for a while and then poured a glass of water.

Cautiously, I put a Pringle in my mouth and started to crunch it. I let it get soggy and dissolved. And then I swallowed it. I took a small sip of water. So far, so good. I could even taste it, a bit. I could taste the saltiness.

By the time Jo had ruined Meg's glove, the whole stack had gone.

I braced myself. But I didn't feel sick at all. I wanted to keep those Pringles. My body wanted to keep some food. My arms were looking like sticks. Some nice, fat Pringles were a good thing. I shook out another stack onto my table.

The night nurse, attracted by my light, came to see what was going on. She smiled hugely when she did. She peered in the can. 'Well done!' she said. 'Feeling sick?'

By now I knew not to nod or shake my head. The wires bit into my neck. I shook my finger, no.

'Your mom left some dip in our fridge. You want it?'

I shook my finger, yes.

She brought that and a Coke with a glass of ice and a straw. 'Your mom said this was your favourite meal,' she said, laughing. 'We tell them to bring in the patient's favourite meal if they're taking a long surgery like you did. Most of them bring in fried chicken or pot roast we can microwave. She brought in Pringles and onion dip.' The nurse laughed. 'Your mom,' she said, smiling, 'is quite a character.'

I rolled my eyes. I wrote, 'Tell me about it,' on Donald.

I used to make sandwiches with Pringles and onion dip. I'd hold one concave and then roll the next one in the dip and put in on top and then the next one and the next one and the next one until it all looked too good and then I'd lick off any bits oozing out, crunch the whole thing into my mouth and wash it down with Coke.

And with care, I did this.

That first lick of onion dip was amazing. The flavours were strong enough for me to taste, and that was like a miracle. It was like in the Wizard of Oz, when Kansas is all in black and white but then Dorothy flies her house in the tornado to Oz and opens the door to a world in colour. My sense of taste, with the hospital food, had been on the greyscale, but suddenly it went into full Technicolor.

The taste and texture of a tiny bit of the onion as it crunched between my teeth! The sour cream rich on my tongue! The garlic and chives were pungent enough to waft up the back of my throat and inform my nose I was eating something delicious. And that was just the first lick... I opened my jaws and crunched into paradise.

I ate a whole tube of Pringles and half a carton of onion dip and drank a small glass bottle of Coke.

I burped but I didn't get sick. I went back to sleep like a rattlesnake with a tummy full of mouse and when I woke up again, they took out my IV.

They called mom and told her. She came in carrying an Egg McMuffin and an orange juice. I wolfed it down. Lunch was a Wendy's burger with fries. She had an extra large pizza delivered before she left, and by the morning I'd eaten it all.

That was it. I was on the junk food diet.

I had a thought the next morning. If I hadn't had such horrible taste in food, I wouldn't have wanted an Icee at seven in the morning and we wouldn't have crashed. Or if I hadn't been so deceitful and had gone with Bethany, like I'd said I would. Or if I'd had my mom drive me to school, instead of wanting every single second of Kim's attention I could get, or if I'd only had one ballet class a week, instead of being selfish and greedy and wanting more…

But thinking that way made my head hurt. After a moment, I decided that thinking all those 'if onlys' and 'what ifs' might make me go properly crazy. I told myself, 'If I start thinking like that, I will never stop thinking like that and I will literally go insane.'

And so I stopped.

# Chapter Ten

## Soundtrack: 'Help Me' – Joni Mitchell

I'd had another card from Kim that afternoon and that morning, after I'd had a shower and done my makeup and hair, I changed into one of my older, shorter and more casual nightgowns-with-matching-panties and settled down at my desk with the little notebook I'd fought to keep and a pen. I was going to write Kim back. It was only polite.

> *Dear Kim*
> *Thank you for all the cards. It's nice to hear from you.*

That was easy.

> *What did you get on the French test? I hope all your classes are going well. How is the play coming along?*

After that last sentence, I had to breathe really deeply for a few moments. Writing that hurt like getting an arterial blood gas taken, and when they do that, they stick a five-inch needle through your groin. I didn't really want to know about the play. I wanted to pretend that everything to do with theatre, film and…most of all…music…just didn't exist.

I got up and wandered over to look out my window at the window on the other side. It looked grey outside.

> *It's weird being in here. I can never tell what the weather is doing.*
> *I've stayed on the ENT ward, so everyone else is old. I sleep so much that I thought I'd been here for months!*

I thought about everything that had happened to me since I'd come into the hospital and how little of it would mean anything to Kim.

*Is Bethany back at school yet?*

I'd asked mom about when I'd have to go back to school. She'd said, 'Not for a long time. Don't worry about it.'

*God knows when I'll be back. I don't think I can go back like this, so...*

I tried to think of something to say, something actually interesting, something that made me attractive as a friend.

*I'm reading a lot and I've lost so much weight that they're letting me eat all the junk food I want. Last night, I had a huuuuuuuge pizza all to myself.*

That was the best I could do. It was rubbish, I knew.

*Please tell Bobby thank you for picking us up that morning. Write me all the gossip.*

That was too weird. I'd never really listened when she tried to tell me the gossip before...I'd never actually taken any notice of the ins and outs of school social life when I was right there in the actual school. And now I wanted her to *write* it to me? I didn't, really. I just wanted her to think, when something happened at school, 'Oooooh, I must remember to write that to Coco.' I just wanted to somehow be there with her, walking the halls and going to the pep club rallies and sitting at the lunch table with the other nerds...I didn't want to fade completely away from her mind. I wanted to make some Coco-shaped space at Burner High that I could then step into, when I went back.

What I wanted to write was, 'Don't leave me. Don't forget me. I love you.'

But what I said was: *How are your boobs and nose? XXXXX Coco*

I went out to the nurses' station and they gave me an envelope and let me put it into the big mailbag at the end of the corridor.

There was a phone in my room, heavy and old, with a short cord. I looked at it when I went back. I could ask Kim to call me at a certain time and she could talk to me. I just wouldn't be able to talk back.

Now, if the situations were reversed, that would have worked. But I couldn't imagine Kim talking for a whole minute, just talking, with nobody asking questions or making the right noises to keep her going.

After I'd nibbled on some bacon and forgotten and tried to drink orange juice again (man, was it painfully acidic without the orange flavour – it was like drinking battery acid), just as I was getting bored, a girl a little older than me walked into my room, pushing a little trolley.

She had library books, a xeroxed TV schedule and things for sale – candy and toiletries and magazines. I rummaged around in my drawer for my purse and bought chocolate and then looked at the books.

'Sorry,' she said. 'There's not much current stuff.'

There were about five hundred Georgette Heyer novels, with soulful looking damsels and strapping Regency bucks on the covers. They looked dreadful, but in desperation, I picked one up.

'When do you come back?' I wrote on Donald.

'We come around twice a week,' she answered. I picked up two more of the Georgette Heyer novels and got a TV schedule – they were free.

When mom arrived, I was already deeply involved in *Friday's Child*. The wild young Lord Sherringham had married an impoverished girl he'd known all his life, just so he could get his hands on his inheritance. Would he realise that he actually loved her and that they could be happy before he gambled away his fortune?

Written down like that, it looks absurd, and it was, but it was also…really, really, really *good*. The dialogue was amazing and the characters were so…funny…and…real…and when mom started talking to me seriously, I wanted her to shut up so that I could get back to my book.

'…so I told him, yes, I would come back to work.' Mom paused and looked at me speculatively from under the heavy fringe of her auburn wig. I was meant to react, I suddenly realised, but I didn't know how I felt about mom going back to work.

Part of it was that I hadn't been listening, so I'd probably missed some of the finer points she'd made, but part of it was that I didn't know how much I minded, if mom left me alone in the hospital all day.

I looked down at my finger, about a quarter along in my book, and the other two fat books waiting on the corner. I thought about the *I Dream of Jeannie* and *Bewitched* reruns I'd spotted on Channel 41's schedule. And then I put down my book and grabbed Donald.

'Do it,' I said. 'It would be good for you.'

The relief on her face would have been worth it, even without the *I Dream of Jeannie*.

So that was my new life. I saw mom every morning. Then she'd go off to work and I'd…I'd chill.

I was supposed to be walking the wards. I'd been given stretching exercises and a route I was supposed to walk twice a day. The stretching exercises were useless, though, they didn't stretch me at all. Even with a solid week of lying still, my ballet training made them totally easy. If Madam had come into the hospital, she would have been horrified by how much extension I'd lost, but the Physio staff were very impressed with how hard they thought I'd been working – which was really not at all. I only stretched when I had a cramp.

As for walking the wards, forget it. Not only did the whole blue tube and four blue buttons thing make me feel like a freak, but I had zero motivation.

After mom left, I'd take some pain meds and have a nap. When I woke up, I'd ring for chip and dip and cola and kick back for some quality TV viewing, ringing for more meds when I got bored and reading myself back to sleep, only waking up when mom returned with my dinner.

Doctor Kular started to frown over my charts. 'Your recovery has slowed down,' he kept saying. I kept shrugging. I didn't care about my recovery. I cared that I was going to miss the beginning of a British war movie that was about to start on Channel 41.

One afternoon, I'd just brushed my teeth after my snack and was wondering whether to start another book or have some pain medication when I saw something bright go by my door. I put on my slippers, got Donald and peeked out into the hall.

It was a Mylar balloon. They were new at the time, and this was only the third or fourth one I'd ever seen. It was shiny and danced on a red fabric ribbon. My friend Mandy was holding the other end.

There were six of my friends in the corridor and they looked really small, standing by the nurses' desk. It had been ages since I'd seen another young person.

I ducked back into my room and frantically brushed my teeth and put on lip-gloss before I got into bed. I'd already thrown my snack things away, but I got the crumbs off my desk and put my feet under the blankets, smoothing them over my knees and making sure my hair wasn't doing anything weird.

One of the kids who had come to see me was Rob Savage.

I was insane for Rob Savage. It was his forearms, and his chiselled jaw and his totally out of control curly blonde hair. Not to mention his clear green eyes.

A week before the accident, I'd had an audition to be his girlfriend.

That's how it felt, anyway. There were three of us in the running, he'd said, and he wanted to go on a date with me to see if I was the one. He took me to Worlds of Fun.

At the end of summer, a theme park is a bittersweet place. We both had season tickets, and some money for snacks. His father drove us and on the way, we chatted merrily about which rides we'd go on first and which were the best. We both liked roller-coasters.

I considered acting really frightened on some of the rides, so that he'd hold my hand, but rejected it as a cheap trick.

Then it got dark. We strolled along with cherry sodas in the lamplight, towards the little cars that went through tight turns in the shrubbery. Other couples were going the same way, because at night, everyone would drive their little car into a turn and stop and kiss.

I thought if Rob didn't kiss me soon, I might actually die.

My heart beat in my ears. He reached for my hand, and I quivered all the way up my spine. I wanted to pull him closer. I wanted, really, to drag him to the nearest bench and kiss him until he couldn't breathe. It was absolute hell being ladylike and waiting.

He was saying something. I tried to concentrate, not on his sexy, slightly thick lips or his amazing cheekbones and eyes, but on his actual words.

I found this very difficult.

He was talking about his future. He was talking about the farm he was going to inherit from his uncle and how he worked there every summer and went out there most weekends to help out.

Which must have been how he got his beautiful forearms. Honestly, they looked like they were carved out of wood...the lines were so flat and the muscle so lean...

I realised I had once again failed to listen, and made a heroic effort to concentrate.

We slowed right down and he looked deeply into my eyes. He said, 'That's what I want more than anything in the world. I want to make the farm a success and keep the land in the family.'

I was clearly called upon to speak at this point. I looked deeply back into his gorgeous green eyes. I said, 'That's wonderful.' And I meant it. I thought it was great. Everyone should have something that means that much to them.

He put his arm around me then, and led me to the queue for the cars...well where the queue would have been if it wasn't so late in the season and the day. We walked right onto one of the little cars and he pulled me close, automatically taking the wheel himself without discussion.

As we got over the stupid bit, with the little fake Eifel Tower, he asked me, 'And what do you want to do?'

I said, 'I want to sing...and act, and dance.' My leg was touching his leg.

He put his arm around me and I leant into him, making my lips available. We got to a turn and he stopped and kissed me.

I became complete mush. I was butterscotch sauce. I was a chocolate bar, left in the sun. I was sweet, hot and absolutely formless.

Then he drove a bit more. It was utterly blissful. I leaned my head on his shoulder as we turned two or three times, going that little bit further so that we could make out a little bit longer before someone disturbed us.

Rob put his arms around me and I *inhaled* him. When the car behind us finally arrived, he had a dazed expression that I found deeply satisfying.

'Um,' he said, wiping his hand across his forehead, as he drove a few more turns at speed. 'You want to sing...professionally?'

I considered licking the side of his neck, but thought that might be too forward. I settled for wrapping my arms around one of his. He could steer with one. His hand came to rest on my knee, setting me on fire in the panty area.

We stopped. 'Yes,' I answered, between kisses. 'I want to sing professionally.'

He stopped kissing me and looked at me seriously again. 'What about family?' he asked.

'What about them?' I said, keeping it short, because my tongue had better things to do.

'No.' He disentangled himself and I felt a sudden chill where he'd been pressing against me. 'I mean,' he explained, 'what about starting a family?'

I was fourteen years old. He was fifteen. I blinked at him. 'Uhhhhhh,' I said. 'I don't think I've thought that far ahead.'

He nodded, like this wasn't exactly news to him. 'I want to have lots of children,' he said. He started driving again.

I wanted him to kiss me some more, so I lied. 'Oh,' I said. 'So do I.' I didn't really mind children; some of my little cousins were okay.

He looked at me again. 'How's that going to work? Won't you be on the road and stuff?'

I still wanted to kiss him, but I couldn't let this go. 'I could take them with me,' I said. 'Carly Simon has kids.'

He snorted. 'She doesn't sound like much of a mother to me,' he said, as if he didn't even know who Carly Simon *was*. That alone should have made me find him repulsive. That, plus the male chauvinist pigdom he was displaying.

But it didn't. I still wanted him to touch me again, kiss me again. But even in my butterscotch sauce mindless haze, I could tell this wasn't going to happen, that I was, somehow, losing him because I couldn't hide my feminism.

I let my long brown leg trail over and rest against his jeans, hoping he would change the subject.

'And what happens when they need to go to school?'

He was driving through the course as quickly as the little lawnmower engine would let him and discussing the childcare issues of professional singers. This was not going the way I'd hoped. I pushed away, over against the window. 'I suppose, *if* I become a professional singer, and *when* I have children, I'll figure something out,' I said.

He shook his head. 'Figure something out?' he snorted. 'You're crazy.'

It wasn't the first time someone had said that to me. At the time, I thought he meant that I was crazy for wanting to sing for a living. That I was crazy for thinking I was good enough.

And that was fair enough. I knew it *was* a little crazy. It was still going to happen, though.

I thought, at some point in the year, I would sing so well that he might believe me. Maybe then he would like me again.

We got to the end of the ride, and walked back up the hill to the entrance. We still had time to walk behind the Tivoli Theatre, where there were benches in the bushes, but I knew that wasn't going to happen.

I had failed my audition.

But here he was, with all my best friends, coming to see me in the hospital. Perhaps I'd become more interesting, or perhaps I'd been forgiven for having my own ideas about life.

If Rob Savage wasn't freaked out by my hardware, I might still have a chance with him...

# Chapter Eleven

**Soundtrack: 'Embrace Me, You Child' – Carly Simon**

My friends came into my room, laughing and chatting. Then they saw me, and everyone got quiet, all at once. Mandy let go of the balloon and it went up to bump on the ceiling.

Bobby got it down, and handed it to me with a fixed smile. I tied the balloon to my bed.

Jack Clary's eyes looked terribly sad, right away. The second I finished tying the balloon, he took my hand and squeezed it.

I got Donald and wrote, 'Hi, guys!' I pointed to Kim and waved her over for a hug. She was shaking and let go of me super-quick, like she'd only hugged me because she had to.

Rob went behind my bed on the other side and leaned against it. I could feel the hip of his jean against my shoulder and I ran my hand down his leg, patting it hello.

Nobody noticed that I'd groped Rob's leg. Nobody was noticing anything I did. They were all staring at my neck.

Karla, always a sensitive girl, started to sniff and then to sob. Shanice comforted her. Shanice's cousin was Mandy, and Mandy looked at Karla sobbing on Shanice, turned to me and scowled.

'They said you were *better*,' Mandy said accusingly, as if I was pulling one of my attention-getting stunts and hurting Karla's feelings on purpose.

I wrote on Donald. 'I *am* better,' I said.

She waved her hand up and down me. 'Clearly,' she said, 'you are not.'

I shrugged. 'I was worse,' I wrote.

Mandy looked sceptical. Then Kim started to cry, too. Bobby pulled her face into his shoulder and patted the back of her head.

We didn't really have a word for being gay back then. The hurtful terms were 'queer', 'homo' and 'fag'. None of us wanted to call Bobby any of those, even in our minds, though he got called them a hundred times a day at school. And, perhaps because we were so geeky and actually having sex with *anyone* seemed very theoretical, we didn't care about each other's sexual orientation. So I hadn't thought much about it before.

But when I saw Bobby taking care of Kim, something about his posture suddenly made me see something. Bobby wasn't cold. He was gay.

It was seeing him every day that had hidden it. Now that I hadn't seen him for a while, his whole being kind of screamed it at me. I think I would have actually said, 'Aha!' if I could have talked.

Jack had gone to lean on the other side of my bed. I had Rob Savage on one side and Jack Clary on the other and had finally understood why Bobby hadn't enjoyed kissing me.

My day was turning out to be fantastic.

Jack Clary was lean, brown and devastatingly cool. I loved him and he loved me, but not like that. I mean, we made out, all the time...Jack was the Baptist preacher's son and sold dope in a small, friendly way, sneaking out of the house and doing the rounds of the older teen hangouts.

Sometimes he'd come and get me in his Volkswagen Karmengia and we'd go out to the lake and get high and fool around...but it wasn't serious. He always had a proper girlfriend and I had very clear limits. No hands inside clothing. Nothing unzipped or unbuckled on his part.

It wasn't like our relationship was going anywhere. But we liked it just where it was.

Jack and I told each other everything, stuff nobody else wanted to hear. We might not talk to each other for a month and then we'd stay up all night together, our parents thinking we were somewhere else, like home in bed. I once made it back into my room just as my mother came in to wake me up...she'd been really impressed that I was already dressed...

Then we'd be in school a day or so later and walk past each other and he'd ask me to give him five and walk on, like he barely knew me.

Mandy could often make me feel like a total dweeb. But with Jack and Rob flanking me, nothing could really hurt me. 'But you're still in *bed*!' she said. 'It's been over a *week*! And your letter sounded fine!'

I couldn't tell Mandy that I'd died or how sick I'd been in Intensive Care or anything like that. Talking about that stuff would make Kim feel terrible. So I wrote, 'I *do* feel a lot better.' I erased Donald, because this hadn't impressed Mandy much and wrote, 'I should be able to talk in February.'

When she nodded, Mandy's dark blonde hair bounced attractively on her shoulders. 'And when can you sing again?'

I looked at Kim, and she looked at me. I could see she knew and that she was dreading everyone else knowing. It was going to be horrible for her. Bobby was standing by, though, and it was as good a time as any.

'I won't,' I wrote.

Mandy scowled again. 'What do you mean you won't?'

I erased Donald. 'My voice box was crushed,' I wrote on Donald. Mandy read it out and everyone winced.

I erased Donald and just got it over with. 'I'm not going to be able to sing anymore.' Mandy read this out, slowly, word by word, a little furrow between her expressive eyes. Then she reached out for Donald and erased him herself.

Bobby's face went white under his tan.

Mandy plonked herself right down on the bed, as if her legs had given way. She said, 'I'm so sorry, Coco.' She always said the exact right thing. She was the prettiest of us all, and the most popular, too. (She would have been even more popular if she'd stopped hanging out with us, but she hadn't.) Mandy was actually on the cheerleading squad. She reached out her hand and took mine into her own warm, soft grasp.

Then everybody kind of cuddled up to me. Rob and Jack sat on either side of my pillow. Shanice and Karla crawled onto the bottom of the bed and held onto my feet. Bobby and Kim came around the other side to sit, and Bobby laid his hand on my thigh.

We all sat there for a second.

Then I wrote, 'How is Bethany?' on Donald and showed it to Bobby. He rolled his eyes.

'She has totally lost the plot,' he said. 'She came back to school and wouldn't speak to anybody. Not even the *teachers*.'

Karla sniffed again but managed to say, 'Her whole family has to go to a psychiatrist. Together.'

Bobby rolled his eyes. 'She'll only wear this one black turtleneck. She washes it every night.'

I wrote, 'Does she still play for rehearsals?'

He rolled his eyes again. 'Yeah, but she's so *weird*. I went over and talked to her. I was like, "Sooooo, how's it going?" and she was completely freaky. She was like, "Why are you talking to me? Do you want to tell everyone what I said?" And I was like, "No, I've been your friend since the *fourth grade*, Doofus," but she said, "You can tell everybody that I didn't have anything to say." It was like that the whole time.'

Mandy snorted. She said, 'Bobby, you've told that story twenty times.'

He shrugged. 'Yeah? So?'

'So Bethany was right,' Mandy said. 'You really *did* want to tell everyone what she said.'

'Oooo, cold.' Jack chuckled. I tried to look up at him and smile, but the wires hurt too much.

Bobby put on a face of outraged innocence. 'No way,' he said. 'I really just wanted to talk to her. But she's super freaky.'

I wrote, 'Bobby would <u>never</u> gossip,' on Donald and showed it to Mandy, who read it out for me.

Everyone laughed and Bobby pretended to pout. 'If you

weren't in the hospital,' he said. 'I'd get you for that.'

Then the plump nurse with the black hair came into the room. 'Okay, monsters,' she said kindly. 'Time to go.'

I got hugs from everyone. Rob was last and he held me very gently. He said, 'When you are back at school?'

I wrote, 'February.'

He winked at me and made the gun thing with his fingers. He said, 'See you in February.'

Oh, God, I thought. I hope so.

Just as he walked out, Kim ran back. She held my hand and said, 'I'm sorry.' She was still shaking. She said, 'I am so very, very sorry.'

I grabbed Donald. I wrote, 'Don't be silly. It wasn't your fault.'

But she ran away without reading it.

Before I could think about what a disaster that was, my eyes pulled shut. I'd fallen back down the well of unconsciousness.


The next morning, my world totally changed.

The first sign of it was an unfamiliar smell of bleach. It was five am and an orderly was already mopping my bathroom.

I heard that strange percussive sound of a nurse in a hurry and someone new appeared over by my door.

It was a woman in her forties in an old-fashioned nurse's uniform of starched white cotton layers. Her hair was honey-coloured and she wore it in a braided bun. Her starched white cap had a blue stripe and she was consulting a watch pinned to her chest and hanging from a small silver strap. 'Good!' she said briskly.

'Now mark it off here.' The orderly peered up at a bit of laminated card, which hadn't been by my door the day before. It was now stuck to the wall and a long string with a grease pencil hung from it. The orderly ticked off a square.

'I'll check these twice a day,' the nurse said. 'And every day, I'll choose one random room to inspect.'

'Yes, Ma'am,' the orderly said. She was the kind of woman you automatically ma'am-ed.

I poured myself some water. I always woke up thirsty and with a horrible headache. 'Ah,' she said to the orderly. 'The patient is awake. Let's look at her bed.'

She nodded to me and flung back my blankets. 'This is not good enough,' she said. 'These sheets must be changed daily, and if there's an accident or a spill, the rubber liner must go down to the laundry.'

'We just wipe down them liners,' the orderly said. 'And we only change the sheets once a week or for somebody new.'

'That's not good enough,' Nurse Starchy said. 'Infection rates are good on this ward, but we shouldn't take chances.' She looked at the orderly. 'I can assure you that the laundry know how to clean rubber liners.'

The orderly looked sceptical. 'If we get them back,' she said. 'We used to never get them back, so we started wiping them.'

'I shall be keeping a very close eye on the laundry inventory,' Nurse Starchy said. I don't know if the orderly believed her, but I certainly did.

She bent and looked under the bed. 'The floors in this ward are excellent,' she said. 'Now let's get the rest of the surfaces up to their standard.'

'Yes, Ma'am,' the orderly said, a bit bucked up and surprised by the praise. I was delighted to hear about the clean sheets. It was horrible sleeping on a growing collection of Pringles crumbs. They turned to go and I stretched out my hip flexor and my back, wincing and making my trach whistle because this made my head hurt even worse.

Nurse Starchy had turned to look at me. Now she marched back and slid out my chart. She flipped a couple of pages and frowned. She took a small silver thing from her chest pocket and screwed it until it became a pencil. Then she made notes on the margins of my chart, made the 'harrumph' sound and emphatically slid my chart into its slot on the bottom of my bed. It made a clanging sound that made me wince again.

'Miss DuLac,' she said. 'Do you have a headache this morning?'

I shook my finger up and down.

She raised her eyebrows. 'I'm not surprised,' she said. She took my water jug and glass and came back with a clean glass and a clean, full jug. 'Drink as much of this as you can,' she said. 'I will see you later.'

# Chapter Twelve

## Soundtrack: 'Waterloo' – Abba

Breakfast service was fast. Usually, the attendant that did breakfast was rather chatty, but that morning it was tray down and 'Good Morning' and gone. The tray was picked back up, too. Usually it was left for the orderlies to do when they tidied up the room.

That morning, the room did not get tidied. It got *cleaned*. I had to get out of bed to let them change it and I wandered into the hall, planning to sit on one of the leatherette sofas. But they were being cleaned, too.

The nurses' station was all dusting and flying files. Nurse Starchy herself emerged from the ward storage room wearing an oilcloth apron. She had a full bin liner in each hand and put it on a metal cart that already held two others.

Cathy – the nurse with black hair and teenagers at home – trotted past.

'What's going on?' I wrote on Donald.

'New Head Nurse for ENT,' she said. 'Wants to get us shipshape.'

Nurse Starchy stuck her head out the storage room door and looked at Cathy who squeaked, 'Gotta go,' and trotted back to the station. Then Nurse Starchy's eye came to rest on me. I had the feeling I was about to get tidied, too.

I was right.

A few hours later, mom had come and gone. It wasn't one of my Physio or clinic mornings. I buzzed for a nurse, ordered pain meds and asked for my dip and a bottle of Coke.

I was grappling with a Pringles can when Nurse Starchy walked in.

The *Bewitched* theme was playing on the television. She

99

switched it off. Just then, the nurse arrived back with the cup of pain meds, a carton of onion dip and the familiar, wasp-waisted glass bottle.

Nurse Starchy raised her eyebrows and the nurse stopped dead. Then Starchy pointed to my desk and the nurse put everything down. Rapidly.

Nurse Starchy cleared her throat. 'Why,' she asked, 'isn't this girl on the children's ward?'

The nurse, who I'd only seen a few times before, stumbled over her words. 'Um, er, the stent is, well, and...' she trailed off.

'The nature of her injuries means that the operating staff want to keep a close eye on her recovery?' I thought I saw a hint of a smile as Starchy translated.

'Yes, Ma'am.'

'You may go.' I'd never seen a nurse move so fast.

I looked at Nurse Starchy and she looked at me. 'Do you have any clothing in those drawers?' she asked.

I shook my finger, no. I wrote, 'I have nightgowns.'

She sniffed.

I thought, I'm in bed. I wear nightgowns. Duh.

She opened my chart again, walked to my phone and called my mother at work. 'Does Coco have some sweats or jeans? Could you please bring a selection with you this evening, along with T-shirts, socks and footwear suitable for walking – tennis shoes would be ideal.'

She said goodbye, hung up and then crooked her finger. 'Come with me,' she said.

We walked down the hall and across into the staff storage room. I'd never been in there before. It was surprisingly large. I thought it would be a rectangle, like a cupboard, but it was a square, like a box room. Down one side was a counter with a sink in the middle. There was a microwave oven and a little refrigerator on the counter. Starchy opened the fridge.

It was full of bags of blood and fluid and bottles of medicine.

On the door were bottles of Coke and tubs of onion dip.

I suddenly realised I'd been a bit of a jerk.

Nurse Starchy pushed the door shut. 'I don't mind you storing your snacks in here,' she said. 'But, from now on, you don't waste valuable nursing time. You get them yourself.'

I nodded my finger up and down. Rapidly. I wrote, 'I'm sorry,' on Donald.

She put her arm around my shoulders and led me back out into the hall. 'I would like to you help out a bit around here,' she said. 'To make up for all the time you've wasted.'

She didn't ask me what *I* would like. I suddenly saw that wasn't going to be a priority any more.

'You're also,' she said, with a brittle smile, 'going to end your promising little addiction to pain medication.'

I sighed, making my trach whistle. I had been busted.

'Enjoy,' she said, 'Enjoy your last lazy day. Tomorrow will be different.' She patted my shoulders and pushed me off in the direction of my room.

I'd missed the entire first section of *Bewitched* and I had an ominous feeling about the coming day. But I also felt better, somehow, than I had in a long time. Someone in this place knew *exactly* what she was doing.


Dinner that night in the hospital was fried chicken. For me, that is. KFC that my mother brought in. Nurse Starchy was on her way home when she came by my room. My hospital dinner rested on a metal instruments cart on the far wall...Salisbury steak with carrots, mashed potatoes and the famous green gravy.

Nurse Starchy was wearing a blue woollen cape that exactly matched the stripe on her starched cotton cap. She looked just as crisp and fresh as she had at five am. Mom and I did not. I had a grease spot on my nightgown and my hair was a tangled mess. Mom's eyes had big black circles that showed where her concealer had worn off.

Starchy introduced herself and my mother automatically started to stand up. I could tell it wouldn't be long before she called Nurse Starchy 'Ma'am.'

They had a little discussion about the sweats, jeans, T-shirts and sneakers that mom had brought in for me. Mom had remembered to bring bras in, too.

Then Nurse Starchy went over and looked at the hospital dinner.

'Do you leave this untouched every night?' she asked me.

'She won't eat it, Ma'am,' my mother answered for me.

Nurse Starchy pretended that she couldn't hear my mother. I put down my drumstick, wiped my fingers on some napkins and got Donald. 'Your food sucks.'

Nurse Starchy raised her eyebrows and I erased Donald. 'I don't like your food,' I wrote instead.

'It is carefully nutritionally balanced,' she said.

'It's horrible,' I wrote.

'Why is it horrible?'

'It tastes like poo.'

Again the raised eyebrows. I folded my arms. I wasn't taking that one back. It was really horrible and so...ugly...that I often couldn't get the fork into my mouth, even when I tried.

'She's a picky...' my mother started, and trailed off when Starchy refused to acknowledge her existence.

'Do you eat your mother's cooking?'

I thought about mom's cooking. I hadn't had mom's cooking in ages. Pot roast with brown potatoes. Steak. Green bean casserole. Chicken pies. Real, homemade hamburgers. Even just plain old macaroni and cheese. My mouth watered.

I wrote, 'I love my mom's cooking.'

Nurse Starchy turned to my mother. She said, 'It's hard enough being a working mother without having a child in the hospital.'

My mother nodded mutely. Suddenly I could see how utterly

exhausted she was.

Nurse Starchy turned to me. 'Will you eat peanut butter toast for breakfast?'

I nodded my finger up and down for yes.

Nurse Starchy said, 'Why don't you stay home tomorrow morning and make some dinner for you and Coco? You can put it on plates, wrap it up in plastic and heat it up tomorrow night in our microwave oven. I'll bring in some peanut butter from home, and Coco can have peanut butter toast for breakfast.'

Mom blinked. She hated being told what to do, after years of Dad. I could see her begin to swell up with indignation. But then she deflated again and nodded. She rubbed her forehead as if her head hurt and left a line of chicken grease. And then she asked, like a little girl, 'But what do I do with the plates all day?'

'Have you got a cooler?' Starchy asked.

Mom nodded.

'Stick some ice in the cooler and leave it in your car.'

And so my junk food diet came to an end. Not only did my mother start bringing in food that she'd made, the whole family started making two extra plates and freezing them. On Sunday, they took them all to Grandma's and, after church, mom came home with three weeks of dinners. I was eating Aunty Jana's burritos, Grandma's beef casserole, Uncle Danno's ribs and Auntie Bella's spinach cannelloni. It was like Thanksgiving dinner every night.

And, as it turned out, I needed the fuel.

# Chapter Thirteen

## Soundtrack: 'Lady Marmalade' – Patti LaBelle

The next morning, I was awoken by the smell of bleach. The orderly made quick work of the bathroom, ticked off the square with the grease pencil and marched off to her next room.

I had known her as a slow, mournful kind of presence, sweeping large circles with a big fluffy duster. And now she was like a brown tornado.

I used the sparkling bathroom. I showered and got dressed and did my makeup.

It was weird wearing clothes, even though I'd pulled on my favourite soft-and-faded jeans and an old red T-shirt. My Tre-torn sneakers had a red tick on the side and mom had washed them. My toes felt strangely cramped, but they still fitted. I just wasn't used to wearing shoes anymore.

I wandered out to the nurses' station, where only one person sat, going through a mound of charts and making some kind of table on a piece of pink paper. She only glanced up when I came.

'Don't go far, Coco,' she said. 'Her Majesty is on her way in.'

I saw the orderly who had been in my room greet another orderly in the hall. They were smiling, and laughed and shushed each other for a while before they trotted off to do more rooms.

'What's with the orderlies?' I asked.

The nurse blew upwards and her fringe flopped out and back. 'Don't get me started,' she said. She looked up, with her finger on the table to keep her place.

'The porters get paid twice as much as the orderlies,' she said, 'because they do heavier work.'

Did they? I wondered. The porters were usually just moving things around on wheels. Orderlies had to lift beds and shift heavy furniture and equipment.

But I wanted to hear the rest, so I just nodded my finger and she went on. 'Well, because of this "women's liberation" stuff –' she actually made quotation marks with her fingers – 'they've gone to court to say that they should be paid the same.'

She looked sourly at where my orderly came out into the hall on her way to yet another room. 'The court case is today.'

I wrote, 'Thank you,' and let her get back to her work.

Then I went over to my orderly. I had to book to catch her before she had finished filling her mop bucket with soapy water for another room. I wrote, 'Good luck in court,' on Donald and showed it to her.

She wore her hair slicked back into a tight bun, and she'd always kept her mouth tight, too. But now she smiled and you could see she'd been a beautiful girl. She said, 'Thank you, honey.' She lowered her voice, saying, 'I think we're gonna win!'

It made me laugh and my trach whistled. And then she had whisked into another room.

'Ah, Miss DuLac.' Nurse Starchy was walking down the hall with papers in her arms, a flowered oilcloth bag over her arm and her navy cloak billowing behind her.

She reached into her bag and brought out some Skippy peanut butter. I preferred Jiff, but somehow I didn't want to mention it right then. *'Bon appetit,'* she said. 'I'll see you in thirty minutes.'

With my toast, I got some paracetamol instead of my pain meds. I was afraid it wouldn't do the job on the pain in my neck.

But it did.

And I didn't know how I felt about that.

Patient Volunteering.

Nurse Starchy had figured it out with Physio when she'd been in Orthopaedics. Why should patients be expected to just wander around aimlessly? Where was our motivation? If we were given tasks, and meant to feel part of the team, then we would be walking the wards with *purpose*.

I got a badge.

And I got a list of things to do.

The first thing was to run a bunch of old charts down to Records. It took forever to book charts into Records. You had to fill out a quadruplicate form for every single blessed one of them and you could only get the form from Records because they were all numbered. So nursing staff had to sit down in the Records hall and write out hundreds of forms and hand each chart in one at a time with the appropriate form to be checked and double-checked and then get a receipt for each chart and take the receipts up to the Ward and file them.

The nurses in the ENT ward wanted to be with their patients, not messing about in Records. So, there was a slight backlog. Of eighty-seven charts.

It took for-fudging-ever. And then I lost Donald in them, and we had to find him again before I could go back to ENT.

I had my hospital map folded in one of my back pockets, but it was fairly easy. Over to Neuro, where the patients made the ENT lot look normal, and then straight down to the basement. Then back up, through Neuro, and home. Or, I could go through Orthopaedics, go down and then walk a little ways on the basement floor. It felt rather exciting to choose.

Then I got to have a Coke on the sofa with Nose Guy. He was volunteering, too. He had learned how to talk with his oesophagus, belching the words. It wasn't easy and he wasn't exactly chatty, but I found out loads about him.

Like most people on the ward, he had cancer. He'd been a smoker and they'd had to cut out his whole larynx and some other stuff, too.

There was a bunch of building work going on that side of the ward. I hadn't really noticed before, but from Nose Guy's sofa, you could see it all very plainly. They'd got to the digging-down-to-make-foundations stage and they'd gone down really far.

Nose Guy used to be a site foreman. He told me that the soil was really soft up on the hill of the hospital. 'Alluvial deposits,' he burped. Then, slowly, he burped that the river used to run closer to hospital site and it had dumped soft, sandy dirt for thousands of years.

It was kind of interesting, watching the crane work and thinking about having to move ten thousand years of silt to get down to solid ground. No wonder Nose Guy liked sitting there.

Then my break was over.

I had to help somebody get to X-Ray, wait for them, and help them find ENT again. Then I did the same thing for somebody else. Then I did the same thing for somebody else.

While I was resting again for lunch, watching *Bewitched* with some chip and dip, I thought about the somebody-else-somebody-else thing, and when I went back for my afternoon shift, I wrote it out on Donald. 'Why don't we take all three of them down next time?' Erase. 'They can take magazines and then we can all come back together?'

Cathy was on duty. She said, 'That's a great idea. We've got four to go to down to the Lab this afternoon. Should we do an X-Ray run every morning and a Lab run every afternoon?' I nodded my finger in agreement, but she looked at me. A how-much-can-you-handle kind of look.

I wrote, 'What?' on Donald.

'How are you feeling?'

I'd been a bit tired and sore, but the break and some more paracetamol had perked me up again. 'Fine,' I wrote.

'Could you push a wheelchair? He's not fat.'

'Sure.'

'Then take five of them.'

It hadn't been great, that morning, walking around with a big gauze bandage around my neck and a blue tube whistling in the middle of it. But I'd been pushing a trolley full of records, or at least an empty trolley, and nobody looks much at anybody pushing a trolley in a hospital.

And then, later, the people I was helping were pretty weak and I didn't even notice what onlookers thought.

Now, I was in quite an attention-getting crowd.

Two of my Lab gang had IV stands. The man in the wheelchair was missing lots of bits, and had bags strapped to him. One was a lung drain. Another was his catheter bag, and I didn't like to think about the third one. One person looked fairly normal, but had a silver trach tube and a Mickey. And another person looked fairly normal but had a lot of scars on her neck and spoke with a Dalek machine.

When we got out of the lift to walk to the Lab, everybody stared. I mean, jaws dropped, eyes popped and people couldn't stop looking, even though they really, really tried. We were right-eously freaky. And the public reaction made all of us, even the guy in the wheelchair who was hardly even there, smile like lunatics. Which made us look even worse, as a group.

The Lab was really close to the entrance, so there were lots of people going to the gift shop and the café. It was crowded, but we had a nice little space carved out around us, because we frightened everybody else.

I thought to myself, 'This is what it's like being a Hells Angel.'

We were all done pretty quickly, actually. We were just getting ready to go when the guy with Mickey waved his Mickey in front of us.

He wore expensive-looking pyjamas and a wine-coloured dressing gown. His slippers were wine-coloured leather. Mickey said, 'Let's go to the Gift Shop. I'll buy.'

We looked at each other. I wrote on Donald. 'Hands up if you want to go to the Gift Shop.' Everyone raised at least one hand.

Mickey got a money clip out of his dressing gown pocket and

peeled off ten-dollar bills, giving one to each of us.

I wrote, 'Really?' to him.

He wrote, 'Absolutely,' back.

And off we went. I didn't even think twice about doing it.

# Chapter Fourteen

## Soundtrack: 'Can't Get Enough' – Bad Company

The lady Dalek was not a small woman. She wasn't buried-in-a-piano-case fat, but she was heavy. She was the first one to choose something – she walked right to the big chocolate selection boxes and bought herself a fancy one. It was the kind of thing that new fathers would buy new mothers, with lots of gold lettering and red ribbon. It cost the whole of her ten dollars.

She didn't open them up and start gobbling, though. She just stood by the door of the shop waiting for us, her Dalek voice dangling from her wrist, and her arms wrapped around her chocolate box. She had a dreamy smile on her face, as if someone had actually bought her a posh box of chocolates and she was deciding whether or not to give him a kiss next time she saw him.

The barely alive man wanted to go to the magazines, so I wheeled him over. It was a huge wall of magazines, and I just guessed that he'd want the manly section, with the hunting and fishing and car magazines.

He didn't. He pointed up and over. I wheeled him over and then started pointing myself, in a kind of weird mime act.

I pointed to the television magazines.

He shook his head and pointed higher.

I pointed to the cooking magazines.

Higher.

Gossip magazines?

Higher.

I hesitated for a moment. *Playboy*? Really?

The barely alive man nodded with energy I couldn't have imagined he had. I got it down and handed it to him. Then he pointed to the magazine next to it. *Penthouse*. The models showed their bits in *Penthouse*. It was disgusting.

I looked at the nearly dead guy for a moment. He was totally thrilled. I got *Penthouse* down as well.

Mickey was suddenly at my elbow. He wrote, 'I'll wheel him to checkout, if you want to shop,' and showed me Mickey. His dressing gown and pyjama sleeve rose slightly when he did, and I could see his wrist.

I suddenly realised how thin he was. He was much thinner than I was. That was really, really, thin.

I wrote, 'Thanks,' and a smile flickered and died on his face.

He took the barely alive man away and I went shopping.

I had *Glamour* and *Vogue*. I didn't want to read anything about music or show business...but I'd seen *Car and Driver* when I'd parked Nearly Dead Guy. I picked it up...beautiful, mouth-watering pictures of cars and lovely roads. No naked women draped over any of them, no naked women in the ads.

It looked like the unthinkable – a car magazine a woman could read. Suddenly, I so wanted to be in a car again.

Considering that I'd just died in a car accident, it might have been a strange choice, but I bought it. I had seven dollars left and I spent it on candy...on chocolate bars. I bought some Rolos, I got a Three Musketeers, I got Zagnuts, Snickers, some Reese's peanut butter cups and Hershey kisses.

I was having trouble carrying all of it to the checkout, where Mickey and the nearly dead guy were just coming up to the front of a short line. The two IV patients were in the line, too, and the clerk looked harassed.

Nearly Dead Guy handed up his girlie magazines and the clerk hesitated a moment, then rang them up and bagged them in brown paper. Nearly Dead Guy gave his change back to Mickey, or tried. Mickey waved it away.

Mickey ordered something from behind the counter, using Mickey.

The clerk hesitated for a longer moment. I could only see the back of Mickey's head, but I could tell he was getting tense. He pushed Mickey at the clerk and tapped the top of it with his free hand.

The clerk rolled his eyes and sighed. Then he reached behind him and selected a carton of cigarettes. He pushed them to Mickey and Mickey slid the ten dollars to him, opening the carton and starting to stow the packs away in his dressing gown. He used his pockets and also put them all around him, above the belt. It was amazing how quickly they vanished.

He'd done it before, I suddenly realised. Then Mickey wrote something else on Mickey and passed over his change. He got three lighters and they disappeared, as well.

One of the IVs was a grown woman, but she bought a teddy bear and a doll. I wondered if she'd got them for her kids or just to keep her company, but I didn't want to ask.

The other IV was an older man who looked a bit like a teacher. He bought a copy of *Guns and Ammo* and a bunch of beef jerky.

I got my stuff and one of the new plastic shopping bags, so that I could hook the handle over Nearly Dead Guy's chair, and we all wheeled back to the ward, walking fairly quickly, ready to tuck into our goodies.

We all kept thanking Mickey.

He waved our thanks away, just like he'd waved the change.

I was tired by the time I'd seen all my charges back to their rooms, and my neck had that uncomfortable-feeling that I'd learned meant pain was on its way. I'd just flopped onto my bed, thinking about a shower, but I got back up and went out to the nurse's station for some paracetamol.

I suddenly noticed things I hadn't noticed before. All along the wide corridor, there were groups of sofas and chairs and potted plants. And in all of the groups, there were big ashtrays. Two doctors were standing, looking at a chart together, and they were both smoking. Cathy was leaning against a wall, a little further down, sucking on a cigarette.

Almost everyone else in my ward was there because of cancer. Cancer from smoking had lost them their larynxes. But here were the people who were supposed to be helping them, and they were smoking, too.

Some visitors walked by me, smoking, and one dashed over and put out his cigarette in the ashtray by Cathy.

It made me feel like I was choking. It was all in my head...I couldn't smell the smoke, and I couldn't really feel it...but it was suddenly really, really horrible. I wanted to run around the hall and pull the cigarettes out of everyone's hands.

I got my paracetamol and thought about it a long time in the shower.

Nurse Starchy got my mom a wheelie desky-tably thing, too. We had dinner together that night almost like regular people, telling each other about our days.

Even though I was tired that night, I couldn't sleep. I slept, but then I woke up and I couldn't get back. I put on my dressing gown and went out in the hall, to ask for some proper pain meds, but no one was at the desk. I wandered down to Nose Guy's sofa and saw the crescent moon. The moon was in just the right position to look as if the construction crane had hoisted it into the sky.

I wrote 'hoist' on Donald, and went back to my room for my pad.

'The crane has hoisted the moon to the sky.'

Too many 'the's.

'I saw a crane hoisting the moon to the sky.'

Better. Much better, actually.

'Pain is a smoke that steals...'

No not steals. The 'fog steals on little cat feet.' I was stealing steals. Or was it 'comes'? 'The fog comes on little cat feet.' Carl Sandberg was the poet. We'd read it in third grade. It was 'comes'. I could have 'steals' if I wanted it. But now it looked stupid.

'Pain is a smoke the walls exhale.'

Good. Very, very good.

And ow. Ow, ow, ow, ow, ow. I had forgotten to get my paracetamol in time.

Back I went to the nurse's station. I wrote, 'Ow,' on Donald and got some paracetamol with codeine, a nice compromise between the taking-enough-away-so-you-can-live-with-it pain relief of the plain paracetamol, that had worked during the day and the pain medication I had liked a little too much.

I swallowed them at the water fountain, went back to my room and used the toilet. By the time I got to my bed, my dressing gown seemed very difficult to remove. I was asleep before I'd actually lain down.

The smell of bleach woke me up. I grabbed Donald and managed to intercept the orderly while she was marking off my toilet on her chart.

I wrote, 'How did the court case go?'

She beamed. She said, 'We won, baby girl.'

I felt so happy that I danced around in a little circle and she laughed. She said, 'We gonna have to share shifts with the men, now. Some big old black man might be in here, cleaning for you.' She looked at me, to see how I'd take that news.

I shrugged. I wrote, 'You'll have to teach him how to do it right.'

And that made her laugh again.

I heard her out in the hall, telling the story of our conversation to another orderly – I mean female porter. There were no orderlies any more.

I made my toast and got showered and dressed before rounds. My deodorant was running out. I made a mental note to get down to the Gift Shop that day and get another one. I had all my allowance money in my drawer – I got a couple of dollars a week and mom had kept giving it to me, even though I was in the hospital.

I was hanging out, waiting for rounds so that I could start my day, when I heard shouting in the hall.

Then I heard something metal being kicked over.

I thought it was something about the porters' dispute and I ran outside, ready to...I don't know...save somebody or something.

It was over at Nose Guy's sofa. And it wasn't anything about the porters. It was Doctor Morris and Mickey.

Doctor Morris had opened the window to the building site and pushed Mickey out the window until only his knees and feet were still inside. Morris was shaking Mickey, holding him out above the sickening drop of the new foundations.

'Do you want to die?' Morris shouted. 'If you want to die, just nod your head. I'll drop you right now and save us all a lot of trouble.'

The baby ducks were wide-eyed and horrified.

I was, too.

Suddenly, Nurse Starchy was there. 'I think he's learned how you feel, doctor,' she said calmly. 'Let's get the patient back into the building, now.'

She got on the other side of Mickey and Kular went over and held the window wider, so that it wouldn't hit Mickey on the back of his head as Starchy and Morris pulled him back in and sat him on the sofa.

Doctor Morris was red in the face and shaking with anger.

'Do you think I'm stupid?' he asked Mickey.

Mickey was shaking, too, with fear. He shook his head no.

'Do you think I can't see a nicotine stain on a trach tube?' Mickey didn't have his Mickey. I had a feeling it had fluttered the fourteen stories to the base of the building site.

He shook his head, no, again.

Morris got right in Mickey's face and shouted, so loudly that the whole corridor rang, 'STOP SMOKING!'

Then he marched away, the baby ducks scuttling to follow.

Nurse Starchy got Mickey under his arm, in that secret way nurses have that helps you to stand up.

'Well,' she said. 'Now that you've decided to stay in the land of the living, let's see about some breakfast.'

I waited for her to come back. When she did, I'd already written, 'It was my fault. I took him to the Gift Shop.'

Starchy erased Donald. 'It was not your fault,' she said. 'He's a grown man. He's just *acting* like a teenager.'

She put her arm around me. 'You'll be wise to that trick next time,' she said. 'Won't you?'

# Chapter Fifteen

## Soundtrack: 'Angie Baby' – Helen Reddy

It was all getting rather tricky. I enjoyed my work as a Patient Volunteer. But it was making me...well...*well*. Healthy. Fit.

And this was a problem. Because the physios and the nursing staff started talking to the doctors about me getting out of the hospital and going back to school.

Burner High – it was...it was truly horrible. Not for everyone, I gathered, but certainly for me.

The problem was cultural. I did not fit in at Burner High. My mother did not fit into Burner society. And I knew, with rock-bottom certainty, that we never would. We bought the house in Burner because my dad had to live in the city he policed. Burner was a little rural enclave – part of the city that never really got built up, because it had old mines running underneath it. It was ten minutes from the Country Club Plaza one way and ten minutes from one of the best school districts and richest suburbs in America the other way. But it might as well been a hundred miles from both of those places. It was, not to be too delicate about it, Hicksville.

Dad stuck us there and then moved out. Which was so typical, it wasn't even funny.

I didn't get taught the word 'homogenous' at Burner High, but it should have carved above the door. When the rest of the city was integrating their schools, bussing black and white kids around so that everyone had the same level of education, Burner left the city school district and became its own school system so it could stay 99.97 percent white.

Cars were pickup trucks and station wagons. Hair was crew-cut or backcombed and sprayed stiff. You voted Republican. You listened to Country. You ate meat and potatoes. You went to church (denomination optional, but Protestant preferred). One of the worst insults a Burner woman could give was to wrinkle her nose and say something or someone was 'different'.

My generation was changing all this, but it was slow. Change was always slow in Burner.

Except in the landscape. The old mines were dug in the Wild West days before paperwork. They were poorly structured, and sometimes collapsed, sinking whole areas of town into ragged holes. We called those 'cave ins', and they were frighteningly common. I remember, just down from my house, there was a pasture for two horses. One day, it was a pasture, the next day, two horses were balancing on the edge of a huge hole, looking nervous.

So, with the rural culture and the homogeneity, Burner was like a parody of every high school movie you ever saw. Jocks and cheerleaders ruled one way, hoods the other. If you fitted in, life was really good there...evidently. If you didn't, life was total hell.

My life was total hell mainly because people really *wanted* me to fit in. If everyone had just ignored me, I would have been fine. But people in Burner were good, Christian and kind. So kind that they never left you alone. They tried to help.

And so, I got...bullied isn't the right word for it. I got *noticed* and *commented upon*. People seemed really interested about what I wore, ate, said, did. I mean, there were the jerks, like the football player, who preyed on weak targets like me, but I could ignore them. It was harder to ignore someone who thought they were saving you.

There was no way in hell I was going to walk into Burner High unable to speak with a big hole in my throat. I would have been the target of every do-gooding soul in the whole place. Whenever the topic came up, I would have nightmares and trouble sleeping.

The University of Kansas Medical Center kept agricultural hours. They woke you up before six am and it was a rare patient awake for the ten o'clock evening news. I stopped sleeping in nightgowns and started wearing sweats to bed, so that I could get up and wander around. I'd sit on one of the leatherette sofas and look out at the city and the big night sky, to try and get sleepy. It took hours.

Nurse Starchy had written in big red letters across my chart – MINIMUM PAIN MEDICATION: PRONE TO ADDICTION. Sleeping pills were *not* going to happen. I sat with my notebook and tried to make sense of the pictures in my head, playing with the words I'd used, moving them around and changing them until, suddenly, a line I'd written seemed *right*.

I was sitting on the sofa that night, or maybe the next one, when I heard something I hadn't heard in a long time…teenaged boys. Laughing.

Between ENT and Intensive Care, there was a ramped corridor that led up to Orthopaedics, the arm and leg people. I cut down that way sometimes, coming back from delivering charts to clinic. The laughter was coming from up there.

I was so bored that I didn't even worry what my hair was doing. I crept up the ramp.

It was a wheelchair race. They'd set up two 'Wet Floor' signs near the nurse's station in the Orthopaedics corridor. Near me, two boys in wheelchairs were lined up, rocking back and forth on their wheels and looking intently at a boy on crutches, between the signs. He raised his arms and the boys grew utterly still for a moment. Then he dropped his arms and they were off.

It was terribly exciting. I crawled onto a leatherette sofa, next to a big metal floor ashtray, and curled up to watch.

What I noticed, straightaway, was there wasn't enough room for them both to turn around their signs at the same time. Whoever made it first to the signs would have a huge advantage in winning the race.

They'd obviously already figured that out, because they were jockeying for the middle of the floor. They didn't actually crash into each other, but they came close.

They both had brown hair, and they both parted their hair on one side and swept it over. And they were both muscular and fit. But that's where the resemblance ended.

One was really big – huge bulging muscles, thick neck, and thick thighs. The other one was leaner and longer. His fingers were finer and his face was more defined. They looked like two drafts of the same drawing, but I knew which one I would have turned in for an art assignment.

Just then, the meatier one gave the pretty one a huge shove that pushed him briefly off course and surged forward into the gap between the signs.

The boy in the blue dressing gown laughed as the pretty one, grinning, spun through the gap second. The pretty one was so much better around the signs that they were neck and neck as they started back down the corridor. Now a couple of boys I hadn't seen before leaned out of their rooms – they were both pale, their faces almost matching their light blue pyjamas.

I forgot I wasn't supposed to be there. I forgot I was in a hospital. And I forgot I couldn't. I tried to shout, 'Come on!' to the pretty one. I was kneeling up on the sofa and shaking my fist. I had no idea how I'd got in that position.

The finish line had to be before the beginning of the ramp. If they went over it, at the rate they were going, they'd fly into ENT and break their necks.

The pretty one was winning, winning and then, at the last minute, the meaty one put on a huge surge and nipped the win.

All the boys whooped and I found myself applauding.

And then I found myself surrounded.

It was like a sea of boys. They were sitting on the sofa with me, leaning over me from in front of it. The meaty one and the pretty one wheeled up and pushed into the crowd, the meaty one saying, 'Now, now, boys, she came to watch *us*, not talk to *you*.'

The boy in the blue dressing gown had already said, 'Hellooooo,' and one of the pale boys had asked my name.

I looked around for Donald and pulled him out from under the boy in the blue dressing gown. I wrote, 'I can't talk.'

They all leaned back, just a little, and gave me a bit more room. They took time to check out my trach tube. Then the blue dressing gown boy solemnly took Donald and wrote, 'What's your name?'

And that just cracked me up. I grinned and wrote, 'I can hear, you idiot, I just can't talk.' They all started to laugh, although the poor blue dressing gown boy said, 'Well, I didn't know,' in such an injured tone that I patted his arm.

His eyes were nearly as bright blue as his dressing gown, and seemed to take in everything at once. He had the warmest smile I'd ever seen.

'I'm Des,' he said. 'And that's Bob One and Bob Two.' The pale boys had the same name, too. Freaky, I thought.

The meaty one leaned forward and put out his hand. 'My name's Mark,' he said. 'But you can call me Stud Muffin.'

I wrote, 'Or not,' on Donald and then erased it. 'I'm Coco.'

There was the usual stuff about how they'd like to drink me and that I was pretty hot and asking where my name had come from. I didn't really even listen to anything like that anymore – boys kind of *had* to do it and it didn't mean anything. I noticed that the pretty boy had wheeled off to the nurse's desk where he got some meds in one of those little paper cups.

'That's Ed,' Des said. 'He doesn't talk to girls right now.'

I looked at him, a why-not look. Des put his arm on the back of the sofa behind me and leaned over, lowering his voice. 'He's had his heart broken.'

'She was a total bitch,' meaty Mark said.

Just as I noticed Des smelled really nice, an Orthopaedics nurse appeared. 'It's midnight,' she said. 'And you're all going to turn into pumpkins. Your pain meds are by your beds.'

They scattered and she looked at me. It took me a while to realise she was looking at me, because I was still thinking about how nice Des smelled and how pretty his eyes were and wondering why I could smell Des when I could hardly smell anything at all. Then I realised the nurse was looking at me.

'Bounce,' she said. 'Or they'll come back. They might be sick, but they're still boys.'

I bounced. I bounced all the way back to bed.

That was...really not that bad, I thought, lying in my nice, clean sheets. It was like being with my cousins. It was...nice.

I wondered why I could be with other kids at home and in hospital but not in my school. Maybe...I started to think...it wasn't them. Maybe it was me. Maybe I was so uptight and worried about fitting in at school that I was horrible to be around. Or maybe it was like a chemical explosion. Me + them = unpleasantness. Both fine on their own. Just not together.

The next night, I went back to the Orthopaedics corridor. It was silent and still and I crept away.

The day after that, I was hauling charts down to records and checking them in. It was *such* a pain that I only did it once every two or three days, waiting until one of the nurses begged me.

When I got there, another patient volunteer was there, and making a total mess out of dozens of quadruplicate forms. It was the pretty boy they'd called Ed, and he looked like he was about to tear his nice brown hair out by the handfuls. The clerk was smirking at him.

The records clerk could be a bit of a twonk. He didn't mean to be, but he had zero people skills. Last time I was down there, he'd bought me a Pepsi. Today, when I kind of waded around Ed's mess and given him the five he'd asked for, he offered me another Pepsi. I got Donald and wrote, 'Could you stretch to two?' nodding at Ed and he laughed and said we were going to bankrupt him. But he went off to the soda machine.

I put my own trolley further down the line of chairs and asked Ed, 'Can I help?' He was so flustered, he didn't want to look at

Donald at first. He still hadn't made eye contact with me. But then he saw Donald and he looked up.

I was expecting...I don't know...gratitude or a smile. He scowled at me. He said, 'Thanks, but I'll be okay.'

I sat down and watched him for a bit. What he'd done was detach all the copies before he'd got them signed in. So now, he was trying to match up all the pink, yellow, green and white copies to each other and the charts, so the clerk could sign them. I'd made the same dumb mistake myself, the day I lost Donald in the mess.

It was extra hard for him because of the wheelchair.

Some of what he needed was behind him. One was actually underneath him.

So, I ignored what he'd told me and got those bits and handed them to him.

And he threw it at me.

Not just the bits I'd handed to him, the whole lot of paper. Luckily, there weren't any of the metal-edged chart holders in the mix. He made a kind of roaring sound and just hurled it all in my direction.

For a bunch of paper, it hit pretty hard. I stumbled back a bit and then he was saying, 'God, I'm sorry, are you okay?'

We were in an absolute sea of multi-coloured paper and his face was so... It was the first time he'd properly looked at me, and he looked horrified, like he'd hurt me terribly badly. And that struck me as funny, and I started to giggle, wheezing air in and out of my trach tube.

'Oh my God!' he cried. 'Are you...can you breathe?'

He thought I was having some kind of a seizure. He thought he'd fatally injured me because he'd chucked a bunch of paper at me. That made me laugh so hard I couldn't catch my breath. I had to bend over and hold onto my stomach.

'Just breathe!' Ed said. 'Help!' he shouted. 'Help! Emergency!'

This made me sober up a bit, and I reached my hand out in

the 'stop' gesture to shut him up. He finally figured out I was laughing and stood there, fuming.

My stomach hurt from laughing so hard. I had to wipe tears away from my eyes. Then I saw the mess of paper, which was seriously going to damage my Pepsi perk.

I put Donald safely to one side and gathered up all the paper I could in my arms. I put all the pink pages on one chair, all the yellow ones on another, all the green ones on a third...

Ed caught on quickly and started to do the same...

By the time the clerk came back with our Pepsis, we'd reassembled about half of Ed's records. We kept working and in about ten minutes, they were all back in quadruplicate, matched to their charts, and ready for the clerk to sign in. Then we did mine.

We hadn't said much.

Ed wasn't much of a talker, and I'd kept Donald clear of the mess.

It was lunchtime and my way back went through Orthopaedics. We walked together and Ed managed the buttons on the lifts, so that I didn't have to wrestle my trolley through half-closed doors. When we got there, Ed dropped off his green copies to the nurses and then we just stood for a minute, looking at our feet.

Finally, I got Donald and asked, 'Where's Mark and Des and the Bobs?'

Ed shrugged. 'Mark went home. Des is pretty sick – they think he's got bone cancer. They moved him to Oncology. And the Bobs had their operations and are in their rooms.'

I waited a bit longer, but he wasn't going to say anything else, so I made a little bye-bye wave with my hand and put Donald on my trolley.

'Wait,' Ed said.

I looked at him.

He said, 'I saw you last night.'

It felt really embarrassing, that he'd seen me looking for the boys. He'd watched me being all lonely and sad. I felt myself blush.

Ed said, 'I can't sleep, either.'

I got Donald again and wrote, 'I'm not allowed sleeping pills.'

He grinned with half of his mouth, kind of twisting his face. 'Yeah, I figured,' he said. 'I liked them too much, too.'

We looked at each other again. He said, 'Anyway. If you come by tonight, I won't hide.'

And I got it. I understood it straight away. He didn't want me to think he was interested in me like a girl. But if I wanted to be friends, he felt like he could manage that.

I'd been warned off by guys before. That was nothing new. What was new, though, was that I saw that even though Ed was beautiful and kind of shiny, and not interested in me like a girl, he really needed a friend. And that the friend he really needed was somebody like me. I don't know how I knew it, but I did, and I knew it right down into the core of me.

So, I stuck out my hand and we shook on it.

# Chapter Sixteen

## Soundtrack: 'Ain't Too Proud To Beg' – The Rolling Stones

After lunch, I had to go to clinic. For myself, for a change.

I hated going to the ENT clinic. I hated thinking about my throat. I hated looking at it. I hated discussing it. I hated everything to do with the area between my chin and my chest.

I especially hated my trach tube. It was the grossest thing in the entire world and still remains one of my greatest fears. I know people who have suffered real medical traumas, terrible stuff like repeated electric shock treatments, who could deal with everything else but the trach tube. They are horrible, nasty things.

In clinic that day, Doctor Kular thought it would be interesting for me to see him change my blue plastic surgical trach tube for a stainless steel civilian model like Mickey'd had. So he arranged to do it in front of a large mirror in his office.

All that showed on my neck was a small plate of turquoise plastic with a large hole in the middle and two little holes either side. It sat in the hollow above the two bones of my clavicle. The large hole was the breathing one and the small holes had tape threaded through and tied off neatly. The tape went around the back of my neck and held the large hole in place.

And that's what I had thought it was, at first, just that. But now I knew better and really wasn't looking forward to this demonstration.

It was all mom's fault. Mom was perky and interested and ready to get the best out of the medical team ('Oh, is *that* how you take a blood gas? How fascinating.') and I had my own whole brave and stoic act.

Then they found out I was rather bright.

Anyway, with one thing and another, and with the volunteering, the hospital staff got the idea that I was terribly interested in their work.

It's very hard to tell people who assume you're interested in their work that you're actually not.

So I was in front of the stupid mirror. Behind the nice little turquoise plate was a huge tube connected to the large hole, a tube that Doctor Kular pulled out and out and out of my throat, covered in strings of mucus.

I was left looking at the slimy bare hole in my neck, rough, red and raw-looking. And then Doctor Kular fitted me with the stainless steel version which felt very, very, heavy.

The reason it felt heavy was that it came apart. It had a little secondary tube, which you could undo and pull out. This came with its own little bottle brush and every day, one of my new grooming joys was to take this out and scrub it clean of mucus, blood and goo and then pop it back in.

I got a whole demonstration of this from Doctor Kular.

It was just him and me that day.

The whole legal side of medicine was much more relaxed back then, but I'm sure even in 1974 underage patients shouldn't have been left alone with a doctor. But by this point, the staff kind of saw me less as a patient and more as part of the ENT team.

So it must have come as quite of a shock to Doctor Kular when I started to cry.

It was just *so* horrid, though. It was just *too* horrible and gross. And I *wasn't* happy about the change or pleased that I got to take this nice shiny trach tube home to clean myself. I did *not* think the cleaning brush was 'nifty'. I thought the whole thing was horrible and I didn't want anything to do with it.

But I didn't have Donald.

So, I burst into tears.

Doctor Kular's mouth dropped open. 'What's wrong?' he asked wonderingly. He thought he'd planned this wonderful treat for me, and here I was, not enjoying myself at all.

He tied off my new tapes in a bit of a huff, and then, when I was back on my chair by Donald, he asked again, 'What's the matter?'

I wiped my eyes with the back of my hands. 'It looks so horrible,' I wrote. Reluctantly, I showed it to him.

'You liked the plastic one better?' he asked, and his voice was indignant.

I shook my head, no, even though the wires pulled. 'I don't want it at all,' I tried to explain. 'I don't want a trach tube!'

'Well!' he bridled. 'You'd better be glad you've got it. You'd be dead without it.'

Suddenly, I remembered that he had given it to me. I'd been told I was lucky an ENT surgeon had just happened to be walking by. I realised I must seem really ungrateful. I tried hard, sitting on one of Kular's mismatched office chairs, to feel grateful.

But I kept remembering the calm coolness of death, how effortless it had been, how happy I'd been to go.

I hadn't *asked* for any of this, I remembered. I hadn't *asked* to come back.

Doctor Kular was actually waiting for me to tell him what I was thinking. And even though it was quite complicated, I thought I should try and tell him...that it was only fair to tell him.

I wrote, 'I didn't actually want to live.'

Kular looked at my slate and at me. His face showed outrage. I shrugged.

My shrug made him shoot up off his little insect stool. He walked as far away from me as he could get. When he spoke, I could tell he was trying to control his temper. In a low voice, that shook a bit, he said, 'We've been working our butts off for you.'

That isn't my fault, I thought. You picked your job. I didn't pick any of this.

Even though he was seven or eight feet away from me, he was still...I guess listening isn't the right word in the circumstances...but he was paying attention. He was waiting for me to respond.

I looked down at Donald. How could I explain what I was feeling? I didn't want to hurt his feelings any more, but it wasn't fair, expecting me to be all perky and happy. I couldn't keep pretending what they did to me didn't bother me. I had to be more honest...

When mom had been trying to keep Dad from leaving us, she asked him to go to counselling. He only went once, but she kept on going. One of the things she learned, and rather relentlessly used in our own relationship, was that when you were arguing with someone, it was a good idea to say how you were feeling.

I got the stylus. I wrote, 'I feel sad.'

Kular blinked at me. 'You feel *sad*?' he said. 'Getting a new trach tube has made you feel sad?'

'The whole thing makes me feel sad.'

Kular closed his eyes and shook his head, as if he was trying to dislodge a bee in his hair. Then he came over and sat down again.

'What whole thing are we talking about, here?' he asked. It reminded me of my dad.

I wrote small and forgot about full sentences. 'Hole in neck. Can't talk. Can't sing. Can't act.'

Doctor Kular read this out loud, very sarcastically, and rolled his eyes.

Then he grabbed my shoulders and brought me back to the mirror. 'I don't know,' he said. 'You could always play Frankenstein.'

There was a moment when our eyes connected. For just a moment, I could tell he regretted what he'd just said. I could have, I guess, written, 'What did you say?' on Donald and he would have apologised and it would have all been okay.

But it just hurt too, too bad. I couldn't hold in the hurt. It was like I had this whole reservoir of pain that I'd been pushing back inside myself since I'd been on Bob's lap, the morning of my surgery. And Kular's stupid joke was like a bomb that blew up the wall I'd made.

All that pain came crashing over my defences. There was nothing – I had nothing left to hold any of it back.

I was never going to sing. I was never going to act. And I looked like a freak, too.

I ran.

I took the stairs, huffing up the three flights, making my new tube whistle. I ran down through Orthopaedics, down the slope, past the nurses station and to my bed. I cried until I was nearly sick, until mucus ran from my new, smaller trach tube and choked me, and I had to go and clean the damn thing out at the sink. I had left the nifty brush in Kular's office, so I just used hot water.

I wanted to stomp it flat. I wanted to throw it out the window.

But I just cleaned it and shook it dry and stuck it back down my neck.

When I came out of my bathroom, Nurse Starchy was sitting on my bed. She handed me a box of tissues and Donald.

'Tell me,' she said. 'Exactly what happened.'

So I did.

I didn't think twice about ratting out Doctor Kular. Telling Nurse Starchy what had happened didn't seem like a big deal to me. But by the time my mother had come back from work, I realised it had all become a very big deal.

One of the medical secretaries had typed up my statement, and I'd had to check it for accuracy. Doctor Morris had called my mother at work and asked to meet us both in my room. Nurse Starchy even offered me pain meds.

I didn't take them. But I couldn't settle on anything. I couldn't read. I couldn't watch television. I just kind of wandered around my room, replaying the argument a hundred times in my head, reading over my statement, wondering if I'd lied or exaggerated or been horrible in any of about a million ways.

By that time, I was kind of over it. He'd said something horrible, the way you do when you've had your feelings really, really hurt and you want to hurt back. And that was…stupid…of him, and probably wrong, since he was a doctor and everything.

But he was only a baby duck. I couldn't blame him for being cross. He'd assumed I saw him like some kind of hero and actually, I thought he was a bit of a jerk.

And maybe that wasn't fair. Maybe I *should* have felt really grateful to Doctor Kular, but you know, I just didn't. And if I didn't, I shouldn't have to pretend all the time…should I? Or *was* I really horrible and ungrateful?

I went to the window and tried to look at something other than bricks and blank glass, but of course I couldn't.

And that was the problem, I realised. They all *liked* it here in the hospital. They'd all *chosen* to be here in this building. And I hadn't chosen it and I didn't like it.

I knew when mom had arrived. I could hear her shouting before she was even level with the nurse's station. 'She's just started to get a bit of confidence back,' she said, 'and that *dickhead*…'

I could hear Nurse Starchy's voice, and she must have said something about my mother's language, because the next thing my mother said was, 'You don't think I should call him a dickhead? What about…' and here she really roared the words, '…a total bastard?'

I started to giggle. I put my hands over my mouth, but that didn't help. Luckily, my new trach tube didn't whistle as loudly as the old one.

Mom blew into my room and pulled me onto her lap and into a big hug.

And although I'd been feeling okay, and had even been laughing the moment before, something about being in my mother's arms kind of stripped away all my okay-ness. Underneath the okay-ness had been lurking a whole lot of not-okay-ness – that whole reservoir of pain...it was still there. I started to cry again, and that was when Doctor Morris walked in.

It was the first time I'd seen him in real clothes. He seemed frighteningly official in a suit and tie. But he walked right in and sat on the bed next to us and when I looked into his eyes behind his clean-as-air glasses, it was just Doctor Morris again.

He said, 'Coco, I need you to be very grown-up right now.'

I stopped snivelling and got off mom's lap. She sat down in the chair. Doctor Morris motioned me to get into bed and sit up against the pillows and he gave me my desky-tabley kind of thing.

He put a form in front of me. It had the word 'Misconduct' in the heading on the front and as many coloured carbon copies as a chart transfer.

Nurse Starchy came in and stood by the door, watching and listening.

Doctor Morris took off his glasses and pinched his nose where they rubbed. His hands and his fingernails were as clean as his glasses. I'd noticed his wedding ring before, white gold.

He sighed. He said, 'This isn't the first time a patient has complained about Doctor Kular.'

That's because he's a dickhead, I thought.

Nurse Starchy folded her arms and looked up at the ceiling. She was, I realised, aching to say something and fighting to keep quiet.

'Maybe,' Doctor Morris said, 'maybe Doctor Kular should just do research. Maybe he shouldn't deal with people.'

'Good idea,' mom said. She slapped the arms of her chair. 'He's a complete...'

Doctor Morris turned around and looked at her, and she got uneasily quiet, too, just like Starchy.

Doctor Morris put his glasses back on and looked at me. 'The thing is,' he said, 'we've never had an ENT resident who's such a gifted surgeon.' His eyes were steady and calm. They made me feel steady and calm.

He said, 'I think Doctor Kular can learn about people. He feels terrible about what he said to you...'

Doctor Morris stood and went to look out at the bricks on the other side of my window. He was thinking.

I've always admired people who can think in front of other people. I find it really difficult, myself. I'm always too busy wondering how I'm looking and what the other people are thinking about me.

Doctor Morris just took some time out to think – he seemed to do it easily. He said, 'I think it would be easier to teach Doctor Kular about feelings than it would to teach someone with good people sense to perform surgery like Doctor Kular.' He turned to me. 'But I might be wrong.'

He sat down again and took my hand. 'So I'm asking you to tell me. Do you think he's so...clumsy...that he's going to...hurt people more than he helps them? Did he do that to you?'

It was my turn to try to think in front of other people. I had to think about Doctor Kular.

I totally believed in Kular. I completely trusted him to make me as much better as anyone possibly could. He was a jerk, of course, and in a way, I hated his guts. But if he was in charge of the buildings, all the floors would match up and all the elevators would go to every floor.

I looked up. Nurse Starchy was watching me with her cool, intelligent eyes.

I got Donald. 'No,' I wrote. And then, grudgingly, 'Kular is a good doctor.'

Doctor Morris sighed again. 'He's not a good doctor,' he said.

'Not quite yet.'

He looked at Nurse Starchy. 'What I would like,' he said, 'is to hold onto this. Maybe store it in Coco's charts. And then, if Doctor Kular doesn't learn his lesson, we can find it again.'

Nurse Starchy rolled her eyes. 'I would like you to annotate the complaint to that effect,' she said. 'I'd like you to say that *you* decided to hold it in abeyance with the patient's cooperation.'

Morris grinned. 'Okay,' he said. 'And Coco can initial that.'

Mom, who'd been sitting there, listening to it all, suddenly spoke. She said, 'Wait a minute. Is he just going to get away with it?'

I wrote on Donald, 'He's really sorry.'

Mom snorted. 'Let him come here and tell *you* he's really sorry. He should apologise.'

Nurse Starchy smiled. 'That's a good idea,' she said. 'I'd like to see that.'

Doctor Morris finished writing and I initialled the complaint. Nurse Starchy took it and my chart off to the desk to add my complaint to my chart.

'Thank you,' Doctor Morris said to me. And to my mother, 'I've taken Doctor Kular off roster for a few days. But I'll ask him to come by tomorrow. You can make him grovel.'

Mom's eyes glinted hard and sharp. 'Don't worry,' she said. 'I will.'

I didn't want to eat anything. I felt too tired. Mom left early...I think she felt tired, too.

Nurse Starchy offered me pain meds again, and this time I said yes. I knew if I took them, I would find the opening of the well and crawl inside for a while. I really needed to do that.

But first I needed to do something else. I asked the nurse, someone I'd never seen before, if she could get a message to Orthopaedics, and tore off a bit of my pad.

*Dear Ed*
*I've had a bad day and they're giving me pain meds. Sorry to let you*
*down, but I'm going to try to sleep.*

I hesitated. I'd almost written, Love, Coco, but I thought that might freak him out.

*See you later, I hope,*
*Coco*

I took my pain meds and crawled into bed properly. I felt…okay, actually. Kind of relieved it was all over.

And then, suddenly, Ed was there, sitting on my mom's chair. 'Hey,' he said.

I fumbled for Donald, but he said, 'You don't have to say anything.' He held my hand. His was warm and dry and there was absolutely no chemistry when we touched. Even all tired and drained out of emotion that night, I wondered if that was because he'd warned me off, or if the warning off was unnecessary because we didn't have a spark anyway.

His eyes were calm and held a lot of affection. And that made mine fill up with tears.

'I just wanted to tell you…you aren't some kind of a freak. You're not a freak at all. Des thinks you're really pretty and funny and Mark thought you were hot.'

The well was open and pulling me in but I could feel his words going into me like medicine goes into an IV.

'Well, Mark thinks everybody's hot,' Ed said. 'But Des is seriously picky, okay?' He shook his perfect hair out of his eyes. 'So don't worry about that douchebag doctor. He's just a dick.'

I felt my lips curve into a smile. And then I was gone.

# Chapter Seventeen

## Soundtrack: 'I Can Help' – Billy Swan

I woke up early. Early in KU Med in the 1970s meant that it was still dark outside. And I couldn't go back to sleep.

I got up and had a shower – I'd been too tired to have one the night before – and towel-dried my hair and put on makeup and got dressed. It still wasn't six am – I knew because they turned the lights up at six am.

I stood by my window and could hear birds through the glass. Somewhere I couldn't see there must have been trees. I realised I really had to get out of that room. Now.

I slumped down onto the fake leather sofa where it was even too early for Nose Guy to suck his coffee. If I looked across the building site, I could see the shapes of birds, flying against the pale morning sky. I was hungry for the sight of birds flying.

The Night Shift nurses were leaving and the Early Shift was coming on. Then the Lates would come in at two. The Day Shift overlapped Earlies and Lates. Starchy was supposed to work nine to five, but she might as well have worked Early and Late doubles every day. I was astonished when I found out she had a husband and a son. I don't know when she saw them.

Nobody knew I was sitting there. I could watch all the nurses, see the Night Shift stretch their backs and hear them all talk about who'd had a bad night and who was more comfortable. It was interesting seeing how they were with each other when nobody was watching.

Then one of the Night Shift handed a tape player to one of the Earlies. I noticed it was the exact same kind we had at home. Then I heard my name, and before I could do anything about it, the Early nurse pushed play and I heard my own voice.

I was singing 'Ave Maria'…it must have been for a wedding.

All the Earlies clustered around our tape machine, listening to my poor, lost voice.

I felt like I'd been scalded with hot water. And then I couldn't feel that any more. I was too angry to feel anything else besides boiling hot rage.

I tucked Donald under my arm and marched over to the nurses' station. Somebody hit the stop button and lots of people just walked away, leaving one poor Early holding the machine. I held out my hand and she gave it to me.

I went back into my room and put the tape machine in my underwear drawer. My hands were shaking.

Why had mom brought it in? I paced to my window and back again. I was too angry to cry. I was too hurt to make any sense out of it. It seemed like an unforgiveable betrayal, but mom wouldn't do that to me. Would she? What had she been thinking?

In the middle of all this, I realised I was glad she didn't come by in the mornings any more. If she'd walked in then, I think I might have hit her. I paced and swore, hoping I'd calm down before she came in the afternoon.

I was now trapped in my stupid room. I wanted to storm past the nurses, down the stairs, and out of the front of the hospital. But I couldn't deal with any more expressions of pity on their fat old faces. I wanted to escape out the window and fly away to live with the birds.

'Miss?'

I spun around, ready to kill whoever had dared come into my room. But it was only the orderly, who had now become a porter. She stopped dead when she saw my face.

'I'm sorry,' she said. 'You must be...' and she backed towards the door clumsily, nearly spilling the water in her mop bucket.

It made me feel terrible.

'Don't go,' I wrote on Donald. I showed it to her and she read the words out loud.

'You sure?' she asked me.

I nodded and then winced because the wires hurt when I nodded and I hadn't had my paracetamol yet. I put my hand on her arm and pulled her back into my room.

She smiled at me. She said, 'I hope you don't think I'm being forward, but I've got something to ask you.'

I gave her a go-on kind of look and she took a deep breath. 'You're always writing in that notebook of yours,' she said. 'And your mama said you get good grades in English.'

I had no idea where this was going, but I gave her another go-on look.

'So, the girls and…well, the men, too…they wondered if you could write the thing to the papers.'

She'd lost me. I had no idea what she was talking about. I gave her a 'huh?' kind of look and she sighed and put down her mop bucket.

'You don't know what I'm talking about, do you?' she said. I started to shake my head, no, caught myself in time, and wrote, 'No, sorry,' on Donald.

'Okay,' she said. She smoothed her already perfectly smoothed hair back off her forehead with the back of her hand and said, 'Okay,' again. 'You know we won the lawsuit?'

I nodded and winced.

'You gotta remember to do your finger thing for when you nod,' she said.

I nodded with my finger.

'So the hospital has to pay us what they pay the menfolk.'

I nodded with my finger again.

'Now the hospital say that's too much money and they're going to lay people off. Did you know that?'

That was horrible. That was just another way to make the women lose. I shook my finger no, hard. I wrote, 'That's not fair,' on Donald and her face broke into her big smile.

'I knew you'd see that,' she said. 'I told them you'd see it, straightaway.'

I started writing, 'There's still the same amount of work to be done,' on Donald just as she said, 'We've still got to get all the same work done.' I showed her and she smiled again.

'You're smart as a whip,' she said.

She said, 'If we lose staff, we're going to have to start cutting corners. And that's not good.'

Nobody wants a dirty hospital, I thought. Nobody wants people waiting for hours to get wheeled down to X-Ray. I shook my finger, no, again.

'But, baby girl, nobody knows about any of this,' she said. She smoothed her uniform down over her hips. 'If people knew about it, they wouldn't let it happen, but they don't know.'

I was so dozy with the pain of the tape machine and the pain in my neck and the early morning, I still didn't see what she meant. So, she explained. 'We want to let the newspapers know and the radio people and even the TV news. But we don't know how to write it up.'

'You want a press release?' I wrote on Donald.

'Yeah,' she said. 'One of them things. Will you do it?'

We'd learned how to write press releases in my Communications class during my last year of Junior High. I shrugged. I wrote, 'I'll sure try,' on Donald. She hugged me and went into clean the bathroom.

I sat down on my bed, feeling a little tired, and a nurse crept in with my breakfast tray. It was the Early who'd had my tape player.

She said, 'I'm really sorry. Your mom told us to make sure you didn't hear it, but we thought you were—'

I held up my hand, in the universal shut-the-hell-up sign and she slid a piece of paper onto my table. I had four people to take to X-Ray that morning. And it was biscuits and gravy again.

I went by Orthopaedics about twenty times that day. I saw one of the Bobs, but I never saw Ed. After dinner, and after my mom had gone home (neither one of us mentioned the tape player, although I was sure the nurses had called her about it), I got Donald and wandered up the slope.

Ed wasn't on the sofa.

I thought about just going back down to ENT and working on the press release, but something made me go to the nurse's station. I used Donald to ask where he was.

The Orthopaedics Night Shift looked at each other. 'He's in bed,' one of them said.

'He's not feeling well today,' the other one said.

I used Donald. 'Where's his room?'

'I'm sorry,' the first Night Shift said. 'We're not allowed to give out that information.' Then she pointed to it with her pen and winked at me.

Ed's room was just like my room, except that where mine had a big blank space, he had a roommate, one of the Bobs, looking pretty flat and grey.

Ed was lying on his side, staring at the wall. I nudged him and he looked over his shoulder. 'No offence,' he said. 'But go away.'

His wheelchair was by his bed and there was another chair, too.

His pillow had that hot, creased look they get when you've been crying on them.

I wrote, 'No,' on Donald, and showed it to him. He batted it away.

I sat down in the other chair and drummed my fingers on Donald, just to irritate him. He hunched his shoulder like it wasn't going to bother him. But I kept on drumming until he jerked himself around on the bed to face me.

'I know you think you can help me,' he said. 'I know you think I can talk to you about stuff. But you can't, and I can't, so just GO AWAY.'

I just sat there and blinked at him. He clearly needed somebody to talk to. And I wasn't going until he did.

'I swear, I'll ring for the nurse and tell her you tried to kiss me,' he said.

I held up Donald. 'Ring, then,' I said.

He stared at me for a moment and then flopped down onto his back. 'God!' he said. 'This is like the forms all over again. You aren't going to leave until you help me, are you?'

I held up Donald. 'No.'

He snorted a laugh, but it fell off his face. Tears trickled out of his eyes and into his hair. 'If you weren't a girl, I'd hit you.'

'If I wasn't a girl, I'd let you,' I wrote, let him read it and then erased it. 'A fight would do you good.'

'Oh, I'm in a fight,' he said. He rolled over and looked at me. 'I'm in the fight of my life, apparently.'

I just looked at him.

'That's what my surgeon says, anyway. We're fighting to keep my leg. Together. Me and him.'

I wrote, 'Is he a dickhead?'

'No. He's okay.' More tears trickled out and Ed wiped them away. 'I just don't really give a shit. They can cut it off for all I care.'

I didn't understand, and it must have showed and Ed lost whatever patience he'd had with me. He rolled on his back again. 'Look,' he said, 'you're not going to get this. Football wasn't just something that I *did*. It was what I *was*.' He sighed. 'I don't really care about *walking*.'

He closed his eyes. He said, 'You don't understand. Nobody understands. Except the people who do and they...they don't want to be around me anymore.'

I wrote, 'But I really do understand,' on Donald, but he wouldn't look at it.

He said, 'Just leave me alone, Coco.'

I was fuming. He thought he was so *special*. That nobody else had ever had anything taken away from them. I wanted to write, 'Shit Happens,' on Donald, and rub his face into it until the plastic came off on his nose.

And then I remembered.

I flew down the ramp to ENT, jerked open my underwear drawer and got the tape machine. I was back by his bed in moments. I took a deep breath. I rewound to the beginning. And then I pushed the button.

It was only mono, but the sound really bounced off all the tile and linoleum. My voice soared up, filled the room, echoed down the hall. The power. The passion in it. The prayer of it.

Ed pulled himself up. I didn't have to tell him it had been me. My face did that.

I pushed stop and looked at him for a long, long moment.

And then I did what he'd wanted. I went away.

# Chapter Eighteen

**Soundtrack: 'Kung Fu Fighting' – Carl Douglas**

I got five notes from Ed that night. Two I got before I went to sleep and three were waiting for me in the morning.

They were a lot alike. They all begged for forgiveness and had spelling mistakes.

I'd already forgiven him, but I thought it would do him good to stew for a while. It would give him something to think about besides his own problems.

The ENT nurses were already dotty about him. They'd worked the whole thing up into some kind of big romance. Every last one of them told me how good-looking he was and how sweet he'd been and how sorry he was. It was kind of sickening.

But I knew nurses by now, and I was pretty sure Ed was getting the same thing at his end, from the Orthopaedic staff. The thought made me smile.

When I was taking my morning X-Ray crew (three ambulatory, one wheelchair) back, I took pity on him and went the Orthopaedics way. It was the first day I'd had enough meat on my bones to look decent in my favourite jeans and my hair wasn't too horrible. The Bob who had been pretty flat and grey the night before was more pink and was sitting up in the hall. I asked him to give me five as I went by. Ed had wheeled himself down by the sofa.

I was planning on milking it…acting all cold and making him grovel. But it would have been like kicking a puppy. My X-Ray crew stopped when I did, looking at him and at me. I wrote, 'Idiot' on Donald and held it up and Ed nodded.

'Agreed,' he said. We shook hands, briefly, and I kept walking.

Nurse Starchy came to see me during lunch. I looked up from

making my Pringles stack of gooey dip to find her at the end of my bed. 'Do you mind?' she said, nodding towards my chair. I shook my finger, no.

I had made a really huge stack of dip and Pringles and they were going to disintegrate if I didn't eat them, so I went ahead and crunched into them, despite Starchy's look of disgust.

They were, as always, truly delicious. I rolled my eyes to indicate delight and she shook her head in disbelief.

'Anyway,' she said. 'I'm not here to discuss your food preferences.'

She leaned forwards. 'I don't know if you know this, but the insurance your dad has for you doesn't actually pay for a private room.'

I knew where she was going with this right away. I was going to have to share with somebody. I sighed, making my trach tube whistle.

'I'm sorry,' she said. 'I've been keeping it private because you were so…'

I looked at her with interest as I swilled my chip and dip stack down with coke. I was so what, exactly?

'So…down,' she said.

I was still down, I thought. I just hid it better, now.

'But you've dealt with a number of conflicts lately, and dealt with them very well, I must say. So I feel you are resilient enough for roommates.'

I rolled my eyes and she levelled a finger. 'Don't get all teenaged on me, Coco,' she said. 'I don't have a bottomless budget, and I do my best.'

I wrote, 'Sorry,' on Donald.

She said, 'I'm sorry, too. I'll only give you nice people.' Then she patted me on the shoulder and left.

Everything is always about money, I thought. Some things are really more important than money. Which reminded me…

I got my pad with my right hand while I made another

Pringle's stack with my left.

*How Much For Hospital Hygiene?* I wrote at the top of the page.

*Support staff at Kansas University Medical Center were previously classed into two roles. Female staff, who undertook most of the cleaning duties, were called orderlies. Male staff, who ~~did~~ primarily moved patients and equipment, were called porters.*

*Recently, under...anti-discrimination legislation, the two roles were...*

It started with an A. It meant combined and made the same thing. Why didn't I have a dictionary?

Ah! I remembered.

*...the two roles were amalgamated. But now hospital...*

What was the grown up word for the bosses? It started with an A, too. Really, I would have been okay with just the 'A' section of the dictionary...

*...administration wants to cut jobs.*

*This is heart breaking for the former orderlies, who have fought so long for equality. But it will also mean lowering standards of cleanliness in our...no...in the city's biggest research hospital.* A 'research' hospital was a really big deal. That's why there were so many baby ducks following Morris, because it wasn't just a teaching hospital, but they did cutting-edge stuff. I'd learned all about that from reading all the plaques on the walls when I hung around waiting for other patients in X-Ray and Clinic.

*Some people suspect ~~they are just being dicks~~...the administration are acting punitively, and many fear that female workers will be over-represented in the job cuts.*

*Interviews with staff, patients and photographs available.*

My orderly's name was Maybelle Jenkins. I put what I'd written in an envelope for her and left it at the desk before I did my labs and shopping run. I actually needed some stuff for myself, and took some of my allowance out of my underwear drawer. I was out of deodorant, I wanted some candy to take up to Orthopaedics that night, and Donald was wearing out. I'd been there long enough to need a new magic slate.

Since I had an actual friend and might have roommates, I didn't want to be unable to hold up my end of a conversation.

When I look back, I can't remember which roommate I had when or who was my first. I think my first roomie was a Mexican woman having a biopsy on her larynx. These days you'd only be in for a couple of hours for something like that, but back then it was a two or three days.

This lady had a *huge* family and they *all* came to visit, *every* day. They brought in gorgeous tamales, menudo in wide-mouthed thermos flasks, tortillas and beans wrapped tightly in foil and Tupperware and covered in spotless dishcloths to keep warm...it was heavenly. They shared it all with me.

One of the ladies made a cucumber and tomato salad with vinegar and another one was really good at cooking green beans and another one did this soupy rice thing with peas... I just inhaled it all. It all had great texture and much of it had such strong tastes that the flavour came through, even if I couldn't smell it.

The ladies were all short and round and I was so tall and thin. They found it very amusing watching me snarf their cooking. It just kept coming and I kept doing it justice. Finally, I asked if I could take a plate to Ed and they started giving him stuff, too.

I was rather bummed when the biopsy came back clear of cancer and the Mexican Lady got to go home.

There was quite a bit of discussion on the ward about me having roommates. Some people thought I shouldn't be shielded from the realities of life, unless I wanted to move down to the children's ward. But even they didn't want me to have the really old people who'd come in to die.

In the end, my room was always the last one to be filled. Some days, I was on my own. Some days there was someone there.

Because of this, I got some emergency admissions. And that's how I ended up with dead roommates.

The first one really was sad. Agnes had outlived all her family except one son, who could only come for a half an hour on Fridays and Mondays. She seemed to keep holding on for those visits. But at last, she died without him. I could hear her last struggling breaths behind the curtain, the murmurs of one of the nurses, helping her to leave.

But the next one, Mrs Walker, had lots of family and they were all very cheerful about her going. They were staunch Baptists and used to say, 'Goodness, Mother, ain't you gone to glory yet? You know how Daddy doesn't like to be kept waiting!' when they came in. But they'd have armfuls of flowers and presents and hug and kiss her so hard that you could tell they loved her tons and were very glad to see her again.

They'd chatter and tell her all the news and keep reminding each other that she was tired. She couldn't even look at her water glass but one of them would jump up and make sure it was nice and cold and raise her up and put the straw in her mouth. They thought the world of her, you could tell. Her great-grandkids kept drawing her pictures. Every visit they'd take the old ones down and tape the new ones on the wall.

It made me get a lot more zealous about maintaining my own display of cards and flowers and teddies. Some of my flowers had gotten kind of gross and I threw them away. I moved the older things to the back and the newer things to the front. My rich great aunt and uncle from Texas had just sent a huge basket of flowers and plants that looked great, and other relatives had sent cards.

It was when I was doing all this that I noticed Kim had stopped sending me a card every day. I looked and realised she only sent one a week, now and didn't actually say much inside.

When I realised this, the Baptist family was twittering away about somebody's dog and how lovely it was. I felt...strange and empty inside, listening to them and missing Kim. I felt a loneliness that was worse because it was only mine, because other people had lives with dogs and grandchildren and a quilting circle and neighbours and I had one this one thing and it was fading away from me.

Every night when they left, they'd say, 'If you pass in the night, tell Daddy we love him.' There was absolutely no idea in any of their minds that Mrs Walker would face some sort of terrible trial or blank darkness. She would be walking into glory to be with her loved ones and her Lord. 'Bye, Mama. Bye-bye, now.'

If I hadn't heard Agnes die, I wouldn't have known what the sound was that woke me. But as I lay there and listened to it come again, I suddenly realised that Mrs Walker was dying. I sat up and groped for the light, but by the time I had it on, she'd given one last sigh and was completely still.

I couldn't help it. I looked at her as I went by her bed to the door. Her face was turned to where her family always sat and though her eyes and were open and staring, she still had a sweet, faint smile.

The night desk was an island of light in the dark ward. There was only one Night Shift there, a smiling, moon-faced thirtyish woman, who favoured scrubs and a white cardigan. She looked up and asked me if I was having trouble sleeping.

I did my finger no and then realised I'd left my magic slate behind. I gestured to use her pen and paper. Suddenly I felt terribly vulnerable. What if she said no, to go and get my magic slate? I couldn't go back in my room alone, I just couldn't.

But she didn't say no. I wrote, 'Mrs Walker's gone to glory.'

The nurse said, 'Oh, honey,' and leaned over the counter to give me a cuddle. 'Come sit around here,' she said. 'We'll get you some hot chocolate.'

She talked to her colleague and they rang for a porter and made me some cocoa. When I went back into my room, everything about Mrs Walker was gone. All the flowers and cards were gone. The pictures had been taken down from the wall and the cabinet with all her flannel nightgowns and matching robes was gone.

Even the bed was gone. There was just a smooth pale yellow wall and an expanse of clean linoleum.

I wasn't worried about Mrs Walker. Her guide had come to take her and she'd gone along willingly. All that was left was the troublesome meat.

But death from the outside was a whole lot scarier than death from the inside.

I lay there for a long while, looking at the empty space, and thinking about it. At last, the moon-faced nurse got the okay to offer me a sleeping pill, but I didn't want one. I felt very, very sad, but I also felt I was learning something, just by being in the room where Mrs Walker died.

Another roommate was young and pretty. She was only thirty-two and had two children and a handsome husband, who took the morning off work to come and settle her in and came back about a half an hour after he had finally left for work to bring her some flowers and a teddy bear. Her name was Janice.

She, too, was in for a biopsy, this time on the back of her mouth, where there was something that looked like it might be a tumour. She'd been smoking since she was fourteen. She'd stopped both times she was pregnant, but started up again once the babies were born. They were eight and six, a boy and a girl, and there was a picture of them looking at her as if she was the whole world and a bag of chips.

The whole smoking thing was really starting to bother me. Doctors walked along looking at charts with a fag in their hands. Nurses leant against the wall for a quick smoke. My mother had lost a lot of weight and to keep it off, she smoked. She smoked 'Eve' cigarettes. They were blue with flowers around the filter.

'You've come a long way, baby,' their jingle ran, 'to get where you've got to today. You've got your own cigarettes, now, baby. You've come a long, long way.'

It was one of the first times I could tell that advertising was playing with our emotions to sell us stuff. My mom felt like she was more liberated as a woman, because she was smoking poison with flowers around the filter.

But nobody really thought Janice had cancer. She was too bright and bouncy. Her blood counts were good. They were just making sure. So, she had a nice nightie and went without dinner and then was nil by mouth from ten o'clock on. In the morning, she had to change into the hospital gown and they gave her the pill and put in an IV. She had to wear her cap and take off her nail varnish. They were going to make her take off her wedding rings but I talked them into just taping them on and she was grateful. She kept saying it was nice having somebody there who knew the ropes.

She was gone a really, really long time. And right before she came back, a screen was wheeled in, and the stuff they need for big drains and catheters and one of the big IV stands and an oxygen tank.

'What's wrong?' I kept asking. 'What happened?' But I knew they couldn't tell me. They drew my screen around me when they brought Janice back. I could hear her crying. She seemed to be trying to talk but you couldn't understand anything she said. The nurses said that they'd tell her husband exactly what happened. Then she shouted, 'No! No husband!' really loud, but it sounded wrong – very weak consonants and all through her nose.

Mom and I were quiet that evening as Janice slept. I'd opened my screen but hers was fully shut. Nurses flitted in and out. They seemed upset.

Late in the night, Janice knocked over her water. I could hear it and then see the puddle on the floor. She was calling, 'Nurse!' again in that weak, weird consonant-free voice. I put my light on and pushed my own button. When one of the Night Shift came, I pointed and she went to straighten Janice out. They had to change the bed, so they just brought in a new one. It was easier to lift her over than to try to move her out. She got a new gown. I kept watching what went in and out.

My whole body was tense with wanting to help. I fell asleep that way and woke up with my hands in fists.

It was getting lighter. I checked my clock – four twenty. And then I heard what had woken me. Janice was crying.

I didn't know what to do. Get the nurse again? But sometimes when you're in hospital and crying, you really don't want some nurse either being bracing or shoving you full of drugs. I wanted to call out to her so badly that for the first time in ages I made my trach whistle trying to make her name.

I pulled up my magic slate. A new one, with a larger writing area and a somewhat more sober design of airplanes. I wrote, 'Do you want a hug?' on the slate and went over to Janice's curtain. I took a deep breath and stuck my arm in.

There was an immediate catch in the last sob, a kind of gasp. Then I could hear her laugh, the way you can sometimes when you've been crying hard.

In that odd vowel-ly voice, she said, 'Sure, if you think you can stand it.'

I opened the screen.

Her entire face, from her cheekbones down, was just a flap of skin. Her slack mouth drooled open and her chin lay against her neck. Above this horrible mess, her eyes looked at me question-ingly. She was ready for me to wince and turn away.

The utter horror of her face was nothing to the pain in her eyes. I swallowed and took the two steps and then I put my arms around her. She cried again, and patted the back of my head. She said, 'You're so brave. You're so brave,' over and over.

I wrote, 'Welcome to the freak ward,' on my pad and her mouth moved in a way I think was meant to be a smile.

She patted the bed and I sat down. I pulled up my plastic and then wrote, 'What happened?'

'Cancer,' she said, only it sounded like *canfer*. 'All in my lower mouth, my jaw. They took it all. They took my whole face.'

I shook my head and winced as the wires pulled. 'Your eyes are still pretty,' I wrote.

When her husband came in, I was ready to kill him if he showed by any blink of an eyelash that she wasn't still a beautiful woman. I would have stabbed his jugular vein with my breakfast fork, I swear.

But he was absolutely wonderful. He kept telling her how they thought they'd got all the cancer and that she wouldn't have to have chemotherapy. As if the fact that her face had disappeared was too trivial to mention.

She was so relaxed after he'd gone that she kept falling asleep. The doctors had to wake her up at rounds.

The next morning they moved her to Plastic Surgery. I never saw her again.

I couldn't really anticipate any of that was going to happen, and I couldn't really prepare myself for sharing my room. But I could get a new magic slate. So that's what I did.

# Chapter Nineteen

**Soundtrack: 'Already Gone' – The Eagles**

Ed and I didn't know what had happened to Des after they moved him to oncology. Nobody would tell us. It bothered us, a little, and we talked about it most nights. Both Bobs had gone home. Ed saw Mark sometimes in clinic – they liked to keep an eye on radial fractures. But Des had just disappeared.

We went down to Oncology and asked the nurses if they could get in touch with him, but although they were nice to us, they didn't actually tell us anything. They wouldn't tell us if he was an outpatient, or if he'd been transferred to another hospital. We got a bad feeling about Des.

I'd only met him once, and Ed had only known him for a couple of days, but we both had really liked him. Something about how people talked about Des bothered us.

We knew his school was on the Missouri edge of the city – Raytown or somewhere like that. Neither of us knew anybody on that side of town, and we couldn't get our parents to help us find out what had happened to Des.

My mother was utterly useless at helping me with social things. She couldn't even help me keep the friends I actually *had*.

If email or texts had been invented then, it would have been easy to keep in touch with Kim. But it wasn't. There was only the telephone, and I looked at it about fifty times a day, wanting to call her.

One night, I asked my mother to call. Mom got on the phone, spoke to Kim's mother and got Kim on the line. I wrote, 'How are you doing?' on my magic slate.

'Coco wants to know how you are doing,' my mother said. She listened while I fidgeted uncomfortably. Speaker phones hadn't been invented yet, either...at least not for ordinary phones.

'Well, I guess she's just concerned about you,' my mother said to Kim.

I wrote 'What did she say?' on my magic slate and showed it to mom, who pursed her lips and turned away a bit. I could hear Kim's voice, the tone of it, but I couldn't make out any words.

It was so frustrating I wanted to scream. I wanted to throw the slate at my mother and possibly throw my mother out the window, like Morris had with Mickey.

'I'll let her know,' my mother said and *hung up the phone*.

'What did she say???' I wrote again.

'She's fine,' my mother said. 'She's just getting on with things. She misses you, of course.'

'Tell me her WORDS,' I wrote on Donald.

But my mother just shook her head. 'I don't remember exactly,' she said. 'You're both very chatty.'

It was lucky I didn't have a roommate at the time. I had to go into the bathroom and slam the door twenty times just so I didn't explode.

So, there was no way my mother was going to help me find Des. Even though I was pretty sure he'd died.

He had been so alive, though. He had been so young and had looked so well. Flirting with me, getting Ed to do the wheelchair race. He had been...one of us. If Ed and I had formed a kind of sick-teens-club, we had, at least in our minds, one other founding member. He was gone, but he was still there, bigger, maybe, than if he'd been around.

Ed had little brothers and sisters. His mom came once a week on Mondays and his dad came on Thursdays and the whole family came to see him on Saturdays, downstairs in the cafeteria. The rest of the time, he got phone calls...just from his family. Never from his friends.

'At least you have each other,' the physio said.

'It's so nice you have each other,' the nurses said.

My mother said, 'You can talk to Ed, can't you?'

Like that solved us losing everybody else. And like being friends with each other was easy. It wasn't.

Ed was two years older than me. He'd been a high school star. Captain of the varsity football team, even though he was only in the second game of his junior year when he was injured. Dating the head cheerleader.

I was just the kind of little dweeb he'd never have deigned to notice before. And he couldn't really hide that, so I couldn't exactly forget it.

So it wasn't like we fitted together just perfectly.

And we weren't equal in other ways. I was a whole lot sicker than Ed. But he had to do more stuff about his injury than I had to do about mine.

In those weeks, Ed had four surgeries. He had plates, springs and holes drilled into his bones. He had to be stretched and wear external cages that bolted into the one inside his leg.

Sometimes, he could be a patient volunteer. Sometimes, he was doped up to the max in his bed. Sometimes, we made mad massive shopping trips with all of our people from both wards. Sometimes, I held onto his arm and we watched *I Dream of Jeannie* while he tried not to throw up lunch.

He actually liked the hospital food, and he'd liked his school cafeteria food, too. It gave me a very poor opinion of his mother's cooking. But even though he always tried to eat everything on his plate, all the medical stuff was making him thinner. Then one day, we had ice cream for dessert and he...he went crazy for it.

So my mom started to bring him ice cream from Baskin Robbins. Rocky Road. Rum and Raisin. Dark Cherry. Butter Brickle. He liked all the weirdest flavours. I was vanilla all the way, myself.

I felt like the well one for a while. Then, I started to sniff and cough.

I couldn't get over my cold. I got worse and worse.

I had to start going to respiratory therapy every day, where they put me on a slant board and pounded my ribs to make me cough up all the day's mucus at once. It was utterly exhausting and it didn't work all that well. My breathing got so bad, they stuck me in bed with steam and oxygen hooked up to my throat. My IV went back in again, with antibiotics and hydration running into me.

Luckily, Ed felt well enough to get around at that time. He used to wheel down to ENT and hang out. He even took some of my crew around with Nose Guy.

One day, we wrote down all the stuff we could about where we lived and our phone numbers and our schools. We were scared that one of us would just disappear, like Des.

And that was pretty clever of us, because two days after they pulled my IV, they decided I'd be better off at home.

I had a selection of scarves I could breathe through and had experimented with tying them in various ways until I was sure I could hide my buttons and trach tube. I was ready to face the world.

It seemed like a bit of a joke, having to be wheeled to the entrance, when I'd been making trips down there as a Patient Volunteer sometimes twice a day. A porter wheeled me and mom used another wheelchair, just to get all my cards and teddies and clothes and stuff down to the car. It was a female porter and she said they'd only had the meeting about my press release the day before and that they were going to use it.

I was still a bit weak from the infection, but I felt…fine. I felt absolutely fine in the hospital. I was one of the most well people I knew in hospital, usually much more well than Ed, even though what was wrong with him couldn't kill him. I was better at eating and washing and walking around than any other patient I knew. Until I gave five to the female porter and stepped out the door, I felt like I was doing really well.

Then I went outside.

The pavement that led down from the entrance was more slanted than the floors I was used to, and I nearly stumbled going down the very slight concrete slope. There wasn't a handrail. My knees felt spongy and weak.

Everyone seemed to be moving ridiculously quickly. I had to creep along. The joins in the paving stones looked incredibly dangerous and I got nervous every time I had to walk over one. Stepping off the curb down onto the road to get to the car was absolutely terrifying. Mom was hopping up and down it, loading stuff into the car and I had to lean over and hold onto the hood and kind of crawl.

When I finally managed to open the car door and get inside, I sighed with relief. Mom seemed totally unreasonable when she asked me to put on my seatbelt. It felt like she should first let me have a nap.

It got worse when she started the car. There was too much colour in the non-hospital world. Too much noise and movement. Every time I saw a tree or some grass, it was almost disturbingly beautiful. I saw a squirrel and had such a strong emotional response to it that my eyes filled with tears. It was absolutely beautiful, that squirrel. The wind moving the trees made me feel intensely grateful, though I didn't know what I was grateful *for*, or who I was grateful *to*. I just had this big feeling. And then there'd be a shiny plastic McDonald's sign or something that hit me almost like a slap. I had to turn off the radio. It was all way, way too much.

It was only a few minutes, even on mom's favourite highway-free right-hand-turns-only route, but, by the time we got home, I felt exhausted. I was glad it was late afternoon, and that the sun was fading. Everything was slightly less dazzling without the bright sunlight.

The walk from the driveway to the door was endless. The

path actually seemed to be getting longer as I went along. Mom unlocked the door but went back for the bags, so I opened it myself.

'Surprise!'

It was Kim, Mandy, Bobby and Jack and…quite a few people in the dining room. The last time I'd been in here, I'd been coughing up my voice box. Now, someone had put up crepe paper streamers and balloons. Everyone ran over and hugged me. I nearly fell over.

My mother came in beaming, talking about how I hadn't suspected a thing.

People started giving me presents and asking me how I was. I pulled out a dining chair and sat down, holding onto the table. I thought I might pass out. The work of staying upright on the chair was making me sweat.

Music was pumping out of the stereo. Everyone was talking. My poor old dog was running around in circles, glad to see me but distressed by the influx of people. Mandy. Karla. Shanice. Bethany…looking normal and not wearing a black turtleneck and talking to Bobby.

They were walking around, getting punch and crisps. In the living room there was a cake. It was a birthday cake. I'd seen a hundred forms the day before with the date on top. How could I forget that today was my birthday?

The living room was four steps away from where I was. I knew there was no way I could get to the living room.

My mother came by with a tray of ice-filled glasses. I pulled her sleeve and she frowned at me. 'Why aren't you with your friends?' she asked.

I wrote on my slate, 'I need to go to bed.'

'But the nurses said you always stay up late!' She leaned down to my ear. 'I think you should stay for a while and open some presents.'

My friends were all talking to each other at the top of their lungs, over the sound of the music. I stood up and wavered on my feet. It was just too bright. They all moved too fast and talked too loud.

I went over to Kim, who was standing nearby. I knew she'd had to organise everyone. 'Thanks for this,' I wrote.

She bit her lip and then opened up her arms. I kind of fell into her. I felt like if she only kept hold of me, I might manage to stay at my party for a few more minutes. I might manage to deal with all the noise and the colour and the whole too-much-ness. Maybe she could hold my hand like she used to when we were kids, and we had to go somewhere new.

But then she kind of patted me and straightened me up onto my own feet. Bobby had come over and was talking to us. His words came so fast, I couldn't keep up. Something about timing.

I looked back at my chair. I thought if I sat down, I'd never be able to get up again. I looked into the living room, where Karla was throwing popcorn for Jack to catch in his mouth.

Kevin G, who lived just down the road, was giggling his infectious, high-pitched laugh. My mom was pouring drinks in the corner. Cokes and more pink punch.

I wasn't breathing through my mouth, of course, but it was kind of hanging open. I was so tired that my jaw had gone slack. I pulled it shut with a snap, just in case somebody looked at me, so that I didn't look totally out of it. But nobody was looking at me.

The party wasn't really about me. It was about all of them, so that they could feel like they'd done the right thing.

The last time I'd been in this room, nobody had listened to what I needed. Nobody was listening now, either.

I really needed to lie down.

So, I went through the kitchen and down to my rooms. I didn't stagger, but my knees buckled a little with every step. I touched the honey-wood of the kitchen table. I pushed myself along on the refrigerator door handle and the pantry shelves.

My room was dusted and fresh. I had crisp, ironed sheets on the bed and mom had laid out some warm pyjamas.

I wanted to brush my teeth, but my toothbrush was still packed in the suitcases by the front door. I wanted a shower, but the idea of taking one while everyone was in the house…it seemed impossible. I washed my face and hands. I enjoyed having a wee on my own home toilet.

I pulled down my blinds and shut and locked my door. And then I unwound the scarf, crawled into my jammies and went to sleep.

It was completely dark outside when my mom shouted at me to unlock the door, that she couldn't check on me and she was worried. She kept talking about it for a good long time and I think she threw in some sobbing.

But you get used to noise in the hospital.

I just rolled over and went back to sleep.

# Chapter Twenty

## Soundtrack: 'Pick up the Pieces' – The Average White Band

My cousin Kathryn was taking me shopping. It was her and her little sister Charlotte. We were going to the mall to find Kathryn some new jeans. Then we were going to see a movie at the huge multiplex cinema.

I had been okay. I got from the car to the food court okay. I ordered my food and ate it okay. And then we started to walk around.

And I got not-okay.

It wasn't really physical. I didn't know it at the time, but my breathing was better through my trach tube than it was going to be for the rest of my life. It wasn't really that I was wearing a nice new furry parka two sizes too small for me, provided by my father and not from the kind of place you can take back for the right size. It was the whole sensory overload thing.

I just couldn't take it.

'Come on, Coco,' Kathryn said, halfway up a flight of stairs. Charlotte was already waiting impatiently up at the top. I felt like I was hurrying up, but my legs were moving soooooooooooooooo slooooooooooooowly. And everything seemed to blur and then...I sat down on the steps, making a spectacle of myself.

My wrists looked too thin, exposed by the too-short sleeves of the parka. My body just looked too fragile to me, all of a sudden. Too fragile in the sense of too easily broken. And suddenly, I saw the tree coming towards us, the sun starting to warm up the earth, the meadowlark swinging on the barbed wire. I saw Kim's look of horror as she tried, too late, to straighten the wheel.

And then I was back in the shopping mall, and Kathryn was

161

standing over me, concerned.

There were benches along the main concourse, where old people sat and rested while the young scurried about and shopped. My cousins parked me on one of those and one of the other occupants looked up and met my eye with understanding. It was humiliating to be stuck there. It was also a real relief.

He was about eighty. He smiled. He said, 'You can get cheap coffee over there,' nodding towards a cookie stand.

I tried to make a grateful expression.

And that's the way it was, every time I left the house. It was all too much for me. I started to look for the places where the old folks sat and watched other people living, and make a beeline for them straightaway. It was like I'd joined a club.

Mom couldn't keep on working, because I had to be super-vised around the clock. She reverted to being a housewife and I reverted to summer vacation behaviour, only without sleepovers and trips to the pool.

I read, of course, and going to the library was one of the outings that didn't exhaust me. I was okay to go to the movies, too, but we couldn't afford to do that much. Although petrol seemed expensive to us that year, it was still really incredibly cheap. I liked mom to take me on long drives to nowhere in particular. I liked visiting my grandparents.

We'd go over in the afternoon and Grandma and Grandpa would have a pot of tea. They'd drink it in big turquoise mugs, with cracked glaze. I always had too much milk and sugar in mine – ice cream tea, they called it. We had cookies – sometimes homemade peanut butter cookies or chocolate chip, sometimes store-bought Oreos or shortbread. Sometimes grandpa would have baked a cake or a pie. After she'd had enough tea, my grand-mother would push herself up and put on her apron and start cooking. Always meat and potatoes and two veg. And I always loved it.

Mom would help and they'd work together cooking and washing up.

I'd sit on the leather sofa next to Grandpa's chair, or maybe help dry or put away, if I felt up to it.

Grandma was, by then, fairly ill herself of liver disease. She was the only person in my life who both cared about me and was truly sensible and sane. She gave very sharp Irish advice, like, 'There's plenty of time to lie down when you're dead,' and 'Show a smile to the world, everyone's got their own troubles.' She believed in doing as much good as you could fit into a day, learning all you could, God and Family.

Grandpa believed in Grandma. He believed so completely that he got all the rest through her.

My father's parents were another story. I hated going to their house, would do almost anything to avoid it. When they came to see me, I felt like screaming and running away.

It's not that they weren't nice to me. They were *too* nice, though my grandfather had that same, 'She's irrevocably ruined,' attitude my father shared about me. That was nothing to do with the hole and wires in my neck. They'd both been like that for a while.

My grandmother was creepy. She liked to get me into corners and whisper things to me. She liked to give me things and tell me not to tell my mother. I had a little chest under my bed of things she'd given me. Sparkly, jewelled things a child would like. A pincushion shaped like a golden poodle and its pink velvet bed. A little golden treasure chest with jewels inset (I'd once made a perfect pipe-cleaner spring on a pencil, after years of trying and I kept it in there). Stuff like that.

During this time, she brought over a sewing machine. It must have cost a fortune. It had all kinds of bells and whistles. It could embroider and smock and who knows what else. And it sat on our living room carpet.

It wasn't that I didn't sew. All girls my age could sew and I sometimes made myself a skirt or made a cushion cover or something. Mom was pretty good at sewing and made her own curtains and many of our clothes. We had a 1950s electric Singer that was nigh on indestructible.

But my father's mother sewed *all* her own clothes, and could crochet and knit as well. She had just bought a sewing machine and got me one exactly like it. It could do everything, things I'd never even consider trying to do. Things I would never in a million years *want* to do. It was the kind of sewing machine a dressmaker would save up to get, for her business. I'm sure it could have flown a space mission, if you read the instruction manual carefully, and used the right thread tension.

I tried to look grateful, but all I could think of was what we could have done with the money it cost. Paid the gas bill. Bought sacks and sacks of food. I looked at mom, who was thinking the same thing. She made a 'go on' movement with her head and I embraced my grandmother, who seemed very pleased. And then they left.

Not long after that, Dad arrived for an unscheduled visit. He asked me if I'd tried out the sewing machine, and when I confessed that I hadn't, insisted we set it up and go for it right then. Mom found some fabric in the utility room and I had to learn quickly how to make three or four different stitches, while Dad looked on. It felt like an exam. Then, telling me to use the thing, Dad left and I collapsed back onto the sofa.

Again, no mention of money for the gas bill.

Money was a bit on my mind.

While I'd been in the hospital, Dad had gone ahead with the divorce.

As you can imagine, my mother was a bit distracted and she hadn't put up much of a fight. She'd just gone along with whatever Dad wanted. I think she just wanted it to be over and not to have to think about it anymore, and I don't blame her. She had enough on her plate.

So, when Dad picked mom's lawyer for her, she thought it was nice of him. She thought it was kind of him to come along to her meetings with the lawyer, too.

It wasn't until she arrived at the divorce hearing and Dad and both lawyers sat on one side of the table and my mother sat all by herself on the other side of the table, that she realised she'd been tricked. She was so upset that she spent the hearing trying not to cry. She felt humiliated and stupid. And she signed whatever they put in front of her, just so she could run away.

So, although my mom had been married for 17 years, and all that time she'd kept house for Dad and looked after me and had never had a job, Dad managed to get out of paying her any maintenance.

Dad paid the house payment and a hundred and fifty bucks a month for me, which even back then wasn't an awful lot. It covered my food, books and entertainment, but it didn't really stretch to clothing (he'd told my mother that he'd take me shopping twice a year, but he never did). This was supposed to continue until I graduated from university. Then, of course, mom had the expense of running the big house: the utility bills, and trying to keep up with the garden. The whole thing was set up so that she would fail, and so that she would learn how crap she really was.

It wasn't really a divorce settlement. It was part of the long war of their relationship. It was another way for my father to try to convince my mother that she was wrong and he was right. About money, about driving, about me, about everything.

Since mom was at home looking after me, we were seriously broke.

The only way we were eating at all was through the kindness of Grandpa's rich brother, my great-uncle, who was sending us 200 bucks a month, and even that didn't stretch all that far. You know all those tins and packets in the back of the kitchen cupboards that nobody ever eats? We were eating those. I remember making pancakes, and all the flour had little bugs in it...but I'd used it anyway and eaten what I made, without telling mom about the bugs. I knew we couldn't afford to throw the flour away.

It was unusually cold for the time of year. Usually, the real chill set in around February, but this year it had begun in October. By Thanksgiving, at the end of November, we had snow flurries and the heating bills were astronomical.

Mom was the first one to move out of her room. She just closed the heating vents upstairs and treated it like a large wardrobe, visiting it once or twice a day to get dressed. She got the sleeping bags out of the barn and put a thick quilt on the floor in front of the gas fire. As soon as I was tucked up under my electric blanket, she'd turn the heating down to nearly nothing and stay in the living room. Before long, however, I'd closed up my rooms, too, and joined her. We'd roll the sleeping bags away and hide them behind the sofa during the day. We used my electric blanket over us. We sewed loops onto our hand-pieced quilts and hung them over the doorways to stop draughts.

Then someone found out and the gas bill got paid and we moved back into the rest of the house.

My godparents had invited us for Thanksgiving dinner. So we didn't buy a lot of groceries that week knowing we'd be given a great deal of the leftovers.

Thanksgiving dinner is a really big deal. My family always has a huge turkey, a huge ham, enchiladas and/or burritos, sweet potatoes, mashed potatoes, roasted potatoes, green bean casserole, broccoli with cheese sauce, roasted squash, corn on the cob, beans, gravy, dinner rolls, everybody's competitive wine selections, muffins, and then the pies. Pumpkin pie, apple pie, my mother's pecan pie, mincemeat pie, cherry pie, lemon meringue pie, Mississippi mud pie, blackberry pie, Key Lime pie, cheesecake, chocolate cream pie and my cousin's pumpkin puffs. And then things to go on the pies: ice cream, Cool Whip, squirty whipped cream.

A share of the leftovers would feed us for more than a week.

But it began to snow. mom's car didn't have proper snow tires. She had radials, which were good for light snow, but this was a real dumper of a storm. Grandpa rang, though, and said that he'd pick us up and take us. This was kind, because it was miles out of their way, but they had snow tires and chains and should be fine.

However, when morning came, the snow was still falling. There was nearly a foot of the stuff. I wanted to go out and play in it a bit, but we were frightened of what would happen if I got too cold and wet. So I just looked at it. Mom didn't wait for Grandpa to ring to say he couldn't make it. She rang and forbade him to try.

There's a parade in New York every Thanksgiving morning. We watched it on TV and felt cold, hungry, lonely and miserable. Finally, the hungry bit took over and we went to see what we could make for our Thanksgiving dinner. Poking around in the depths of the frosted-up freezer, mom unearthed two ancient T-bone steaks. I found two large potatoes without really big eyes. We had some tins of corn and green beans.

While it was cooking, we got rather silly. Mom got out all our best stuff for the table. We had white linen tablecloths and damask napkins. We had lead crystal wine glasses and heavy silver knives and forks. We had candelabra. We even had candles to go in them. It was just the food part we were lacking.

When it was all ready, the table looked amazing.

Our dining room was the first room you walked through. It was an extension with big windows all the way around three sides. In the summer, we had a hedge, which provided privacy from the busy main road in front, but it wasn't evergreen. In the winter, we either shut the curtains or did without privacy.

Well, the room looked wonderful against the snow outside. Everyone who drove by looked at the candles glowing off the panelled walls and the big island of the gleaming white table.

Which gave us another idea.

We decided that we should be dressed a bit better if we were to be a shop window for fine dining. Mom turned the oven down. We ran to our rooms and chose from our small selections of evening gowns. I put up my hair. Mom wore her best wig. We put on jewellery and makeup.

Then mom broiled the steaks with garlic and salt and cut up bacon and onion for the green beans while I made up some Kool-Aid squash and decanted it into a carafe.

The food was good and we laughed a lot. Every time someone drove by, we'd raise our antique crystal wine glasses and toast each other, very seriously, with the Kool-Aid and then we'd collapse into giggles once they'd passed.

We'd had the crappiest autumn imaginable. But we still had each other, and for that, we were both really, really thankful.


That night, while we were watching an old black and white film in front of the fire, the phone rang.

Mom said hello and then said, 'But…' and then listened for a while. 'Okay,' she said. 'We can try it.'

She turned to me and said, 'It's for you.'

Ooooookay, I thought. Phones had cords back then. I had to walk across the room and put the big old receiver up to my ear. 'It's me,' Ed's voice said. 'Do you have a pen handy? Just tap the mouthpiece with it.'

Everybody had pens next to their phones. I grabbed one and tapped the mouthpiece a few times.

'Good,' Ed said. 'Now tap once for yes and twice for no. Have you got that?'

I tapped once.

'I think you said yes,' Ed said. 'Am I right?'

I tapped once again.

He laughed. 'You see?' he said. 'I'm not completely stupid.'

It was good to hear his voice. He said, 'I got to come home. And I've been practicing, and I can drive our station wagon. It's an automatic.'

I didn't have to add anything to that, so I just waited.

'And so I wondered. Do you want to come out to lunch tomorrow? I'll buy.'

I looked out at the snow. I didn't tap.

Ed said, 'Don't worry about the snow. It's going to rain in the morning. It'll be gone by noon.'

Typical, I thought. I was really looking forward to Thanksgiving and it had been ruined by just one dumb day.

'So, do you want to come?'

I tapped once.

'Great. I've been by your house on my practice runs. I'll come over about twelve. Is that okay with you?'

I tapped once again.

I lay back down on the sofa and got my magic slate. 'I'm going out for lunch tomorrow,' I wrote to mom.

'Get you, Little Miss Tappy,' mom said. 'Do keep me informed of your social engagements.'

It made me grin. But then I started worrying about the snow and wanted to watch the weather report.

I wrote, 'Can we change the channel and watch the local news?' Mom didn't usually watch the local news. It really bothered her to see any of Dad's old colleagues, or any of the people who used to come to their parties. But she got up and changed it.

'...hospital administrators deny massive job losses were ever intended...' there was a picture of the hospital and a man in a suit, standing behind a nice wooden desk. 'We never intended to make significant cuts to the number of porters at the hospital,' he said.

'However, this reporter...' a familiar-looking woman in a red coat was talking in the snow outside the hospital entrance, '...feels the administration turn-around has more to do with press and public interest in the story. Nancy Preston, Channel Four News.'

I went over and got the local newspaper from the magazine rack – I never used to read the newspaper, so I hadn't seen it. 'Hospital Cleanliness Too Expensive?' was the front-page headline. I read down the columns...and recognised some of my own words from the press release.

The reporters had interviewed male and female porters. They'd interviewed nurses.

What I'd written had...worked.

I lay in bed that night, Thanksgiving, and looked at my notebook, at the draft of the press release and all the little bits I'd written about the hospital. It seemed like a miracle that something I'd just messed around with on a piece of rumpled paper...it even had a bit of dried dip on the edge of it...had actually changed the world. Maybelle and her friends were better off because of something I'd just scribbled around with.

If I hadn't already come to terms with trying to be a professional singer when I was miles away from New York or Nashville or L.A., I probably wouldn't have had the idea. But it was no crazier than wanting to become a recording star...and people *were* professional writers. And writers came from all over the place, and were all kinds of colours and shapes and sizes and a whole lot of them were women. So...

...so why *not* me?

I decided I'd talk to Ed about it and went to sleep.

# Chapter Twenty-One

**Soundtrack: 'Gimme Three Steps' – Lynyrd Skynyrd**

Ed had to go back to school. He was walking with crutches and had gotten really good at slinging them into the back seat and driving with his left foot. On Monday, when everybody came back from Thanksgiving, he was going back, too.

I thought he'd be thrilled. But he was totally bummed.

We were at Don Chilitos. It was a top teen hangout on weekend nights for Burner, Pawnee Mission North and Pawnee Mission North West. Even Warmon kids sometimes drove to Don Chilitos. They did amazing burritos smothered in cheese sauce and you could refill your coke. The staff didn't blink when I ordered by magic slate and gave us free chips and salsa – I guess because we were so pitifully disabled. I carried the tray with everything on it, so Ed could swing his leg into a booth.

The lunchtime crowd was a lot quieter than it was after games. And nobody was playing Pong on the video game table. After football or basketball games, there was always a queue of people wanting to play Pong. Even *I* liked to play Pong. I'd spent countless quarters of my allowance playing Pong, even though I was rubbish at it.

Ed went to Pawnee Mission North West, so of course he knew about Don Chilitos. I'd found out from my cousins that Ed was this amazing quarterback. College scouts were already after him. He'd helped North West win State as a Sophomore. He'd evidently been really, totally brilliant.

I wrote, 'You'll still be cool at North West,' on my slate, but Ed waved it away.

'Yeah,' he said. And then added, 'Well, kinda.' He stuffed about half a ton of ground beef burrito in his mouth and chewed it moodily.

I waited.

'Everybody's being really nice,' he said. 'Even Julie'—I knew this must have been his girlfriend from his expression of pain— 'keeps coming by the house and wanting to be friends.' He cut another big chunk of burrito and shoved it in his mouth.

I was loving mine. I could taste Mexican food. I'd never been a big fan of refried beans before the accident, but I loved how silky they felt on my tongue and I could taste the garlic and onions and hot sauce and the chili in the queso sauce. Most of my meals didn't taste of anything, but when I had Mexican food it just kind of exploded in my mouth.

Ed didn't even seem to be tasting his burrito. He just choked it down his neck. He was, I realised, angry.

I wrote, 'Why are you so mad?' And he snorted.

He said, 'I don't think you'll understand,' and I just looked at him. I didn't have to remind him about the last time he'd decided I wouldn't understand.

He sighed and pushed his burrito away. 'Look,' he said. 'I was never good at school. I got help with my grades.' He grabbed his coke and started spinning the thick plastic tumbler around on the table. 'My dad's a plumber. My uncle is a plumber. My grand-pappy is a plumber.'

I wrote, 'There's nothing wrong with being a plumber.'

And he sighed. He said. 'I don't want to be a plumber.' He spun his coke glass so hard it nearly went off the table. 'Julie doesn't want to marry a plumber.'

Mark had called Julie a bitch. I suddenly really hated this girl I'd never even met. Ed said, 'She wants to go places, see the world, do interesting things.' He spun the coke glass again, and this time it did fall off the table, spraying ice and coke in a wide arc. Some people in suits jumped back just in time.

Ed started to struggle up to his feet, but before he was out of the booth, a staff member had bustled out of the kitchen with a mop. They told him to stay there, that accidents happened and they got him a refill. Ed hunched over. His face was red and looked hot under his perfect hair.

My burrito was getting cold. I had another bite of it.

'What do you like to do?' I asked. 'Besides football?'

He shrugged, watching the guy mop the floor. 'I don't know,' he said. 'Baseball?'

'What's your favourite subject?'

He looked at me. He said, 'I never had one. When I was a kid, it was recess.'

He was the kind of boy, I suddenly realised, who messed around in class and didn't listen. He would have been passing notes and joking with his friends and chatting to the hot girls, safe in the knowledge that the teacher would have to give him a passing mark, or the school would lose their football star.

I wrote, 'Try paying attention in class,' and he rolled his eyes.

I erased it and wrote, 'You've got a brain, use it.'

He looked at me sharply. 'I'm not smart,' he said.

I tried to snort and made my scarf flap over my tube. I wrote, 'Bullshit,' in such big letters that I had to erase them to write, 'You're just lazy.'

He was looking at me, but he seemed a million miles away, like my words had meant something to him. And so I pushed my luck. I wrote, 'Imagine if the effort you put into ball...' and ran out of space. As soon as he read it, I erased it and wrote '...you put into school work,' but he stopped me.

He said, 'It's the middle of my junior year. It's too late.'

I wrote, 'Too late if you're a great big chicken.'

He was thinking again. I wrote, 'I can help.'

He rolled his eyes. 'You and your helping,' he said. 'You've got a complex about it or something.'

'Your English sucks,' I wrote. He glared at me and I let my face go blank. 'I can help with your English.'

'They drop our freshman grades,' he said, still thinking. 'And I got straight Cs last year. So if I got Bs this year, and As next year, I could have a B average.' He wasn't really talking to me. He was thinking out loud.

I wrote, 'It's your SATs that matter,' on my slate, and his eyes widened.

I erased it and wrote. 'You've got a year.'

'I've got a year.' His voice was expressionless and seemed like it came from far away. He was still looking at my face and not seeing me.

'You've got a year before SATS.' I showed it to him again.

'And if I aced my SATS...' He rolled his eyes. 'Like *that's* going to happen...'

He started to spin his coke, and I took it away from him.

That made him look off in the distance again. '*If* I aced them, though,' he said slowly, 'I could still...go to college.' I looked at him. He was scared, I could tell, but he was also excited. 'It's a big freaking if, Coco,' he said.

I shrugged. 'So?' I wrote. 'What else are you going to do?'

We sat there for a minute and looked at each other.

Ed said, 'This is crazy.'

'Thinking you can be an NFL quarterback is crazy,' I wrote. 'This is just work.'

He erased it, slowly, with his long, elegant fingers. His eyes sparked under his perfect hair, but his mouth was set in a grim line.

'I'm not afraid of hard work,' he said. 'But there's no way, man...I'm...' He looked off over my left ear, like he was watching a movie of the boy he'd always been. 'I haven't cracked a book since I was ten.'

I shrugged again. 'Start now.' I was in the middle of re-reading *Catcher in the Rye* for the twentieth time. It was in my shoulder bag. I took it out, removed my bookmark and slid it across to Ed.

He sat there for a moment, staring at the paperback like it was a coiled rattlesnake, ready to strike. And then he picked it up.

I completely forgot to talk to him about being a writer. I didn't really need any help with that, I thought to myself. I was already doing all the right stuff...writing and reading. I didn't need anybody to help.

On the way home, he was deep in thought. We listened to the radio, and hardly said a word. He was headed through a light when it turned yellow...he stopped kind of suddenly and I was jolted forwards and...

...I saw the tree coming towards us. The sun was starting to warm the earth. A meadowlark swung on the barbed wire fence. Kim's face had a look of utter panic...

Ed said, 'Jeez.' I opened my eyes. I was gripping the dashboard. My arms were shaking. I was sweating.

'You okay?'

I nodded my finger. I nodded it where he could see it, so he didn't have to take his eyes off the road.

I stayed up to watch Monty Python on the Public Broadcasting television station. It was gloriously silly, but mom didn't like it. 'I don't get it,' she said. 'I don't understand why it's supposed to be so clever.'

She always went to bed early on Monty Python night.

I felt...strange...going down the hall to my rooms on my own. The elderly dog was long asleep in the corner of the sofa. The old house creaked and sighed in the night.

It was no big deal. I'd been staying up later than my parents some nights since I was twelve. But...it didn't feel right.

I tried to read, but I was too tired.

And so I rolled over and closed my eyes.

To see the tree coming towards us, the meadowlark swinging on the barbed wire fence, the look of fear on Kim's face...

I opened my eyes again. There was a streetlight just outside the gate, eight feet from my bedroom window. This time of year, the light seemed cold and blue. In the summer, it always seemed yellow. I knew every shadow.

I closed my eyes again and heard Billy Preston singing, 'Nothing from nothing leaves nothing,' saw the tree coming towards us, the meadowlark...

I opened my eyes again. I was sweating.

I thought about waking up mom. It would be nice to be cuddled. Then I thought about writing it all out on my slate and how mom's face looked when she was worried.

It's not like she could help me. Ed was right. Some things, nobody could help.

I thought about the loop of memory and how terrifying it was. There wasn't any actual pain in it, though. There wasn't any of the nastiness. The things about the memory weren't actually horrible, they just made me *feel* horrible.

If I thought about it, and thinking about it made my heart pound in my ears, it was just a tree, and my friend, and a song and a bird. Thinking about trees and Kim, and songs and birds couldn't really *hurt* me. Not really.

Though even naming them in my mind made me sweat and shake.

I prayed a bit, to whatever had come for me when the ceiling went away. I didn't ask for it all to go away. I just asked not to fall completely to bits.

A few tears leaked out of my eyes and I got angry and sat up, moving my pillows behind me.

I was so, so *tired*. But I didn't dare close my eyes.

And then, for some reason, I started to think about the meadowlark, swinging on the barbed wire.

That was quite a *nice* thing to remember, actually, if I thought about it. I lay back down and *made* myself think about it with my eyes open, the pattern of the feathers, the way they ruffled in the breeze, the way his little feet gripped the twisted wire, the way he'd used his tail to steady himself against the current of air.

After a while, I closed my eyes, and kept seeing the

meadowlark, the meadowlark, the meadowlark.

And then it was morning and I'd done another whole day.

I actually crossed off every day on an actual calendar. I looked forward to February's surgery like you'd look forward to a cruise around the world.

I filled the time with reading, and visits to family.

Sometimes I met up with friends, but going out in the world nearly always gave me that memory loop, especially if one of my friends was driving. Over the Christmas break, I'd gone with Kim and a bunch of other people to the mall, to watch a movie. Kim hadn't sat with me in the car, and she hadn't sat near me in the movie, but as we walked through the mall, I caught up with her. I wanted to ask her if she had a memory loop, too, but the moment I started writing on my magic slate, she broke away from me, darting into the flavoured popcorn shop like it was a big emergency.

Mandy had seen, and I asked her, 'Do you think Kim will ever talk to me again?' Even writing the question made a cold wind blow right through my heart.

'Look,' Mandy said. 'She's not not-talking to you. She's not avoiding you, or anything. Not really.'

I looked at Mandy and she had the grace to look ashamed.

'I don't know,' she said. 'I think it bothers her that you can't talk.'

I looked at Mandy again and she shrugged, like it wasn't fair, but that's the way it was. I shrugged, too. For the rest of the day, I didn't try to talk to Kim and she kind of walked *around* me. Near enough to touch my arm or make a joke, sometimes. But not near enough, not really.

I wanted my surgery, not only because I wanted a voice again, but because I wanted my life again. I wanted to be able to run after Kim, grab her and tell her not to be such an idiot, that there was nothing wrong between us.

In the meantime, I suffered the memory loop on my own.

I packed my bag with glee. I sighed with relief as I walked through the doors of the ENT clinic to see Doctor Morris and Doctor Kular. It felt like I'd been on a long journey, but was finally home.

They thought they'd be able to take the stent out through my mouth. That meant they wouldn't have to cut me open again. I was so pleased, I even smiled at Doctor Kular.

It was so great to be back. Most of my fellow patients had either died or gone home, but Nose Guy got an infection and came in while I was there, which was very exciting. We sat together on the leatherette sofa and he burped all the latest information about the construction of the new building.

I was a bit of a celebrity on the ward... Rounds were absolutely rowdy with giving out fives and tens and questions and answers. One of the female junior doctors had gotten a trendy haircut and we all teased her about it. We were laughing so loud that Nurse Starchy came in and told us to be quiet, that my medical team was disturbing the other patients.

I was due to have the thing out on the third day, and on the afternoon of the second day, Bob the anaesthesiologist arrived to talk me through the operation. He'd scheduled himself on the job on purpose, even though he was starting to work more for Neurosurgery.

Everyone was so kind.

I was hip to the drill now. After the pizza mom had brought in, it was nil by mouth. Then the early morning wake up with the old happy pill, change into the green gown and cap, and then Bob would arrive to do the IV. I'd taken off my toenail polish and left my ring at home. I was trying to be good.

I was so excited. I couldn't wait to be all better.

I waved at everyone when I got to the OR. I counted

backwards, this time, from ten. I got to eight, and I was gone.

Recovery seemed overly bright and once again, everything hurt. But now I knew that the drugs I'd been given didn't agree with me, and that this horrid grotty feeling was temporary. I also knew I wouldn't be able to stay awake for long. The effort of pushing my eyes open made them roll back in my head and I slid back down the deep well of unconsciousness.

Then someone said, 'How are you feeling?' to me and I forgot and tried to answer. I expected my trach tube to whistle but instead I heard myself say, 'Oh, just wonderful.'

My hand flew up and encountered my trach tube still in place, but now with a cork in the middle. My buttons were gone.

I said, 'Hey, I can talk!'

My voice was a weak, hoarse whisper. I breathed through my nose and it felt like luxury. All marvellous. And I wanted to just relax now and go back to sleep. I had done it. It was over.

'Coco, stay with us.'

I pushed my eyes open again and Doctor Morris and Doctor Kular were with me in recovery.

Doctor Morris said, 'I want you to say eeeee.' The 'eeeee' was in a high-pitched tone.

I obediently said, 'Eeeee.' Mine was a whisper with a few intermittently growly notes. They weren't overly impressed.

'Once again,' Morris said. 'Eeeee.' This time his 'eeeee' was very loud and clear.

I tried again with the same result. Kular frowned and started to say something but caught Morris's eye and didn't.

'Just rest now,' Morris said.

But I whispered, 'Is there something wrong?'

He came back and took my hand. 'We don't have the vocal articulation we wanted,' he said. 'But that could be swelling from the surgery. Or, you might have forgotten how to talk, in which case we'll send you to speech therapy. You should be making stronger sounds.'

I said, 'I'm sorry.'

Doctor Kular said, with some heat, 'It's not like it's your fault, Miss DuLac. I'm sure you're doing your best. You always do.'

Morris looked at him, startled, and smiled as he quickly collaborated. 'Oh, yes,' he said. 'We're not disappointed in you as a patient. We just expected more from your larynx.'

He still had my hand and I squeezed his. I said, 'Thanks.' I reached out to Doctor Kular and he took my hand, awkwardly, for a second, before dropping it.

He said, 'We'll see you at rounds tomorrow. We've got other patients to check on now.'

He was still such a dick.

# Chapter Twenty-Two

## Soundtrack: 'Black Water' – Doobie Brothers

They wheeled me back to my room where mom was reading on her chair. I said, 'Hi. Been waiting long?' and she jumped up and hugged me. The porter had to tell her to let go so that I could get into my proper bed.

I was able to scramble over from the gurney all by myself.

'How do you feel?' she asked.

'Horrible,' I said. 'And evidently, this voice isn't good enough.'

Mom grimaced. 'It is a little weak.'

'I feel like I've got a sore throat. Can I have some water?'

Mom rang for the nurse.

It was the moon-faced lady, working a day shift. 'Can I have some water?' I asked.

'Hey!' she said. 'Listen to you!' She beamed. 'And no. Not till rounds tomorrow morning. They want to watch you do it and make sure your epiglottis is working properly. It got a bit bruised. But you can have a lemon swab.'

That's what they fob you off with when you want water. I guess I didn't really need water, I had an IV pumping me full of saline solution, but when your mouth is dry you get this feeling like you're so dehydrated you're about to die if you don't get to drink some water. And no amount of reasoning with your body about your urination rate or the volume of water coming down the tube makes it think any differently. I hated those damn swabs.

I sighed. 'Get me about a hundred, will you?' I asked.

But I'd forgotten. Even the taste of lemon in my mouth, which seemed so acute it was nearly unbearable, made my stomach heave.

I began vomiting up gastric fluid and then dry heaving. My little post-surgery routine.

My mother hovered over me, trying to make me comfortable, raising the bed, putting it down, turning on the TV, switching the programmes (only really rich people had remote controls back then), reading to me, turning my light on and off, pulling the blinds shut and open, putting my curtains around me and then opening them up again.

Nothing was right. It all irritated me. I kept telling her to go away and then the next second begging her to turn my pillow to the cool side or help me go to the loo or hold the basin while I heaved or wipe my face with a flannel. Then I'd tell her she'd got my pillow in the wrong place when she turned it, that she was making my IV line pull on the way to the loo, that she couldn't hold the basin properly and that the flannel was too hot, too cold, or too wet. Over and over I told her to go away, to go home and never come back.

'God, I hope you never have to have another surgery,' she said. 'You are such a pain in the ass.'

'I know,' I said. 'I can't help it.' I thought for a minute. 'And you didn't have to mention it, did you?'

'Oh, for Chrissakes.' My mother rolled her eyes.

Just then, my father came around the corner with a bunch of flowers. 'Great,' I said. 'That's the last thing we need.' I'd rather forgotten people could hear me now.

'Hey!' Dad said. 'You're talking. Kind of.' He turned to mom, frowning, 'It's going to get better than that, right?'

I took a breath to speak but my mother held up her hand. 'Let's talk outside, Roger,' she said. 'I need a cup of coffee.'

Mom had just had a coffee.

I looked at the flowers. It was a pot of chrysanthemums, and some of the blooms looked bruised. That was because some stems were broken. I pulled off the broken ones and fluffed up the leaves. But there's only so much you can do with chrysanthemums. They either look okay or they don't. They never look amazing. And these were orange. They'd probably have been grown for Halloween or Thanksgiving decorations.

You'd think, day after Valentines Day, that some pink roses might be more appropriate. But at least he'd tried.

I wanted to slide the pot off my table and onto the side stand, but I didn't trust myself to lift it.

I was dreading my father coming back. I didn't want to see the look on his face that let me know that I'd let everyone down, yet again, by not having more vocal articulacy.

So I rang for pain meds, which they gave me straight into my IV. Then I closed my eyes and went away.

And it felt like about five minutes later that I was home and getting ready for my first day back at school.

I was not thrilled to be back at Burner High. I hadn't been thrilled about going there in the first place.

The priorities at Burner were being popular and fitting in and making a contribution. Even the teachers bought into the nonsense that your social development into a good 'Bear' (school colours = black and gold; school team name = Bears) was just as important or even *more* important than your intellectual development. This put me directly into conflict with the school.

I was there to get an education. They were there to socialise me. They were trying to build a community and I was just driving through, ordering my high school diploma with large fries and extra ice in the Coke.

So, right from the get go, it wasn't going to be pretty.

Add my ordinary social problems, and then drop my loud whisper and healing throat scars into the mix and it was…it was just horrible.

Kim, who had been avoiding being close to me since the day they'd all first visited me in the ENT ward, had somehow decided that she would be my best friend again.

It was kind of weird. She rang me every night, sometimes two or three times and we met before we walked into school together. We stood in the lunch line. We went to after school clubs together. We were inseparable.

And I should have been really happy about that. But I wasn't, because Kim wasn't really *there*. Oh, she was there, she was always *there*. But I had no idea what she was really thinking, or really wanted. She wanted to do what I wanted.

If I wanted her to sleep over, she slept over. If I wanted to spend some time at the library, alone, she left me alone. She was like a doll of Kim. There was the body, fully jointed and able to stand and blink, but there was nobody really home.

We never argued. We never really talked about anything. Except how I should be a bit better at the whole school thing. I should be nicer. I should try harder, I should notice more about what was going on. It was nothing that Kim hadn't been saying for years, but now it was like it was *all* she said.

Kim had bought the whole 'good Bear' concept hook, line and sinker. She tried to educate me. She kept me up on all the gossip. She dragged me to parties. She ensured I went to basketball games and truly got excited about them. But when the news came around that our star point guard had injured his foot on a hunting trip and I asked, 'Who's he? Why is it so important?' she sighed.

I could tell she found me a heavy burden.

She would tell me that Donny and Carla had broken up and I would answer, 'Were they going out? And who's Carla?' and Kim would…she'd go even further inside herself, until she kind of disappeared.

I couldn't blame her.

I was always making her look stupid for hanging around with me. She started finding excuses not to meet up. She stopped sitting next to me at lunch, and then didn't go to parties in my company, and then she stopped talking to me altogether.

I was still invited to things the whole group did together. But everyone was always telling me why I wasn't doing anything right. And so I had this choice – to either spend my time with my friends, being lectured on my inadequacies – or stay home with my mother.

Mandy regularly gave me a bulletin on where I'd recently gone wrong. 'You shouldn't wear your hair like that. The really popular girls wear that kind of ribbon and they don't want you copying. And when somebody holds the door for you, you should smile and say thank you. And during assembly, when they were talking about the sacrifices our soldiers made for our country, you were picking your nails…people *notice* these things, Coco.'

Bobby told me that I really needed to give Kim some space, that she'd been through a lot, too, and the way I'd been leaning on her was unfair. Karla told me that if I was a bit nicer to people, they'd have more patience with my shortcomings. She challenged me to name all my friends' birthdays and I didn't even know Kim's.

Nice senior girls I barely knew took me aside and explained how I could be a better person. They asked me if I went to church and suggested I talk to my pastor about my spiritual growth.

I should smile more. I shouldn't be so sarcastic. I should have a more positive attitude. I should take time to pray each day. I should have more school spirit.

I should sprout wings and fly to the moon.

Doing all of it – doing any of it – was totally impossible.

I talked to Ed. He'd seen me and my friends at Don Chilitos one night. When he came in, he'd kind of grimaced at me with a half wave. He'd been with all his cool crowd from North West, big handsome senior boys. Really gorgeous girls with perfect hair and teeth. Ed had a new walking cast and didn't even have a crutch anymore.

'Did that boy in the cast just *wave* at you?' Mandy asked. 'The really nice-looking one?'

All my friends had their mouths hanging open. I shrugged. 'Yeah,' I said. 'I know him from the medical centre. We got to be friends.'

Shanice and Mandy exchanged glances and rolled their eyes. It was clear they didn't believe me. But on his way out, maybe because they'd had pitchers of beer at Ed's table, Ed was a bit nicer to me. He stopped by my chair and messed up my hair. He said, 'Drive safe, peanut.'

Everyone's mouths had hung open again.

Later, Ed had wanted to know why I hung around with total dweebs and I had explained my social position and that only the dweebs would hang out with me and that's only because they were really tolerant. I told him how everyone kept telling me to act differently.

He said, 'God, Coco. It's not exactly difficult. What did *you* tell *me*? Pay. Attention.'

Ed was paying attention in his classes. He called me three or four times a week to ask me about things he hadn't understood. 'What's the Reformation? I need to stop dangling my participles – what's a participle? What happened in Salem and what's that got to do with fighting communism?'

He'd worked up a study schedule and put in long hours. His uncle built him a desk for his room and his parents moved the television away from the wall his bedroom shared with the living room. His little brothers and sisters brought him a snack every night before they went to bed, so that he would have energy to keep working. That night at Don Chilitos was rare. He spent most of his nights at home, studying.

I marked up his coursework nearly every week. He paid me with dinners and movies. His friends got used to seeing me around, and one or two of them even learned my name. I asked him if he knew their birthdays and he just looked at me like I was insane.

But I knew what Ed was saying was true. If he could get his grades up, I could sort myself out, socially. I just couldn't imagine putting a tenth of that effort into fitting into Burner High.

I said, 'Where's my motivation? Why should I pay attention?'

Ed sighed. 'Isn't there anybody you...' he coughed a little. 'I mean, wouldn't you like a boyfriend?'

Rob Savage had selected his future wife. They were plastered together, kissing in the hall, in between classes. He looked stupid, getting all hot and sweaty over her five times a day, but I guessed she wanted to start a family, too...like maybe before baseball season.

I snorted. 'No,' I said flatly. 'There's nobody.'

This was not strictly true. Jack and I had started seeing each other again fairly regularly, for our normal driving-to-the-lake-smoking-dope-and-groping-each-other-with-clothes-on sessions.

The phone would ring and my mom would say, 'It's Jack.'

We'd known each other since we were about eight and we'd been friends all that time. I went to his birthday parties. He went to mine. In the summer I was eleven, he even came to stay with us for a week.

Mom didn't think anything when I got a phone call from Jack. If I got a phone call from any other boy, she would kind of hop from one foot to the other in front of me, waiting to find out if it was a date. But when it was Jack, she just got on with whatever else she'd been doing.

He'd ask how I was feeling and then he'd ask, 'Are you doing anything later?' He meant a lot later. He meant after he'd dropped off his girlfriend or after his parents had gone to sleep.

He meant midnight.

Sometimes he had a bottle of Boone's Farm Apple Wine.

Sometimes he had my favourite limeade or a coke. He'd idle his car outside my gate and the sound of the engine would wake me up…I guess I was always waiting for the sound of Jack's engine, even in my dreams, even when he'd forgotten to call first.

I'd pull on some clothes and slide up my window. The screen was loose. I could push it out and then slip out, sliding the window shut behind me…leaving just enough space to get my fingers under later. Ever since Jack was fourteen and got his learner permit and his car, I had been slipping out that window to run around with him. I'd just been thirteen when it started – two summers and three winters. I'd slid out into snow on nights the car heater was blasting and I'd shimmied out in shorts and a T-shirt with bare feet and everything in between.

We always went to the same place, down by Pierson Pond. He'd skin up a joint and I'd smoke it with him, maybe drink some wine. We'd listen to music, kiss and hold each other, in a kind of lazy way. Sometimes things would get a little heavy and I'd bring it all to a stop.

But I loved the way he made me feel. And I loved the hazy feeling of the dope and the wine and the view of the sky and the lake. I completely chilled out when I was at Pierson Pond with him. And he could completely chill out with me, too.

Jack was officially hanging out with us nerds less and less. His new friends were cooler, but dumber. His grades were falling. I thought part of him was getting lost – the sweet child who didn't agree with his father's religion, but who had a kind of holiness all of his own. When he was with me, I thought we could still find the nine-year-old boy inside him.

I wasn't in love with him. And I wasn't stupid. I knew I wasn't ready for a full on relationship, not really. I wasn't ready for the emotional turmoil of actual sex. With Jack, I had just what I needed. He was a wonderful kisser. He drove me right to the point of excitement where I had real trouble stopping.

And I could trust him. I told him *everything*.

'I don't need a boyfriend,' is what I said to Ed.

One day, when I was cleaning my trach tube, I noticed that the tape was looking dirty. As I went to change it, I bent over to get something and the whole thing fell out of my neck.

I braced myself and looked in the mirror at the hole. God, I hated my tracheotomy.

Once, I'd asked at clinic how they would close the hole. 'Oh, it will close itself when we're ready,' Doctor Morris had said.

Forget them, I was ready. But I had one little problem. I couldn't breathe through my nose and mouth or talk while the hole was open. So I got a big, square plaster and put it over the hole, sealing the air leak shut. Sorted.

Within weeks, it had healed. I was left with something that looked like a large belly button in my neck, an 'innie'. I kept wearing the scarves.

I went to speech therapy twice a week. I had loads of exercises to do. And once a month, I attended the ENT clinic.

I soon got very tired of saying, 'eeeee.' But slowly, I got better at it. I was trying to train my vocal chords to move. It takes babies a long time to coordinate this, and it was taking me a long time, too. The way I had done it before didn't work. But both of them moved, so if I concentrated, I had an actual voice.

Sometimes.

Kind of.

It was better, anyway.

The end of the school year was coming towards me so fast...and then something happened that I had not seen coming. I got a job.

# Chapter Twenty-Three

## Soundtrack: 'Jackie Blue' – The Ozark Mountain Daredevils

I'd had trouble with Biology at Burner because I'd refused to vivisect a frog. It was one of the few things about the months before the accident that had stayed in my memory. I'd done a dissection of a dead frog, with reservations, in junior high, but when they wanted me to cut up a live one, I spoke out. Mr Carter was about halfway through his introduction when I raised my hand.

There followed a long discussion. I asked what the point of the exercise was, and when he said that it might interest us in a career in medicine, I scornfully laughed. Only about ten percent of Burner graduates even went to university, and that included two-year programmes at community colleges.

Mr Carter didn't like it that I'd laughed. He liked it even less when I asked if this minute possibility was worth the suffering involved in vivisection on this scale (some 15 frogs were due to be tortured that class). Then I said that since doctors were usually wanting to help their fellow creatures, vivisection might actually turn people off medicine.

Mr Carter had mopped his sweating brow with his handkerchief and glanced at the clock. His bald head gleamed. In desperation, trying to shut me up, he said animal suffering could not be compared to human suffering.

I said he'd just told us how similar our systems were to a frog's. Was he trying to tell me that amphibians lacked nerve endings and pain sensors? I asked him to tell me how the frogs would hurt any differently than a human would hurt.

Mr Carter lost his temper. He shouted if I didn't do the vivisection, I would flunk Biology. I hissed that we'd see about that. Mr Carter slammed down a stack of books and kicked me out of class.

I talked it over with the Assistant Principal while he was giving me detention.

To get out of cutting up a live frog, I had to submit a proposal to the school board to allow an essay alternative. Bethany had been doing some volunteering with an animal rights organisation and she put me in touch with them. They got me all kinds of facts and figures and helped me write the proposal. I won. I was allowed to write a term paper instead.

Mr Carter *hated* me after that. I got the lowest marks of my life in Biology – mid-range Bs.

But when I got back to school after the accident, I started getting As in Biology. We'd been doing natural selection and genetics and I loved both the logic and the randomness of the marigolds, eye colour, bobcat tail length and all the other genetic tendencies we'd been mapping.

At first I thought Mr Carter felt sorry for me and regretted giving me grief. But then I started to suspect it had something to do with how my brain had dealt with the trauma.

Some things I used to be able to do, I couldn't. Math had always been hard for me and now it was simply impossible.

I had been included in a school musical dance routine but I'd had to be shown the steps over and over and over and then still messed it up in performance. My ability to remember a dance routine was just...gone. I could still do all the moves, some moves better than everyone else at my school. But I couldn't seem to link them together into an actual dance. Not only could I hardly breathe fast enough to keep moving, I couldn't remember what I was meant to be doing next. It was like a fog descended on my brain, every time I tried.

But I could suddenly draw better. And my skills at logic and in understanding systems had improved. Which is why I 'got' genetics.

One day, Mr Carter asked me to stay back. I was afraid I'd made him mad again, but it turned out to be something different. He was in charge of recruiting students to go to Youth Conservation Corps. Students were invited to go away and work for the government for the summer, helping with Department of the Interior projects and generally making themselves useful. There would be a mixture of top science students from the state, and students from the poorer districts who needed work. Burner was poor enough to count as a poor district and, because of my improved marks and mom's low income, I counted as both a top student and a low-income family.

Getting away from my social failure for the summer sounded wonderful. I said yes straightaway.

Mom was horrified at the idea of me going away, but she thought the doctors would say I couldn't go. She rather smugly said, 'You may go if Doctor Morris thinks it's a good idea.' And then stopped smiling very suddenly when he said I could.

The end of May found her dropping me off at Fort Hays State University.

Kansas is in the middle of America and is known for...well for having a whole lot of nothing. Don't get me wrong, I love my state. I love its rolling hills and its table-flat plains. I love the big blue bowl of the sky above me. I love its prairies and its endless wheat fields. But it's not for everybody.

The trade-off for all this countryside is that there aren't many, say, opera houses in my state. There aren't a lot of art house cinemas. If your favourite band is on tour, you might have to drive over three hundred miles to see them.

Fort Hays was in the middle of Kansas. It made Burner look like downtown Manhattan. The only culture in the place was in yoghurt, and it wasn't even that easy to find yoghurt.

Mom drove me in the day before and then we looked around for something to do. We ended up back at the motel, eating pizza and playing cards. Even the films in the cinema were out of date.

I'd already sewn the badges on my four work shirts and had my construction boots and gloves. I'd been wearing my special work boots to break them in, just like the letter had suggested. I was being good.

Mom dropped me off at a big brick dorm building with a sign that read, 'YCC' on the front. I got my suitcases out of the back and we looked at each other.

She said, 'This feels seriously weird. Just four months ago, I had to be with you day and night because you might die any minute. And now I'm letting you go off on your own.'

She'd lost more weight and was wearing her best wig. She looked great. I hugged her and she felt great, too, soft and warm. I wondered when I'd have another hug...maybe not until she came to pick me up at the end of the summer.

I let her go, and said, 'You'll be free and single.'

She rolled her eyes. 'Oh, yeah,' she said. 'Party animal.' She sniffed and blinked.

I picked up my stuff and walked into the building.

There were about forty of us and I was one of the last to arrive. There was a place to put your stuff and then you had to go into a big room for the welcome talk.

I hated walking into a room full of strangers. I stuck my nose in the air and kind of strode in, my face blank.

'Hey, Peanut,' a familiar voice said. 'What's the matter? Bad smell?'

It was the best-looking boy in the room. Ed.

I'd told him all about YCC and he'd been really interested and had asked me loads of questions. He hadn't ever said he was coming, too.

He was sitting with the older kids, the ones who looked cool. He patted the chair next to him and I sat down.

I didn't know what to say. So I punched him in the arm.

I was wearing a T-shirt and jean shorts. The girls sitting by Ed had coordinated outfits and proper handbags and everything. I got the feeling, straightaway, that it was going to be a long summer.

Our welcome talk went on for the whole day. We were going to work five days a week. The Department of the Interior would usually loan us out to local parks and wildlife management organisations. And then, once a week, we'd have a lecture. There'd be a test after every lecture, we would write a short paper over the summer and we'd end up with three university credits in Natural Science. They would send our pay checks home, so we'd end up with some money saved, too.

One of the girls knew one of my cousins. Her name was Maureen. A rather earnest Christian couple were present and he'd brought his guitar. It killed me not to be able to sing along to his James Taylor and Carol King numbers… He kept forgetting lyrics and I'd have to whisper reminders. It was torture.

Dorm life wasn't any different to hospital life except the food at lunch was actually worse. Every day, we'd have to load up huge barrel flasks of squash and enormous coolers into the back of a truck. We loaded ourselves back there, too. Hard hats, jeans, boots, and work shirts with the YCC badge. I also had asked and been granted the right to wear a bandana around my neck, to cover my scars. Sunglasses and work gloves completed the look. We balanced on coolers or the wheel wells as we were driven to our work sites, even though we were bombing down the highway at 70 miles an hour. It was before Health and Safety.

I learned to put up fence, lay concrete, build stone walls, and did a *whole* lot of painting those first few weeks. All those years of my dad telling me off for doing things badly had made me into a good worker. I was weedy and weak, but I learned quickly and applied myself with a kind of grim determination that provoked admiration.

'You ever used a weedwacker?' the foreman said one morning.

I shook my head. I didn't even know what one was. All the farm kids laughed.

What it was, was a kind of scythe. A shortish handle attached to a semi-circle of steel, open side down. Across the open side of the semi-circle was a serrated blade, kind of like a two-sided bread knife. I was given a hillside to clear and my partner for the task was Ed.

He stood and watched me for a little while. He still wore a brace on his leg when we went to do work, and he was fiddling with it...sometimes he had to adjust it if we had to carry things or if we were working on a hillside, like we were now.

I swung the tool back and forth, chopping at the weeds. It didn't take much time for my hand, even inside my glove, to start to hurt. The weeds didn't look any smaller.

Ed limped over and looked at me. 'Really?' he said. 'You've never used one of these before? At all?'

I just stared at him.

He stood kind of around me, like a golf instructor, and corrected everything – my stance, how I held the thing, the angle I used on the weeds.

'Now try.'

I didn't exactly set the countryside on fire with my weed-whacking. And I got blisters that swelled, burst and swelled up again. But I was actually cutting down weeds. You could tell where I'd done and where I hadn't. When the foreman examined my work, he was impressed. After lunch, Ed and I did something different while another partnership whacked. It'd absolutely kill you to whack all day.

The four of us who had weed-whacked were like celebrities that night. Everyone looked at our hands and kept letting us go first in the dinner line.

Now people use strimmers. Every time I see someone looking fed-up while they're strimming a roundabout or something, I want to go and lift up their ear protectors and say, 'Cheer up, kid, you could be using a weed-whacker.'

My blisters were bigger than Ed's, because his hands were tougher. He said, 'You know, Coco, you did really good.'

I said, 'Shut up.'

'No, really. I don't think I've ever seen you work hard at anything before.'

I thought about ballet and singing lessons and learning lines...but there was no explaining any of that to Ed. He just didn't understand what my life had been like. And there was no point in trying to explain, because one of the boys came up and asked if he wanted to play Frisbee, so he went off with them.

It was like that. People all did certain things. The Christian couple sang and prayed with a few of the other religious weirdoes. The jocks played Frisbee and hacky sack. The girls talked...endlessly...about...stuff. Hair care. Clothes. I can't really tell you, because it all bored me stiff. I used makeup, but I didn't want to *talk* about it.

And, anyway, I always had a book. So, Ed went off to play Frisbee, and I sat in the shade and read something from the library. I was the only person in the group to get a local library card and I'd kind of bonded with the librarian. I'd read all the Georgette Heyer books, and she'd started me on Miss Read and R.L. Delderfield. I'd also read *Diary of a Provincial Lady*. Twice.

One day we got seconded out to a fish farm to help with moving fish eggs into the incubation tanks. We had to get into big square ponds full of bass, croppies, carp or walleye and collect the eggs.

Thing was, it wasn't just the season for fish to lay eggs, the mosquitoes were busy doing it, too. And that meant they needed nice warm blood for their babies. We put on DDT every morning (nobody knew yet that it gave you cancer) but the water just washed it off.

On the third night we sat around the dorm and counted how many bites we had, while we used my clear nail varnish to paint over the spots (this really does help, if you ever get a mosquito bite). I had one hundred and thirty-two on my right leg alone. This was so depressing; I didn't even count the ones on my left leg.

I caught a strand of barbwire in my face, broke my nails, crushed a fingernail, and collected lots of scratches and scrapes. We all got pretty beat up and we never really knew what we'd be doing next.

One day, I'd be stringing barbed wire in the middle of nowhere in temperatures near forty degrees, within a group of ten or twelve. We'd be left with one cooler of squash and another with sandwiches and would not see another human being for the whole day, until the truck came bouncing along the dirt road to pick us up.

The next day, I could be lying alone on my back in a wildflower meadow, looking at the sky and counting hawks. Then I might be helping a hundred seven-year-olds walk around a nature trail and next I might be in an air-conditioned visitor centre, helping them colour in pretty drawings of wildflowers...or I might have been moved to a crew that was shovelling cement out of a mixer. I never knew what was coming.

On weekends we might get to go horse riding or to the lake or to the movies or bowling. We got ferried out to our various places of worship Sunday morning – Maureen and I were the only Catholics and I always went to Mass because you had to go *somewhere* on Sunday mornings. Atheism was not an option. We were allowed something like ten dollars a week. I spent mine on Pringles, onion dip, Coke and *Car and Driver* magazine.

It was a weird, institutional kind of life, kind of like prison or boarding school. We did everything all together. I absolutely hated it. Every time I said something sarcastic, though, Ed would give me a look...I could tell he thought it was an ideal opportunity for me to develop my social skills.

Yeah. Well. It didn't work out like that.

I think the first crack came during our fourth lecture. This one was from the Fish and Game Authority, who were talking about the management of white-tailed deer herds. The speaker was a handsome man in his early thirties, with a very masculine presence. And I would have believed everything he said, except that I had, firstly, been on a deer hunt myself and secondly, had been reading a book on animal rights from Bethany's organisation.

The poor man wasn't prepared for anyone to question him. He was just there to run through the slides and read the notes.

'...and so,' he said, pushing a little button on a cord to change to a slide showing an over-browsed thicket, 'when their food supply gets low, we institute a cull. 'We –' he clicked to a slide showing a man and a boy in Carhart jackets, carrying deer rifles– 'issue extra hunting permits, and...'

My hand shot up. He was surprised. I think everyone else was asleep.

'Yes, miss?'

'Isn't the problem of over populated deer herds really because we've eliminated all their natural predators?'

It was a small room. He could hear me, even over the whirr of the projector. He nodded enthusiastically, greeting someone who actually understood the problem. 'Yes,' he said. 'Very good.' He prepared to go back to his presentation.

'Why don't we just reintroduce the predators? The wolves?'

Suddenly everyone was awake. 'Shut up,' Ed hissed.

The man from Fish and Game heard Ed, too. He must have been a good hunter. He said, 'Now, now. This is interesting.' He used his hands in a 'calm down' gesture to Ed and the rest of my fellow YCCers. In answer to my question, he said, 'It's much easier to issue a few more hunting permits.'

I said, 'Well, yes, I'll bet it is easier. But what we're doing is degrading a whole species. We're weakening our white-tailed deer herds.'

Ed actually moved his chair away from me. You could feel everyone in the room willing me to stop talking.

The Fish and Game man bristled at this. 'No,' he said. 'We're maintaining the same numbers.'

I said, 'You may be maintaining the numbers, but the quality will degrade. Wolves go for the weak and sick members of the herd. Deer hunters want trophies and meat. They go for the biggest and the best.'

I was right, and he knew it. He huffed at me. 'You can't seriously think it would be a good idea to reintroduce wolves. We lease a lot of it for grazing.'

'I think the priority should be conservation, not making money.'

'Look, young lady, you wouldn't have any conservation without any funding.'

'But—' I began.

Our foreman stood up and looked sternly at me. 'I think you may be excused, Coco.'

Honestly? What was the point of having a lecture if you were just supposed to take it all in? Why not just read a chapter of a book? What ever happened to intellectual enquiry?

I slammed the door on my way out. Behind me, I could hear the handsome man from Fish and Game make a jocular remark and everyone laugh heartily.

I had only been *interested*. I had only wanted to *discuss* it with the handsome man. It seemed to me that every time a conversation got interesting, everybody else felt it had to stop. Mandy always said I went too far. But I felt like the people around me never went far enough.

I waited in the lounge all by myself. I thought, when everyone came out, I could explain. They would understand that I wasn't just a troublemaker. I was really *interested* in the *actual ideas*.

But everyone blanked me and went straight to their rooms. Nobody said a word, except for Ed. He said, 'You can be such a jerk.'

'I just...'

He held up one elegant hand. 'I don't want to hear it.'

It took a week for anyone to speak to me again, and then the Christian girl asked me, quite earnestly, if I'd ever thought God might been trying to tell me something when He took away my voice.

That week, my mother called. Grandma had died.

I was devastated. I wanted to come home for the funeral, but mom said no. Before she died, Grandma had said that it shouldn't ruin my summer, that there was no sense in me coming, and that she wouldn't need me there to know I had loved her. *I* needed to be there, for *me*, but I couldn't make mom see it. I pleaded, I begged. But mom wouldn't let me come.

# Chapter Twenty-Four

**Soundtrack: 'When Will I Be Loved' – Linda Ronstadt**

At first I thought it was grief.

I started to feel really, really tired. I'd had a few days off because of Grandma's death, and it started then. When I went back to work, I felt horrible.

I was just dragging myself around. It was the whole everyone-else-in-fast-forward thing starting up again.

And then, I thought it might be because I wasn't eating enough proper food, so I tried to eat more. I started making a peanut butter sandwich at breakfast to take with me for lunch, and made sure to eat some of my dinner and not just fill up on dip.

I drank more juice and squash and less Coke. All of this helped for a few weeks. And then it didn't help very much. And then it didn't help at all.

I was just dragging myself through the days.

I picked up a cold and it got worse and worse and then they took me to the doctor and I got some antibiotics. In three days I was supposed to be better. My cold was gone, but I felt even *worse*.

If I'd just been sitting around the house, I don't think I would have even noticed. But the things we were doing really pushed me, physically. We were doing lots of concrete work at the time, levelling earth, making forms, mixing the stuff, pouring it, levelling it off, putting in texture. It was a whole lot of lifting, carrying, and working quickly.

And it was still over 30 degrees, every single day.

I started to slack. I fell asleep every lunch break and had to push myself hard to go back for more work in the afternoon. Sometimes, when the foreman wasn't there, I couldn't help it. I'd just sit down.

It was driving Ed crazy.

He started calling me lazy and asking what was wrong with me. Pretty soon, the foreman was saying the same thing.

He called me into his office and said I'd been a really good, dependable worker. Now, he said, I'd lost his trust.

I started to cry when he said that. I apologised, and said it wasn't that I didn't want to do the work. It wasn't that I wasn't trying. But I felt really, really tired.

He told me to get to bed earlier. I did. I was still tired. That weekend, I stayed in bed forever. I skipped the picnic. I skipped the movie. I skipped church.

Ed came to see me in my room on Sunday afternoon. 'You've got to snap yourself out of this,' he said.

I pushed myself up on my pillows. 'I feel totally wiped out,' I said. 'In the morning, I'm okay, but I just…' I looked at him, but his face was turned away from me.

Ed said, 'I've worked in teams all my life, Coco. I know you haven't.'

Again, I wanted to tell him about dance, choir and theatre, but I didn't think he'd listen. He said, 'You don't let people down. You just don't.'

I said, 'The show must go on,' meaning that I got it, that I knew this stuff, too, but he frowned at me.

'It's not a joke.'

It hurt. It hurt me that he thought I wasn't trying. I picked up my old teddy bear, and held him against me like a shield. I said, 'Why do you think I'm resting all weekend? I'm trying to get over it.'

His face softened a bit and he finally looked at me. He said, 'I'm really trying to believe you, Coco.'

That next week nearly killed me. We only had two more after it to do.

The foreman had put me on lighter duties. I'd been frog trapping, painting and planting flowers. Every day, I'd be okay in the morning, but start to get really tired after lunch. I evolved all kinds of strategies to try to hide this. Instead of writing up the frog reports as I went, I trapped all morning and filled out reports all afternoon. I planted flowers all morning and watered them all afternoon. I painted all the bits that needed me to run up and down ladders in the morning, and just plodded along the easy bits in the afternoon.

But on Friday, we had to lay some concrete for a path for the local State Park superintendent's house. We were working in one, big crew. I had no strategy for that.

It was very hot and everyone was ratty. And I...I was utterly useless. I fell asleep during lunch, sitting up, right in the middle of my peanut-butter sandwich. After lunch, I was meant to be helping shovel the concrete into the forms. I picked up the shovel and spaded three or four loads into the form. Maureen and the Christian girl were waiting to level it off and we had to work fast, or it would set.

I felt like I was going to faint. I stopped for a few seconds to breathe and then...I just couldn't make myself put my shovel back into the mixer. I stood there, trying to force myself to keep shovelling concrete and I just...I just couldn't do it.

I can't remember the guy's name I was working with. But I remember how cross his face looked. He was working double hard. Sweat was running down his face. And I just stood there.

Then, everyone started shouting at me. The more people shouted, the less I felt like I could move. The foreman stormed over. 'Get in the truck,' he said. 'I'm going to take you to the doctors after this.'

The truck was parked in the shade. I lay down on the hot ridges of the truck bed and went straight to sleep.

Everyone had to work harder and faster to get done even quicker, so they could get me to the hospital. And they had to do it short a worker. And when they got to the hospital, they all had to come inside and wait without going back to shower or anything. Their sweat dried on them in the air-conditioning and concrete dust settled into their skin. They looked like ghosts and everybody stared at them.

The staff rushed me through and hooked me up to machines. They tested my blood pressure and they had this groovy box that measured my blood oxygen without an arterial blood gas. They did an EKG.

Then they let me get dressed again and brought the foreman through so we could both hear the results.

The doctor, a severe-looking woman in her thirties, hadn't said much to me during all the measuring. She didn't say anything to me, now, either. She just talked to the foreman.

'She's fine,' she said, in a flat tone. 'I'm sure nobody likes to lay concrete in this heat, but there's nothing wrong with her.'

The foreman gave me a look that could have burned paint off the wall behind me.

'Why do I feel so horrible, then?' I asked, but the doctor pretended not to hear me.

'All of her vital signs are completely normal. I can find nothing wrong with her.'

I thought about how exhausted I'd felt every afternoon. I thought about falling asleep in my peanut butter sandwich. Surely that wasn't just being lazy.

The foreman grabbed my arm and half-lifted me off the gurney. 'Thank you, ma'am,' he said to the doctor. 'I'm sorry to waste your time.'

He marched me through the waiting room and straight out to the truck, where he clearly had to restrain himself from throwing me into the back of the thing.

It seemed like a long ride back to the dormitory. It seemed like a long dinner. It was certainly a quiet one. Everybody went to straight to their rooms again. I had a feeling Ed would not be visiting.

I was right.

Nobody spoke to me for the whole of the weekend

I blamed all of my misery on Doctor Kular.

What had he been doing down in the Emergency Room, anyway? Why couldn't he have just kept his long nose out of my death? I'd been perfectly fine without him. Every unkind comment, every sideways glance, every sigh from the foreman just fuelled my resentment.

Kular thought he was so wonderful. I'd to see him sweating under the hot sun, trying to shovel concrete mix before it dried on the shovel. This wonderful life he'd given me – gee, Doc, *thanks*.

On Sunday, we went to a lake to swim. There was no question of me being allowed to stay behind.

It was a bit awkward, in the back of the truck, balanced on the wheel arch, totally ignored by everyone else. It was awkward mainly because I kept nearly falling asleep and catching myself at the very last minute. Finally, Maureen said, 'Look, Coco, just stop pretending to be tired. It doesn't work anymore.'

I wanted to cry. I wanted to shout. Instead, I tried to be reasonable. I said, 'I'm sorry, but I feel really...'

But one of the other girls cut in, saying, 'We can't hear you, you know.' And everyone laughed. Oh, it just never got old, that sooooo funny joke.

'Get stuffed,' I said. They seemed to hear that okay.

We finally got to the lake and I just dumped my stuff, shucked off my shorts and T-shirt and walked right into the water.

I hadn't swum since the accident. I'd been afraid to try, after accidentally drowning myself so many times in the bath and shower, when I had my trach tube. But I was so cross, I just kind of went for it.

It was great to be back in the water again. There was a floating dock, anchored about a quarter mile out. I struck out for it with great, lazy strokes. I was completely confident about getting there. It was nothing. I'd swum five, six times that far regularly, down at the lake where my cousins had a cabin.

I was fine until I was about halfway there. Then, something strange happened. I started to hurt. Everywhere. I felt so weak and I could hardly move my arms. I turned on my back and floated for a little while and then gave up, and started doing the back crawl, just rolling over every once in a while to check my position.

I had been, by far, the first person into the water. But other people were already on the dock.

All my muscles were shaking. I was gasping. For a little while, I thought I wasn't going to make it.

There was a little ladder on the dock and I barely had the strength to heave myself out of the water. I half-crawled, half-fell onto the dock and lay there, wheezing. I coughed and goo came out of my nose and mouth.

I tried to say, 'Sorry,' about that, but the people on the dock just looked at me in disgust and swam away.

I noticed that when I'd tried to say, 'Sorry,' I couldn't talk. I tried again and I could only whisper it...it was a really faint whisper...nobody was there, of course, but I'm not sure anyone could have heard me even if they were.

I lay there kind of gasping and coughing for a long time and then I sat up, used some water to clean my face and rolled over.

The sun felt good on my back. My legs were still trailing in the water. I nearly fell asleep that way, only half up on the dock. Finally I managed to roll onto it. I closed my eyes.

A few seconds later, I could hear someone calling my name. I looked around and couldn't see anyone, but then I saw the foreman on the shore. Everyone else and everything else was all loaded up in the truck. It was getting darker and the wind had picked up.

I had slept all afternoon.

The water was cold. I had forgotten how difficult the swim out to the dock had been. I'd forgotten everything except getting to shore and not keeping everyone waiting. God, I thought, don't they hate me *enough*? Why do I have to keep messing up?

I was still a bit groggy. I struck out in my fastest crawl, which was pretty fast, but decided that wasn't fast enough, so did my underwater swim.

I'm sure I didn't invent that stroke, but I don't know if it has a name. I used it when I was in a hurry. It's like a breaststroke, but underwater. In one out of every eight strokes, you surface to breathe, and then dive back down again. I'd discovered at the Country Club, racing against my friends, and had used it hundreds of times. All that lung capacity I'd built up as a singer made it possible. I'd often win against much better swimmers using it, because you're so much faster swimming underwater than you are when you're swimming on the surface.

In the lake that day, I sank down and did seven quick breast-strokes, coming up on the last one to the surface. That all went fine.

However, when I tried to take the quick breath, I couldn't.

I couldn't pull the air in fast enough. I was automatically diving back down under water, in the rhythm of the stroke. But my mouth and lungs had come off stroke and were still trying to breathe in. Too late, I realised what was happening.

By that time, I'd already sucked a whole lot of lake deep into my lungs.

I came up, in an untidy tangle of arms and legs and gasped. But my gasp didn't seem to do anything. Air didn't seem to be going in.

I had no idea what was happening to me. I couldn't think straight. I tried to gasp again, but my flailing arms hadn't kept me above the water, and again, I took in water instead of air.

I coughed so hard I went under again. And just like in the Stevie Smith poem, I waved to everyone watching and instead of jumping in to save me, they all waved back.

Suddenly, I knew I was going to have to try to calm down if I wasn't going to drown.

I rolled onto my back to float. But I kept coughing, and every time I coughed, I folded up, and every time I folded up, I sank. Also, moving my arm in a back crawl was exhausting.

I was still gasping for air, but coughing out, as well and I felt too clumsily dozy to coordinate my swimming, floating, sinking, with my breath. It seemed like every time my lungs were ready for air to come into my system, I had my face in the water.

I kept trying, still horribly aware of everyone waiting for me, until finally that familiar remote feeling hit again and I stopped caring. I stopped caring about the people on shore, about trying to keep afloat and about trying to breathe. It was all clearly an unsolvable problem.

I let myself sink.

But I was not allowed to rest. I bobbed up again almost immediately and again, tried to gasp, got a bit of air in and then had a massive coughing fit. I threw up some lake water and coughed some more, again beating my arms weakly against the water. It didn't feel like I was getting anywhere.

My legs felt so heavy. I tried to circle them in a nice, brisk kick, but it wasn't happening. I went down again.

The next thing I knew, the foreman had me in an arm lock. I wasn't all that far from shore by then. He towed me in.

On the way he asked me what the hell I thought I was doing.

I was too ashamed to let anybody know I'd forgotten how to swim.

So I lied.

I told him there was a leak in my trach tube scar. And when we got to shore, I turned over and coughed out several litres of lake water. It was very convincing.

I stuck to that story for years. My husband was the first person I ever told the truth about it.

We went back to the local emergency ward to have me checked out. This meant that we couldn't go to the cinema that night, because everyone had to go together.

My colleagues had to sit in the waiting room again, freezing wet in the air conditioning, while three or four doctors peered at my neck, shrugged, and told me not to go swimming again until my scars had completely healed.

The x-rayed me to make sure I'd coughed up all the water, gave me some antibiotics, just in case my lungs got infected, and sent me back to YCC.

I tried to apologise, but no one answered. I wasn't even sure if anyone could hear me. My voice was…it was quieter than it had been even a few days before. I tried to speak up a bit and say sorry again, but I couldn't.

I got back into the back of the truck and the foreman said, 'Don't be stupid. You have to ride up front.'

I can't tell you how much not being able to swim hurt. I can't explain how completely worthless and low I felt, as I hugged my horrible secret to my aching chest, while everyone else balanced on stuff out in the back of the truck, getting cold in the night wind.

I couldn't work. I couldn't swim. I was unpopular everywhere I went. Nobody liked me. I didn't like myself.

Dad was right. I *was* useless.

# Chapter Twenty-Five

## Soundtrack: 'Squeeze Box' – The Who

We were finally going home. All the other kids were making elaborate plans to meet up in the year. I wasn't included in any of the plans, of course.

I sat on my suitcase in the lobby of the dorm and watched all the other kids have joyful reunions with their families.

Where the hell was mom?

Then I remembered that when she was really fat, mom used to hate getting out of the car. She'd do anything to stay in the car and hide. I thought maybe she'd eaten too much without me there and had blimped up again. Maybe she was hiding in the car.

So I dragged myself and my suitcase around to the car park.

But mom wasn't hiding. She was posing.

She had lost *more* weight. She was wearing a new pantsuit in plum with three-inch heels on her sandals and a chiffon scarf tied rakishly around her neck. On her new auburn wig sat a pair of enormous sunglasses with gold accents. She was leaning against our new-to-us car and smoking an Eve cigarette with plum-coloured lips. Her nails were long and varnished to match.

'Oh, hullo, darling,' she said, waiting for me to approach. I lugged my suitcase to the car and she bent to kiss me on the cheek. Evidently whoever she was now didn't do enthusiastic public displays of affection.

I was wearing ragged cut-offs and a jersey halter neck with a lace trim that had frayed to bits because I wasn't that good at laundry. My hair was halfway down my back and so wild with humidity that it looked like a two-foot afro. I looked at her. I didn't say anything.

She popped the hatchback open and invited me to lift in my

suitcase.

I crawled onto the passenger seat and let her put it in herself.

It was a two hundred and fifty mile drive back to Kansas City, so she'd checked us back into the same Fort Hays motel for the night. When we got there, I had my first private shower of the summer. Mom had remembered to bring the shampoo and conditioner I liked. I stood under the water for around an hour, while mom went out to find some dinner. When I put on a T-shirt and shorts, I felt nearly human again.

We hadn't really spoken yet, just kind of sized each other up. As mom opened the family-sized bucket of chicken, she said, 'Was it really horrible?'

I ate a drumstick in about a second while I answered. 'No, not horrible. I liked it, at first.'

I then ate two pieces of corn on the cob, a bread roll and a small tub of coleslaw.

Mom paused, holding her piece of chicken, from which she'd taken two or three bites, in mid-air. She watched me, half horrified, half fascinated, as I ate.

I ate two chicken wings, a breast and another drumstick in about ten seconds. I then burped and said, 'How 'bout you? Was it weird being alone in the house?' before eating another piece of corn.

'I missed you, of course,' mom said. 'But I kind of liked living alone. It was the first time I'd ever done it.'

And I ate another breast.

Mom said, 'Um...did you eat *anything* all summer?'

I then launched into a description of the lunches, the sandwich spread provided. Pink stuff or yellow stuff. You could never tell. Once in a while, it was brown stuff. There was absolutely no indication of the ingredients and whatever they were had been processed into a thick paste. I described the thin white bread, the greasy potato chips, and the watery squash. All the time, my hand was automatically bringing food to my mouth. Another two drumsticks. The last bread roll – with honey.

My mother watched this voracious stranger. 'Should I go get another bucket?'

But I was full. I'd eaten an entire meal for a family of four, except for one chicken breast and the beans, which I'd left for mom.

She was tired from the drive and I was just tired. We got into bed and went to sleep with our backs to each other, in a state that felt rather like a truce. But we woke up tangled in each other's arms.

When we got home, mom showed me the checks. I'd made $535, which was a whole lot of money in 1975. I paid mom back for the gas and motels and still had enough to buy any clothes I wanted. I already had four pairs of jeans, all nicely worn in from weed-whacking and fencing. I bought shirts and sweaters, some hiking boots and a short navy-blue, double–breasted, military-looking coat in thick wool. I felt sorted. Everything else, I'd save for doing things during the year.

My hair floated out around me like a tangled dark cloud but I didn't want to pay to have it cut. I got some combs and some clips and let it grow.

When I got back to Turner High, however, all the other girls had started wearing skirts and tights and proper trousers. Their hair looked amazing, with highlights and lowlights and things. They had ladies' blouses and, I discovered in gym, had lacy matching bras and panties like grown-ups.

As usual, my utility wardrobe made me weird. I'd kind of fried my bras in the dryer at YCC, so I'd stopped wearing one altogether. And I preferred big cotton panties, like I'd worn when I was six years old. They didn't ride up my butt and I thought I looked fine in them…as if anyone was ever going to see me in my panties.

I mentioned to mom how expensive and wonderful all the

other girls looked and she sniffed. 'Junior year,' she said. 'Their parents will be trying to marry them off.'

I thought mom was crazy. But by Christmas, couples had started getting serious. There were a whole lot of engagements and plans to marry the summer after we graduated.

To me, this seemed ridiculous. We were just children...at least I was. Sixteen seemed no age to start making these kinds of decisions. But the kids at Burner were already making plans for their 'last summer', which was the summer coming up – the one in between junior and senior year.

I assumed I'd be going to university. Summers stretched out endlessly before me. *I* wasn't going to work for the railroad or the county or the car factory for thirty years or so starting in June of the following year. *I* wasn't going to get married and start paying a mortgage.

The other kids were always reminding each other that these were the 'best years of our lives', something that made me feel suicidal. I found it hard to believe that they really *wanted* to keep living in Burner – that they actually *wanted* to buy houses and have kids and...I don't know...start spraying their hair stiff and eating chicken-fried steak.

I wasn't really able to hide my thoughts on this stuff, so...my social standing went down another notch.

Kim hardly spoke to me. Jack hadn't come to get me since I got back. And I hadn't heard from Ed since YCC. I'd called his house, but he wouldn't talk to me.

If I wasn't completely exhausted, I'd have been lonely. But I had to sleep so much to get through my days at school, I hardly noticed. I spent a lot of time sitting in the halls of Burner, resting up for the next flight of stairs. I came up with so many excuses not to do P.E. that my teacher let me write a term paper for the class instead.

Everyone kept telling me how lazy I was. I didn't know what was happening to me. Sometimes I thought I'd gone insane...

what with the memory loop thing and how exhausted I always felt. Sometimes I just thought everyone was right, that I was a worthless piece of slime.

When I got back to speech therapy, even the therapist was cross with me. 'You have not been doing your exercises,' she said.

'I did,' I said. 'I did them every day. But around the end of July, I forgot how.'

'Forgot how?' She was sceptical.

I shrugged. I said, 'One day I could do it and the next day I couldn't. After a week or so of trying, I gave up.'

'You gave up.' She looked at me sternly over her glasses. 'Say "eeeee,"' she said.

My 'eeeee' was crap, evidently.

'We've lost *all* the progress we made last year,' she said. 'What is the matter, Coco? Don't you *want* to talk? Or do you like all this attention?'

Oh yeah, I wanted to say, I just love coming here. You are my favourite person in the whole world. I rolled my eyes and bit my lip.

'Now, say "eeeee,"' she said. I did, and she got even crosser.

Doctor Morris looked over the top of his glasses. 'Your speech therapist is quite concerned about what she sees as deliberate sabotage of her work. She says you have a very poor attitude towards your therapy and that you're not demonstrating responsible behaviour.'

'That's ridiculous,' I said.

'She doesn't understand why you refuse to make the sounds you could make four months ago.'

'I'm not refusing,' I said. 'I just can't do it. I'm *trying*.' God, how familiar this sounded. I'd said the same thing to the foreman at YCC. I'd said the same thing to Dad, all the time, about everything, my whole life.

Inside myself, I collapsed into a mess of anxiety – I started to shake and sweat. If Doctor Morris thought I was useless, too, that was the utter end. As a project, Coco was over.

'I *want* to get better,' I said. 'I've *tried* to. Really.' As if I didn't feel humiliated enough, I felt myself choke and I burst into tears.

Doctor Morris patted my shoulder for a while. Then he started ringing Psychiatry.

I had lots and lots of psychotherapy. Dad's great police insurance paid for most of it, but the people over in Psych saw me as a fascinating case. Two of them actually volunteered so they could use me as research.

Every night after school I went for some kind of psychological intervention. I had a Freudian psychiatrist, a hypnotherapist, a biofeedback specialist, and a transactional psychologist. In case you're counting, I saw the Freudian twice a week.

I'm sure I did have mental illnesses. In the past 18 months, I'd been rejected by my father, my grandmother had died, I'd been in a horrible car accident and still had post-traumatic stress disorder, even though nobody really called my memory-loop thing that at the time. I'd lost all my friends, and the only real relationship I had was with my mother, who was loony herself.

I'd also suffered hunger and poverty for the first time. Add the fact that I was going through puberty disfigured and that I'd already had anxiety issues before all of this had started and…well…I had quite a bit to talk about. I had, as you might guess, quite a few problems here and there.

But nobody wanted to help me with any of my actual mental health. I wasn't even allowed to talk about my memory-loop thing that was eventually diagnosed as Post Traumatic Stress Disorder. Every person I saw that autumn in Psych just wanted to be the genius who solved the riddle of why I had refused to use my vocal chords properly. Whenever I'd get on a roll, talking about one of the issues I was currently processing, or my growing sense of unworthiness, my therapists would gently redirect me to how it felt to vocalise these issues. Even my Freudian never actually let me just freaking *talk*.

And as for the hypnotherapist, now there was someone absolutely obsessed with 'eeeee.' Half the time, I didn't feel all that hypnotised, to be honest, but there was no way I was going to tell him I was just resting in the chair.

I was so damn tired.

I no longer swung by the bakery in the morning. I sat in the school car park and dreaded the walk up the stairs. The KU Med campus seemed to stretch forever, when mom dropped me off after school. I'd walk and walk and walk and walk and feel like I wasn't getting anywhere, as I went to my endless appointments.

The whole me-in-slo-mo-and-everybody-else-in-fast-forward effect got worse and worse and, for the first time in my life, I had to actually work to keep up with my classes. Sometimes I didn't manage it. I wrote the most God-awful drivel for a History essay and I still don't know how I got a good mark. I used lots of big words and concepts but it was just random thoughts. I would have failed me.

I never did any homework. After dinner (usually a taco stand mom used so often that they'd learned our names) I'd just go to my room and collapse.

I'd never felt so utterly awful in my entire life.

Then, right around my birthday in November, I got a cold. It was a bad cold and turned into a lung infection. My GP told me to see Morris. He never liked me to have anything wrong with my respiratory system without going to see Doctor Morris. I suspected he didn't want the blame if I croaked.

So I drove myself to the ENT clinic, for what seemed like the hundred and fiftieth time and sat forever on the crappy plastic chairs in the puke pink hall. Finally, Morris received me.

He said, 'How's all the therapy going?'

'Well, you know me, I just love the attention.'

Then we both laughed and I coughed until I felt sick. Morris handed me a tissue.

'Clear your mucus,' he said. 'And we'll have a look.'

I spat, blew my nose and binned the tissue, and then stuck my tongue out. Morris grabbed it with the cotton and stuck the mirror down. I hardly gagged at all.

He said, 'Wait a minute,' and let me go, jumping up. I could hear him outside, telling the nice lady to get Doctor Kular straightaway.

Then Kular came into the room and, without any form of greeting, grabbed a square of cotton and a dental mirror. I stuck out my tongue and down it went.

'You see?' Morris said.

'Well, it'd be hard to miss,' Kular replied. He let me go and flipped through my chart. 'Didn't you notice in August?' he asked.

Morris rubbed his balding head. 'I didn't look,' he admitted. 'I spent the appointment dealing with issues from the speech therapist.'

Kular read the notes and snorted. 'Forgetting that even a sixteen-year-old patient might be telling the truth.'

He turned to me. 'Remember when I told you that larynxes have a habit of growing shut?' He made a fist again.

I nodded.

'Yours has. That's why you can't articulate anymore.'

'I don't think I can breathe all that great, either.'

Morris said, 'No. You're down to about ten percent of your airway.'

They looked at each other, hesitating.

I knew what they were going to say. 'Don't tell me,' I said. 'We have to do it all again.'

Morris grinned ruefully. 'Sorry,' he said, and I knew he meant both for the rotten luck and for not listening to me.

I felt this wonderful feeling that I couldn't quite place. It was making me smile, even though I knew it wasn't appropriate in the circumstances. I felt so...happy. That was it. I felt...happy. I couldn't help smiling broadly. I was positively beaming.

Kular shook his head. 'I don't like you walking around with that breathe-way, especially with an infection.' He turned to Morris. 'I think we should sign her in.'

'Oh, of course,' Morris said. 'I wasn't planning on letting her run around.'

'Can I go home to pack my bag?' I asked.

They looked at each other again. This time Morris grinned and Kular rolled his eyes.

'I suppose you'll need to get your nail polish and your lip gloss,' Morris said.

'And my conditioner. The shampoo here is so harsh.' I thought. 'Oh, and I have to pick mom up at work.'

'Be back by six,' Morris said. 'Or I'll send Starchy after you.'

'And don't walk up any hills or stairs,' Kular added. 'You're quite fortunate not to have had a heart attack.'

Still going strong on the old bedside manner, I thought to myself, looking at him fondly. He was *such* a dickhead.

I had to drag myself through the parking garage, but my heart was singing. I wasn't crazy and I wasn't slack. I wasn't useless, after all. I was sick! I was dying!

It was wonderful news.

Mom didn't take it as well.

I was busy throwing things into a suitcase – sweats, T-shirts, sneakers, nightgowns, books, teddy bears, cosmetics. Mom said, 'I just can't do this again.'

Mom was working for a yearbook company. She was working in the factory, in the shipping department.

It hadn't been exactly easy for her to get the job and she liked it, I could tell. She'd gone to put in her application because she'd heard they were hiring, but, as usual, the box which read 'Previous Work Experience' was nearly blank. Still, the guy doing the hiring asked her to come into the office for an interview. It sounded to me like he had meant to give her some tips on how to make her applications look better, but she ended up impressing him.

'What kind of work do you want to do?' he'd asked.

'Anything that will feed me and my child,' she'd answered.

'You have *no* experience? Except for the...uh...reception work at the jewellers? None whatsoever?' My mother had shaken her head sadly.

'I was a housewife for nearly twenty years,' she said.

'So,' he said encouragingly. 'What did you do as a housewife? What skills do you bring to the workforce?'

Mom sighed. 'I can cook and make love,' she said, 'and that's about it.'

Evidently he laughed so long and loud that his admin assistant came to see what was wrong. He hired mom on the spot and she'd been early every day, worked her socks off, stayed late and did any overtime going. She was bright, motivated and charming. She got on with everybody and you never had to tell her anything twice. They'd already put her in charge of a group.

I said, 'You won't need to stop working. I don't need a babysitter anymore.'

Then mom said, 'It's not just that,' and started to cry. 'It's the trach tube and the IVs and more scars...it's so horrible watching you go through all of that...'

I thought she could have been a bit more tactful. After all, I had no choice. But I said, 'I know, I know,' and patted her on her shoulder, because she didn't have a lot of friends to complain to. And Grandma was dead. So she *had* to complain to me.

And then I remembered to pack toothpaste and steal the television schedule from the paper, because the candy stripers wouldn't bring the xeroxed ones around until Monday.

Before I left the house, though, I had a phone call to make.

Ed's mother said, 'I'm sorry, Coco, but Ed—'

I cut into the speech I'd heard her say about twenty times. 'Tell him that he doesn't have to talk to me. He can just listen. And that it really is important.' And that got him to the phone.

I could hear him breathing on the other end of the line. 'My scar tissue has been growing back. I've been finding it really hard to breathe. That's why I was so tired all the time. I have to go back for the operations again.'

His breathing stopped for a moment and then started again.

I said. 'Look, I know I can be a jerk. But I wasn't being a complete pig at YCC. I've been really exhausted. When I sit down and I'm resting, I can breathe just fine and my oxygen levels look great. But when I exercise, they tank.'

He was still there.

I said, 'I know this is a lot to take in. And I know you've been really mad at me. But if you think you can ever forgive me, could you tap the phone once? And if you never want to hear from me again, you can tap twice and I'll leave you alone.'

I listened for a long time. I heard paper rustling and something get knocked over. And then a pen tapped against the mouthpiece. I waited for a whole minute by my Mickey Mouse watch, but it didn't tap again.

I waited, and he waited. And then he said, 'When do you go in?'

'Now.' I then had a big coughing fit, because I'd talked so much. When I'd finished, I had to listen closely to hear that he was still on the line.

Finally, he said, 'If I bring you a bean burrito, will you help me with my Hemingway essay?'

I was so…relieved…tears started leaking out of my eyes and I had to sniff, even though the cold part of my lung infection was long over. I said, 'Sure.'

We listened to each other breathe a little more and then I said,

# Chapter Twenty-Five

'I think you know how to get hold of me, right?'

'Yeah. I've got the number.'

And we said goodbye.

Mom was so upset that she let me drive to the hospital. I could turn left and take the highway, even though I didn't, because I swung by the library to stock up on books.

I felt fantastic. It was amazing how much of feeling completely horrible had been about my mood. It was still difficult to move around, but without the weight of utterly despising myself on my shoulders, it was a lot easier.

I didn't walk up any hills or stairs, because Doctor Kular had told me not to. But I danced a lot.

# Chapter Twenty-Six

## Soundtrack: 'Rhiannon' – Fleetwood Mac

The next day changed my happy mood.

Morris and Kular told me at rounds that they'd be coming by that afternoon with Bob the anaesthesiologist. Although they didn't want to operate while I still had a lung infection, they had something they wanted to discuss about the surgery.

I'd slept well and had a fun-packed day of breathing steam and seeing the respiratory therapists, who put me on a slant board and pounded my back with cupped hands to help me cough up everything lurking in my tubes and lungs. Okay, that wasn't really fun and sometimes I ended up pretty bruised. But on the plus side, I could already breathe tons better.

I was also getting injected with serious antibiotics, the kind that make you go all blotchy. I found that reassuring. Those always seemed to work faster.

My surgical team arrived after lunch.

I'd actually eaten quite a lot of lunch. Chicken, mashed potatoes and gravy. Peas and carrots. After my experiences at YCC, I was a lot more tolerant of institutional food. The catering at Fort Hays State made the food at KU Med seem wonderful in comparison.

Nurse Starchy had been very pleased and had spent some time drawing the relative benefits of the meal I'd just consumed contrasted with chip and dip and Coke. It was typical of Starchy that even though you'd done the right thing, you still got the lecture.

She'd barely gone when the surgical team arrived.

Usually, conversations with surgeons are not lengthy. They tend to stand there for a few minutes or perch on the edge of your bed, if they're exhausted. They don't mince their words and they aren't interested in your small talk. But today Bob took the bed and Morris and Kular actually found chairs and they were talking to me as if they were normal human beings.

Something was obviously up.

I was wearing a T-shirt and sweats and tucked my legs up under me, so I felt more in control.

'I want you to think about what we're going to ask you to do very carefully,' Morris said. 'I want you to talk it over with your mom and think about it for a couple of days.'

I said, 'Ohhhhhh-kay.' And then, 'I thought I already pretty much knew what we were going to do.'

Kular took a breath, but Morris gave him a look and he let Morris do the talking. He was getting smarter.

Morris said, 'The last stent didn't work.'

I said, 'I know.'

'We think it might have been slightly in the wrong position.'

Then Kular took a plastic larynx out of his backpack and did quite a bit of explaining about how vocal chords are attached. I won't bore you with it here. I didn't really understand it then, and I don't now.

I was distracted, wondering how long he'd carried that thing around with him.

Did he have it in the cafeteria at lunch? Did he pull it out and rest it on his tray as he got his money out to pay? He was never going to get a girlfriend if he carried large plastic larynxes around in his backpack.

Gradually, as he talked, I understood that it would be really handy if I could make the 'eeeee' sound *during* the surgery.

Morris said, 'So we thought it would be very useful…'

And I said, 'Yeah, I get it. You want me to be awake during the surgery.'

That's when we all looked at Bob. He said, 'I've been doing this kind of thing a lot in Neurosurgery. I can guarantee you won't feel any pain. You may feel some pulling and tugging, but you won't feel any cutting.'

The chicken and mashed potatoes turned over in my stomach and headed back up my throat for freedom. I had to swallow hard. I put my hand over my mouth, as if that would keep my lunch in and their hands out of me.

Everyone looked at me for a moment. Finally, I was able to take my hand away from my mouth. 'I've got to say, that as an idea, it doesn't really grab me.' And that was an understatement, if I'd ever heard one…

Bob said, 'Okay. Why not?'

I said, 'I just don't want to know what you guys do to me. It's not like I actually *like* surgery.'

Morris reached for my hand. 'I know,' he said. 'I really do understand.'

But Kular snorted. 'It'll be happening anyway. Just because you sleep through it, it doesn't mean it's not happening.' He shoved the plastic larynx back into his bag tetchily and I rolled my eyes.

I said, 'How long have you been carrying that thing around?'

He looked at me, affronted. 'Why?' he asked. 'What's wrong with this model?' He was almost as ticked off as the day he'd called me Frankenstein.

I shrugged. 'It's kind of dorky to carry around a plastic throat in your backpack. It's not exactly attractive.'

Bob turned away, but I could tell he was laughing because the bed was shaking.

Doctor Kular said, 'The issue isn't how I transport my model. The issue is whether or not you are mature enough to cooperate with our surgical plan.'

'*Mature* enough?' Now I was the affronted one.

Morris gave him a look, but Kular muttered, 'It's not like you have a choice.'

I said, 'I don't have a *choice*? I *have* to do this, whether I want to or *not*?'

'No, no,' Morris began, but Kular talked over him.

'I meant the surgery. You've got to have the surgery.'

'I know *that*,' I said. 'I know I can't let my larynx just grow shut. But I don't know that I want to *be awake for a surgery*.'

Kular looked at his watch. He and Morris stood up. 'Think about it,' Morris said. 'The thing is, we're trying to figure out where we went wrong last time and how to do it better this time. And this is our best plan. You don't want to do this four or five times or have us just give up and end up with a trach tube for life.'

The idea actually made me shiver. Goosebumps came up on my arms and I had to rub them with my hands to make them go down.

'I'll stay,' Bob said. 'Let me tell you how we deal with the pain.'

He talked quite a bit and very technically about his work and, in spite of myself, I got interested. I trusted Bob and I knew, if I did this horrible thing, that he would make it as not-horrible as possible.

I thanked him when he left and he wished me luck making up my mind.

Mom thought I *had* to do it. I couldn't make her see that I had a choice. For her, you did what the doctor said was best or you wouldn't get better.

I tried to call Dad and ask *his* opinion, but he was taking a few days off with his new wife. He'd married that woman with the flat hair as soon as the divorce was final. I'd been invited to the wedding, but I couldn't bring myself to go. Now, when I saw my dad, I had to see Nina, too. It wasn't a great motivation.

I didn't know what to do about staying awake during surgery. I felt like a coin that hadn't fallen heads or tails but had rolled to a stop balanced on its edge.

Starchy let them offer me a sleeping pill, but I didn't want it.

Not yet, not while I was still walking around and breathing, however restrictedly. I was on the other side of the hall, this time, not the construction site side, but the roadside, with its old trees and green spaces. I hugged my knees on the wide windowsill and looked out at the moonlight.

It was two or three in the morning. Suddenly, I saw the shape of large wings. An owl came floating by my window, intent on the grass below. It was so close, I could have reached out and grabbed a feather from its furry wings.

One of the freakier things my mother had come up with that autumn was that she thought Grandma's spirit travelled back to earth in the shape of an owl. Mom really missed Grandma. She still sometimes picked up the phone and dialled the number, forgetting Grandma wouldn't be there. Mom had said she'd seen an owl and it had spoken to her in Grandma's voice.

Of course, mom was totally nuts. But still.

It was worth a shot.

The owl swooped onto the branch of a nearby tree, and I decided I would ask it what to do.

I formed the question in my head. 'Should I try staying awake during surgery, to help my doctors? Even though it's really scary?'

And it worked. An answer popped into my mind, in my grandmother's voice.

I nearly fell off the windowsill.

I think that I knew my grandmother so well, I could guess what she would say. And concentrating on the owl made it easier, somehow, to 'hear' her words. 'The Lord never gives you a cross you can't carry.'

I went back to bed, coughed briefly and disgustingly productively, and then slept like a lamb.

Everyone was so proud of me. That's what got me through those next few days, and the preparations for surgery. Nobody had been proud of me in a very long time, maybe since the day Ed and I weed-whacked the hillside.

I'd seen Ed twice. He was even more gorgeous when he was being apologetic than he was when he was all bouncy and full of himself. I didn't know how the Julie girl could resist him. I'd had two bean burritos and we'd sorted out his Hemingway essay and a History research paper.

He'd made me call my friends from school and tell them what was going on. He listened to what I said, and then told me where I'd gone wrong.

'You don't ask how they are.' 'You didn't apologise for calling during meal time.' 'You didn't thank his mother.'

By the third call, he was sighing at me. I said, 'Look, I'm trying. I really am.'

'Try harder.'

I'd done it in alphabetical order. It was Bobby next. I apologised to his mother for ringing in the evening, remembered to say please and everything.

'You see,' Ed said. 'You can be human, if you just try.'

I punched him.

Bobby said, 'Coco? What's wrong?'

'Why should something be wrong?' I asked.

'You never call me.'

That wasn't true. We spoke on the phone all the time, arranging to meet up with the group here or there. I said something about this and Bobby said, 'Yeah, but that's me calling you. You never call me.'

And it struck me that was true, actually. I guess I'd kind of gotten out of the habit of dialling people's numbers. If I thought about it, I hadn't actually originated a phone call myself, except to my mother, for a long time. 'Anyway,' I said, a bit cross that this had been pointed out to me at that precise moment, 'I'm just calling to tell you. I'm back in the hospital. The surgery on my throat didn't work, and they have to do it again.'

Karla had sympathised. Mandy had asked for a great deal of factual detail. Bobby sighed, as if the whole thing was tiresome.

He said, 'Oh, no.' And before I could say that I was actually quite pleased to be getting it all sorted, and not to worry about me, he added, 'This is going to kill Kim.'

I hadn't thought about that. When I did think about it, the thought was so big and heavy that it kind of landed on me and left me gasping.

Bobby said, 'Have you told her?'

Stupidly, I shook my head and then had to hurry to say, 'No. No, she's next on my list.'

He said, 'Don't. Don't call her up on the phone and tell her like that. I'll go over and see her. I'll do it now.'

But...I wanted to talk to her. I never got to talk to her any more. I started to say this. 'But—'

'Coco,' Bobby said sternly. 'You're my friend. But you know what you're like. Let me do it.'

'Okay,' I said.

I told Ed and he said, 'It would have been better if it was your mom who went over.' Then we thought about mom for a minute. 'Well, maybe not.' And then he added, 'Call Kim in a couple of hours.'

And I really should have.

But my grandpa came in with mom and then some cousins came by.

And I forgot.


All the web that held me to Kim. All the love and the memories and the remembered conversations and the time...just the sheer time we'd spent together, literally years of my life...and it was just little shitty things like that that cut through the strands.

I forgot to call.

And I shouldn't have.

The next morning, my hands shook as I changed into the green gown and cap. I looked in the mirror at my neck. Next time I saw it, it would have the blue trach tube and matching buttons again.

My dad had sent a nice bouquet of actually fresh flowers and I smelled the roses and carnations, knowing I wouldn't be able to smell them later. I didn't wear socks, they'd only take them off to see my toenails while I was asleep. Instead, I asked the orderlies for an extra blanket for my feet.

Mom was brave, cracking jokes. She'd stocked me up on onion dips and wet wipes and had already asked the nurses for lemon swabs and cardboard basins. But when she didn't think I was looking, her face was haunted by fear and worry. I felt terrible about that. Why couldn't I just stay well?

Bob gave me a *huge* happy pill. I could barely stay awake to say goodbye and nearly rolled right off the gurney. When I got to the OR, I knew everybody. They were all so nice, signing onto my surgery like that. It was lovely.

And then it all started. And it wasn't lovely. At all.

The problem was not the tugging and the pulling, which was, frankly, horrible.

The problem was that they hadn't thought to rig up a proper screen. They put the instrument table over my face, but the bottom of the stainless steel tray was rather shiny and shiny silver things are what we call mirrors.

I tried hard not to look, and Bob gave me enough dope so that I felt pretty sleepy. Most of the time I managed not to look. But it was impossible to completely ignore something happening eight inches under my eyes.

Kular, with his usual tact, kept forgetting that I was there. He would say things like, 'Swab, swab, why does she always bleed so damn much?' The OR nurse who always looked after me kept patting my toes. She did it so often and so habitually that I'll bet she did it all the time, to everyone, even though they were asleep and would never know.

There's a lot of blue stuff in the neck, it seemed to me, and some yellow things, too. I felt horribly sick every time my eyes flicked up to the tray or glimpsed a scalpel with a tiny bit of me dangling off. They were flinging the scar tissue onto something nearby.

Bob put his hand over my eyes when he could. He kept urging me to relax and finally said something about 'trauma' and 'shock' to the doctors. I heard Morris say, 'Let's get the stent in and then she can go.'

I felt myself start to cry. I'd been really brave, but this was too much. It was so horrible that I couldn't help feeling sorry for myself. Nobody should ever have to be awake during surgery.

After about five hundred years, Kular said, 'Okay, Miss DuLac, let's hear that 'eeeee.'

I obliged.

There was discussion.

And then I woke up in Recovery. There was no once, twice, three times. I was fully awake straightaway. My mouth was dry and tasted nasty. I saw the Recovery nurse walk by and asked for a lemon swab.

All that came out was a whistling sound.

My hand stole up and felt the trach tube. I'd nearly forgotten.

I closed my eyes and tried, but I couldn't go back to sleep.

# Chapter Twenty-Seven

## Soundtrack: 'Dream Weaver' – Gary Wright

I wasn't quite as ratty as usual after the surgery. Mom was worried about me, said I was too quiet. My new magic slate (jungle animals) rested by me in the bed. I didn't even want to throw up.

The fact was, all the fun had gone out of the whole situation. I was pretty good about seeing upsides, but I felt that I'd been fooling myself. There was no upside here. There was only goo, blood and discomfort.

Mom stayed way past visiting hours, just holding my hand while we watched crappy TV. I still had my IV and had to go pee a lot. Mom helped me wheel the stand.

I felt weak, old and tired. When she said she had to go home, I nearly cried.

She looked good, even after sitting in the hospital all day. She was wearing her new jeans and a thick cardigan and boots. From some mysterious source last summer, she'd acquired a shoulder bag, hand-tooled in thick, Mexican leather. She'd stopped smoking when I'd gotten my lung infection, and her skin was clear and soft.

It was dark when she left. I looked towards the windows. It seemed hard to believe that I'd been able to climb up and sit on the sill just a few nights ago. It seemed hard to believe I'd ever moved around just for fun. My bones felt heavy, as if they'd been replaced with lead. Moving my head on my neck was exhausting.

I sighed, the wind whistling through the plastic tube, and tried to watch the television.

And then mom was back in the room, crying. It took me a minute to figure out why she was there and what was happening.

Three young men had tried to mug her. They'd pulled at her bag and asked her for her money and jewellery.

'I hit one,' my mother said, distressed. 'I shouted at them. I said, "Come on!" I've had *enough* and I'm not going to take any shit from little punks like you." And I hit one.' She was crying and shaking. 'I hit him hard and he fell down and the big one said I was on drugs and they ran away.'

One of the nurses arrived with a cup of coffee. 'This has cream and sugar,' she said. 'Drink it, it's good for shock.'

'The police?' Mom asked.

'On their way,' the nurse said.

'They could have had guns,' mom said. 'They could have had knives. I only had four dollars in my bag. They could have killed me. What was I thinking?'

I wrote on my magic slate, 'mom, the bad-ass.'

She shrieked and began laughing as hard as she was crying. 'The look on their faces,' she said. 'They called me a psycho bitch.'

She was laughing and crying. Her wig was askew and her makeup was running down her face. Psycho bitch was probably a bit strong, but I could understand how the muggers had gotten that impression.

I handed her the tissue box.

'I wasn't going to take it,' she said. 'I don't want to take any more *shit*.'

Her hands shook so much that she spilled a little coffee on her shirt. 'Oh, *hell*,' she said furiously. 'That will *stain*.'

The police came about twenty minutes later. They thought they knew who it was and said they'd come by with some mug shots in the next couple of days for mom to identify.

'They were just kids,' she said. 'But it was scary.'

I recognised one of the officers. He'd been to parties at our house. He said, 'Diane. One of those kids has already put two women in the hospital.'

Mom swallowed hard. She said, 'I guess I was pretty stupid.'

He grinned. 'You're one tough mama,' he said. 'But I think this time you were lucky.' He turned to me. 'Say goodnight to your mother, we're going to walk her to her car.'

I wrote on my magic slate, 'Follow her home.' And stared at him as he read.

'That's what I meant,' he said. 'We'll make sure she gets home okay.'

I flipped up the plastic. 'Good,' I wrote. Again, I met his eye. He knew I'd tell Dad if they didn't take care of mom.

His partner said, 'We've got that 1020 under the bridge.'

'Later,' the first cop said.

I wrote on my slate, 'Go use the bathroom,' to my mom, and she did. When she came out, her mascara streaks were gone and her wig was on straight. She had revived under the male protection and the fussing of the nurses. The second cop had practically been hopping from leg to leg while they waited. You could tell he thought this was a big waste of his time. The first cop kept giving him dirty looks.

I could imagine the conversation in the car as the first cop explained to his impatient partner that Major DuLac would not be pleased if his ex-wife was not escorted home safely after an attempted mugging. He wouldn't have had to explain who Major DuLac was. Dad had ended more careers than the recession.

I lay there after they'd gone. Now I would have to make sure mom got to her car before it got dark. That meant she could only be there for a couple of hours the next day. And the next. And the next.

The evenings stretched ahead of me, endlessly. The television mouthed inanities and the fashion magazines mocked my imperfections. The telephone stood there, useless.

I was alone.

And when I got home, I was even more alone.

It wasn't anybody's fault. I'd done it to myself. Bobby was right, and so was Ed. I hadn't made an effort. I'd been letting everybody else do everything. If they didn't call me, I didn't talk to them. If they didn't ask me to go somewhere, I didn't go. I didn't think I had ever asked anyone to go anywhere.

My mom had, back when we were littler. But the whole arranging-things thing started when I was in the hospital. I'd missed that bit.

I was starting to see what Ed meant. I needed remedial social skills.

The first time around, everyone had felt sorry for me, and had made a big effort. But when I'd been better, I didn't make the effort back. They weren't doing it again.

I'd seen myself as a loner and an outsider. Well, now I was, and how did I like it?

I reckon I was completely insane after about two weeks.

I was trapped in the house, in the winter, all alone, with an ancient, incontinent dog. The heating was on, and there was food around, but it was otherwise pretty miserable. We had five or six channels of television. Cable was just beginning to happen and far out of our price range. People were starting to buy video recorders, but there was a big debate over VHS and Betamax formats and we couldn't afford either, anyway.

I went to the library every week. Then Christmas came and Dad and my other relatives gave me some money.

I started my life-long addiction to cinema matinees that year. I almost always went alone (and still do, even now).

Over the summer mom had started going out in the evenings, a very tiny little bit, with her best friend's sister, who was also recently divorced. The sister had convinced her to join a bowling league and mom got into it, even though she was a terrible bowler. I think she liked the shirt.

So, she was gone all day and one or two nights a week. And the house got worse and worse because mom wasn't all that interested in housework at the best of times.

I kept lying to her and telling her I was fine when I wasn't. I think she knew I was depressed, but she was fighting her own little war. She just couldn't help me any more than she was and not go totally insane herself.

One night, my mom was out bowling when there was a knock on the door. It was Jack. He held up a six-pack of beer and a doobie when I opened the door.

The house smelled of dog wee and I was terribly depressed. We got stoned and started kissing, but then Jack stopped. He said, 'This isn't going to work.'

I started to cry, and he put his arm around me and held me. 'I'm not leaving or anything. But we can just be together. You don't have to...you know.'

This made me cry harder. I wrote on my slate about the smell and about the house and about being tired of being poor and sick and alone. He read it, opened beers and rolled another doobie. He sat with me for hours.

I've had good friends since. But Jack was something special. He's gone, now, the drugs took him over and he died. It was far too late when I realised that what I'd had with him had been true love, after all.

My loneliness must have been obvious at the clinic because Doctor Morris gave me one of the buzzing machines so that I could talk like a Dalek. He said that they hadn't wanted to give me one before, for fear I'd get dependent on it and then not try to talk properly. He said that he knew that was stupid, now.

And so I rushed out and embraced the world, freed to communicate.

Yeah, right.

Just because I had my Dalek voice didn't mean that I suddenly had a new personality. I was still lonely, and bitter and twisted and resentful and shy and all the other things that kept me in the house. And anyway, the Dalek machine vibrated my neck to make a voice. Which was fine, but that meant it also vibrated the four wires that ran through my neck. That wasn't so fine – it hurt like hell after a few sentences.

Mom started calling me in her lunch hour at work, and that made a huge difference in how I felt about my day. And then we didn't have much snow that winter, so I could go to the library and the cinema.

I started calling Kim, nearly every day, just to ask her how her day went. Because I couldn't talk that much, I actually started listening. And, finally, she was actually there…her own ideas. Her own concerns. Her own life.

It was as fragile as spider silk, but the things that had always drawn us together began drawing us back again…

I even arranged for us to go shopping in the end-of-season sales at the mall. I had enough money for gaucho skirts now, but they looked horrible on me and I hated wearing tights. I found a long skirt made of brushed denim with a wide, curved waistband. I got some cheesecloth blouses and white cotton camisoles with lace straps to wear under them. I got a pair of nice jeans and some ribbed turtlenecks and a thick, warm, brown cardigan.

Kim helped me pick them all out – very decisive and sure about what looked good and what didn't. She needed some new jeans, but although I let her into the cubicle with me, I had to wait outside when she tried on.

And that felt…painful. But it also felt…true. We were back, in a way, to our real lives, where I wanted her and wanted me…but farther away than I wanted to be. Somehow the ache of wanting her more than she wanted me was nearly comforting…just because it was so familiar.

We never talked about the accident or my health. I knew the spider's silk would break if we did.

Ed called me. A lot. His SATs were coming up and he was nervous. He thought he'd be fine on the math and the science. He thought he'd probably do okay on anything multiple choice. But he was dreading the essays and short answers. He did practice tests every night and kept calling me and reading me his answers.

Everyone kept giving me silk and cotton scarves. I soon had quite a collection. Mom saved up some money and I got contact lenses. I started to look...okay.

My hair finally grew down instead of just out. I just had to clip it out of my eyes. Religious use of conditioner meant it curled and didn't frizz. I had stopped brushing it between washes and that helped, as well.

Now that mom had a bit of her confidence back, she started cooking again. I lost that pasty look I'd had from living on takeaway.

And during this time, I got something else, too. I got a half-sized ring binder. And in it, I started to write poetry.

There was a phrase in a James Taylor song, 'I find myself careening, into places where I should not let me go.'

I thought that was me, and that I was still in some way, stumbling on Key Lane by the tree, trying to find my way home. I was careening from my injury. I wrote 'Careening' on the front of my ring binder and started to play with words, sounds and feelings.

At the library, I checked out books of poetry and found the war poets. Here were people who understood me and the things I felt; other people who had walked closely with death. I loved them.

I read books about World War I. I read Hemingway, Fitzgerald, Rilke and Ford Madox Ford.

I scribbled all of my feelings down on paper.

I started to feel even more confident. I even ran errands at the supermarket or post office while mom was at work. I think it was seeing the vice principal on one of these errands that gave him his brilliant idea.

I got sent a teacher.

Sam White was our French teacher and he was gorgeous. He was refined and erudite and had lovely skin, which tanned to a golden brown. He was finicky about his shirts and smelled lovely. Altogether, he was the most attractive man I'd ever seen.

He was also very kind to us all and French Club had been not just a society for practicing speaking French, but something special for us dweebs. Sam was the only person any of us knew who had been abroad as a civilian. We thought he knew everything.

We tried cheeses, we went to French restaurants, we read Camus and Sartre. We saw world cinema. Sam White was *amazing*.

At first the school had sent a woman I didn't know, a supply teacher. I can't remember what I did to alienate her. It might have been our house, which was shabby and smelly from the dog. It might have been me. I might have been horrible to the poor woman in any one of a hundred ways. I can't remember.

Then Sam White began to visit twice a week, and I sat up and took notice.

We caught up on the previous semester in three or four weeks. I took test after test and passed them all with As and Bs. Then we began racing through the second semester work. We had nine weeks, but I was finished in four or five.

Ed called. He hadn't aced his SATS, but he'd done well enough to be accepted into the University of Kansas. He was going to start a year late, so he could work and save up some money, and so he could have more physiotherapy on his leg. His parents were throwing a party to celebrate and wanted me to come.

A few months before, if anyone had asked if I'd like to go to a big party with a bunch of people I didn't know, I would have...well, I wouldn't even have answered, except with a look. But I said yes.

His dad made a big pot of chili. His mom baked a special sheet cake with Jayhawks all over it, the mascot of the university. I met Julie. She was blonde and blue-eyed. She had a funny, crooked smile and freckles on her nose. Everyone else called me Ed's coach or his 'little friend'. Julie called me Coco and was just...really cool and nice.

I liked her so much that I wanted to ask her why she'd dumped Ed when he got hurt. I felt sure she had some kind of reason. But even I could tell now was not the right time.

I drove myself there. I ate chili and drank a beer – because even though I was only sixteen, everyone treated me like I was Ed's age – and had a slice of cake. And then I drove myself back home. I talked to people with my Dalek voice. And I didn't die. And nobody hated me. It was...fine.

Ed was absolutely radiantly happy. And I had helped.

He took a moment to pull me to one side. He said, 'You know, sometimes I thought Des was the lucky one. I thought having to keep living was too hard.'

I still felt like that. Loads of times. Ed put his arm around my shoulders and kind of hugged me sideways. He said, 'It's not, Coco. It's really not.'

Mom and I started cleaning the house properly again, now that Mr White was coming over. For the first time in my life, I was even given chores. I ran the vacuum cleaner. I dusted. I baked.

As soon as the weather was clear, Mr White had us playing

badminton outside on the front patio. Movement and exercise felt extremely good. I'd never had to think about it before. I'd always been dancing all winter and swimming all summer. But now I had to actually make a plan to move my body. It seemed strangely artificial. It still does. I'd still much rather ride my bike to work than go to a gym.

But, really, there was plenty to do outside. Mom and I had missed the previous summer in all sorts of ways. The grass needed cutting – in fact, it had to be weed-whacked first. The roses needed pruning. The planters needed planting and weeding.

Mom and I got busy.

It was a good time for me. I was outdoors most of the day, every day. I'd do something in the yard and then when I got tired, I'd eat lunch and then take my notebook back outside. Once, a boy came by from school. He'd seen me sitting in the yard, reading and writing. He told me how nice I looked. Gradually, I realised he was flirting. With me.

I went to my mirror after he'd gone and looked at myself. I was whip thin, of course, but more muscled than I'd ever been before, from the summer at YCC. My hair was, frankly, amazing. Nearly black and curling madly down past my shoulders.

My skin was brown and my clothes were interesting and funky. I'd found a pair of sandals with wooden soles that I really liked. I had some silver earrings with turquoise bits. I had wonderful scarves that covered my trach tube and buttons.

I looked marginally better than okay, I decided. I looked at myself carefully, for quite a long time, using a hand mirror to see the bits behind me. The evidence was there, right in front of me, but it took a long while to sink in. I actually looked…good. I looked attractive. I sat down and laughed. It was just air whistling in and out of my trach tube, but I did it long enough for my ribs to hurt.

I hadn't really been trying. I'd just been getting on with things.

# Chapter Twenty-Seven

And that had worked much better than worrying about my looks ever had.

In the summer, I went back into the hospital to have the stent removed. It was the same scene again. In for two days before. On the construction site side this time. Catching up with Nurse Starchy, having my meeting with Bob, seeing Morris and Kular and all the gang. The new students seemed nervous around me and I realised I'd been part of the team longer than they had.

Mom didn't go to work the day of the surgery or the next day, but planned to go back on the third day. She wasn't scared I was going to die. She was just scared I was going to come back a horrid teenager on a drug comedown. I got into the gown and the hat, taped my ring, took off my toenail polish and got onto the gurney. Mom looked up from her magazine and wished me luck.

There were about four or five cards on my table and one plant that mom had brought in herself, just to cheer up the room. Nobody takes your fourth surgery very seriously.

It was the same old Scooby gang in the OR. I waved hello to everyone and they all patted me somewhere. I had my extra blanket and was so glad to be made unconscious that Bob said I was grinning with glee.

I could feel the lights of the Recovery room seeping under my eyelids, but I waited until I felt good and strong to open them. My hand snuck up and found a cork in my trach tube. Ah, I thought, success.

I thought about saying, 'eeeee' to myself, but it felt silly. Also, I found it very hard to tell the difference between a good 'eeeee' and a bad 'eeeee'. Thinking about it, I went to sleep again.

The next thing I heard was Kular. 'Honestly,' he said, 'she can sleep through anything.'

'That's teenagers,' Morris said. 'You should see my nephew. He went camping with us and...'

I opened my eyes. 'Eeeee,' I said.

Morris broke off his anecdote. 'Again,' he directed.

'Eeeee,' I said.

They exchanged glances.

Kular said, 'Hmm.'

'What?' I asked. 'What's wrong, now?'

'Nothing,' Kular replied. 'We just would have liked a little more articulation.'

'But it's not bad,' Morris said. 'It's better than a whisper.'

'Kind of,' Kular said. 'It's a much stronger whisper. And there will still be some swelling, of course, from the surgery.'

'Let me guess,' I said. 'You'd like to keep me in a week or so to see how it goes.'

Morris smiled. 'You're starting to read our minds. You've been here too long.'

I said, 'Tell me about it.'

When I got back to my room, I failed to vomit. I was even nice to my mother.

'If I had known you were going to be reasonable,' she said, 'I would have taken more time off work.'

Two days later, I got a roommate, an opera singer. She had nodes on her vocal chords and Morris was going to take them off. She could have gone to any ENT surgeon in the country, but she came to KU Med to Morris and Kular. It made me feel proud.

I was fully back into my Patient Volunteer role, although my original crew had all died and not many of the people there at the time were ambulatory. I could never get them to be enthusiastic for the afternoon shopping expedition. Still, I had enough to do catching up on their records filing, running samples and taking folks to X-ray and clinic.

Kim didn't visit. When I called her on the phone, she'd talk to me, but not for very long. I called Bobby to ask him what he thought was the matter, and he gave one of his big, deep sighs.

'It bothers her,' he said. 'She just starts to get over it, and then you have to have something else done and it bothers her all over again.'

I didn't know what to say.

He said, 'Just give her some time and some space.'

So I stopped calling Kim. I don't know if Bobby was right or wrong or if I should have tried harder or not. I'd had her back, so now I missed her again.

During this time, the plastic surgery team came to visit. They looked at my scars and asked me what my trach scar had looked like last time and murmured amongst themselves.

'The thing is,' the very handsome and well-dressed leader said, 'necks are tricky. When your trach tube scar has healed, call us and we'll start to schedule. We're going to need two or three sessions, I think.'

'By sessions, you mean surgeries?' I asked.

'Mmm yes.' He looked at me with his head on one side. 'Have you ever considered rhinoplasty?'

'What's that?'

'I think we could improve the shape of your nose,' he said.

'My nose,' I said tartly, 'is not the issue.' I could see his eyes flick down to my breasts and before he could suggest implants, I added, 'Let's just stick to the scars.'

'Of course.' He handed me his card. 'Just give us a call.'

They weren't the only ones planning on getting me back in the operating room. Morris and Kular thought they could use the same technique they'd been using on singer's nodules for my scar tissue.

'Let's just let it stabilise,' Kular said, 'and make sure it doesn't grow shut again, and then we'll see what we can do. If we do a little at a time, we should get away with it and give you more articulation.'

'Great,' I said, trying to sound enthusiastic.

'We'll try and plan it around school breaks,' Morris said. 'Get one in around Thanksgiving and another one at Christmas. We could schedule the plastic surgery for the same visits. We can do everything through your mouth now, so we won't be messing up their work.'

'Good idea,' Kular said. 'She recovers much more quickly now from the anaesthetic.'

Great, I thought. Other kids planned their holidays around activities. I would plan mine around surgeries.

Kular noticed my sour face. 'Have I said something to upset you?' he asked.

'No,' I said. 'I'm just not looking forward to more surgery.'

He snorted. 'Don't start that nonsense again,' he said. 'You're very lucky.'

Really? I wanted to say. Would you like to swap?

Doctor Morris patted my hand and pulled Doctor Kular away.

'We want to leave the trach tube in place,' Kular said at my first post-op clinic visit. 'Just in case.'

'Take it out,' I said. 'I hate it.'

'Oh, come on,' he said. 'It's only for four to six weeks.'

'Take it out,' I said. 'I want to go swimming this summer.'

'Four weeks,' Kular said, smiling at me in his fatuous, smug way. 'We'll make sure it's only four weeks.'

The moment I got home, I took it out.

The next visit, he went to check on it. He didn't seem all that surprised to see the scar healing nicely.

The yearbook factory where mom worked only employed women in the school year, which worked out well for the factory and for the women themselves, who were all mothers. But mom had gone to the guy who'd hired her and begged to be kept on for the summer. 'I need this job,' she explained. 'It's not for pocket money. It's to feed us.'

He'd winced. 'I only have dirty, heavy work,' he said. 'Cleaning photographic plates with acid. Moving equipment and supplies.'

'I can do it,' mom said. 'I can outwork any man.'

She'd come home with her arms stained yellow. She started smoking again and I couldn't find it in myself to lecture her. She joined a volleyball team with the people on her bowling team. Sometimes she came home smelling of marijuana. And who could blame her?

I went camping with Dad and Nina in their new motorhome. They had their little routines. They knew who would do what and liked to make their pitch all smart and sharp quickly. They also liked cooking in the motorhome and not spending much money. Every time they could avoid doing something to save some money, they thought that was great.

I didn't fit in to any of this. I took up room, always had my nose in a book, didn't notice what needed doing and snapped to it, but had to be asked and directed. I showered too long, ate too little or too much or too messily. I'd had enough of minding every penny and was always up for a treat. I never acted quite right. Other teens in the campgrounds were clean-cut and willing and I was…not.

Dad seemed much less guilty about me after the trip. I'm sure Nina had helped him to realise that it was my fault that the relationship wasn't working – that I wasn't suitable to be his daughter.

They were working very hard at being middle class and respectable. And me? I didn't work very hard at anything at all. Although I did start to care about clothes, now that I was gorgeous.

I remember asking Nina, 'How does this top look with this skirt?' because I hadn't tried the combo before and there was no full-length mirror.

They were losing their patience because they wanted to go somewhere and I wasn't ready. But instead of just saying, 'It looks great, you look great, let's go,' Nina said, 'Why do you think anyone's going to look at you and notice what you're wearing?'

And I said, 'Well, I'm nearly six foot tall, with huge hair and a funny voice. Do you really think I'll slip under the radar?'

'You think too much about yourself.'

I thought, 'Well, somebody has to,' but I didn't say it.

I became chilly and polite for the rest of the week. They liked me better that way.

I was able to go back to school. It was nearly…enjoyable.

I was quite confident about how I looked, and that helped a great deal. I didn't take any shit anymore and I wasn't frightened of anyone.

And so, naturally, things happened.

Rob Savage's eye had started to wander from his future wife. In fact, if the rumours were true, more than his eyes had wandered. Bobby gave me a list of names and the probable extent of Rob's sexual contact with each girl on the list.

Rob was now a cross-country runner and I was no longer the only one who fancied him rotten.

One night, after some sort of sporting event, I found myself in somebody's uncle's camper van, headed home. There were a bunch of us riding around in the back and whoever was driving was dropping us off, one by one, until there were just six people left – three boys and three girls.

One of the girls was up front with the driver. One was Kim and I can't remember who she was with. And one was me. With Rob Savage.

We stopped. We drank some beer. Everybody started kissing.

I was kissing Rob Savage, for the first time since the theme park and it was absolutely lovely. He wasn't talking about childcare issues. He wasn't talking much at all, except to tell me how gorgeous I was. The kissing got more intense and he started to undo the belt of my jeans.

I protested and Kim, who had seemed totally engrossed in whatever she'd been doing with the other boy, leaned over and said, 'Go ahead. It's fun.'

And that shocked me.

I mean, I wasn't stupid. I knew Kim had gone with a few boys and I kind of knew that she'd been having sex. I don't how I knew, but I knew.

And none of those boys became a boyfriend and I thought that was...a little sad. And a little...stupid.

I didn't think any less of Kim because of it – it was the kind of thing that could happen to anybody. But I didn't think it was a good idea. And I knew she wasn't terribly happy about it.

So her urging me to do the same dumb thing seemed... unkind. It was probably the first unkind thing I'd ever seen her do. And for the first time in my life, I thought 'no' to something Kim said. I thought Kim (and this was almost unthinkable to me) was *wrong* and more than that, that she was *doing* wrong, urging me to let Rob Savage have access to what was inside my jeans, on a whim, in the back of some boy's uncle's camper van, after some random game.

I don't know what Rob thought. I must have stiffened and I suddenly felt totally sober. I pushed his hands away and did up my belt buckle.

Then Rob began trying to undo the knot on my scarf, to see my scars. I said no, but he kept saying he wanted to see. I suddenly realised that he was much more insistent about seeing my scars than he had been about getting into my panties.

'That's enough!' I said. I stood up and walked over to the little window that separated the driving bit from the campervan and banged it open. I tapped the boy who'd driven on his shoulder to get his attention. He was pretty distracted at the time by what his girlfriend was doing.

'I have to go home,' I said. 'Right now.'

His mouth dropped open. 'Now?' he said weakly and his girlfriend finally realised someone else was there and grabbed some clothes to cover herself.

'Sorry,' I said. 'If I don't get this special medicine in a half an hour, I'll die.' He looked at me and blinked. 'I'll die right here in your uncle's camper.'

Kim said, 'That's a lie!'

And I got right into her face. 'How do you know? How do you know what medicine I need or what's the matter with me? You never want to know anything.'

Kim's face looked like I'd just slapped her. I wanted to slap her. I wanted to slap Rob. I wanted to slap everybody.

I knew I was behaving badly. But I would have behaved much worse than that if it got me home.

Mom pulled into the driveway at the same time we did. She took one look at my face and went to put the kettle on the stove.

We sat on the sofa with cups of tea. Both of us were home earlier than expected. Neither of us wanted to talk about it. We just sat there and fumed together.

And it was nice.

# Chapter Twenty-Eight

## Soundtrack: 'Growing Up' – Bruce Springsteen

When I say I went back to school, I really only went back three days a week. The other two days I took classes at the local community college, to give me a bit of a start on university. Sam White had told me it was possible, and I jumped at the chance. Ed was taking some classes there, too, while he worked in a plumbing supplies shop to save up for KU.

I only saw him for lunch one day a week. I didn't make any other friends at all while I was there. I wandered around, usually lost, and tried to understand what the hell the English professor was talking about. He was Sam White's brother and a Jungian. That meant he looked at literature through Carl Jung's ideas. Archetypes. Commonalities.

I didn't understand much of it. I don't think I was really ready for university when I was sixteen.

On the other hand, I felt I had already absorbed all Burner High had to offer.

I took Psychology that year, and the football coach (who was hired to lift our standings in the conference, not for his teaching) was the teacher.

Sport was…well…essential to American high school life. People wore the school team's colours like football fans wear replica strip. Grown people, even. They had stickers on their cars and key rings. Burner Bears. It was part of their identity.

The population of the entire area is ecstatic when the high school team wins and gutted when they lose.

The crowds can be huge – why would 1500 grownups go watch a bunch of kids play football not very well? And, given that it takes place in the autumn, when it's a bit nippy at night…I've always found it a bit strange. I mean, I know why *we* did it. We *had* to. Even I wasn't ready to risk total social exclusion by skipping games. Everybody, even Jack and the rougher kids still came to game nights. They didn't cheer or anything lame like that, but they stood around. They watched.

Kim was the bear. Not *a* bear, we were all meant to be Bears. But *the* bear. Dancing in a padded furry suit with a big stuffed teddy head. She'd been a letter girl the year before. There were six of them, and they were all my old crowd. Shanice was, I think, the B. I'm pretty sure that Mandy (who had retired from cheer-leading) was an R, and so was Karla. They walked at the front of parades and held the long banner. They sat in the bleachers and led the response to the cheerleaders' cheers. Kim had been the N, I believe. But now she was the bear. Bobby was her handler, who kept her from falling over and brought her diet cokes. It was hot in the bear.

Because of this, Kim's hair was always a bit of a mess when we went to Don Chilitos after the game.

I was deeply, intensely bored with it all. I was bored at pep rallies. I was bored at the games. I was bored at Don Chilitos. I was bored with driving around drinking beer. I was bored with kissing the boys that wanted to kiss me. I was so, so, so, so unbelievably bored.

But it was like I was running on autopilot. You went to the pep rally and learned the new cheers (like my voice added much). You went to the game. You went to Don Chilitos afterwards and then at ten o'clock you drove home, if you hadn't hooked up with anyone. If you had hooked up with someone, you drove somewhere, like Pierson Pond, and explored elements of your sexuality in the car.

It was stupid and pointless – but that was what there was to do.

There were five channels on your TV. There was no internet. Video games meant Space Invaders (which had succeeded Pong) and was something you played at Don Chilitos, because nobody had a computer at home – except for geeks like Ferdinand Porter. None of us could understand what he did on the thing. Phones were big and worked at home and had cords attached to them.

So school sports were very important – your entire social life revolved around them and everybody around you cared about them and talked about them. Which made Coach a terribly important man.

He came into class with a scowl, because he didn't want to be there. He wore a tracksuit and shoes with cleats.

He smelled like outside.

He'd sit at the table and read the sports pages to us out loud. There would be general discussion about the issues in the articles about football, basketball or baseball.

This took up roughly half the class time.

Then he would call the register, chatting with each student as he went through the roll. He spent a little time making fun of me and other geeks as he went through. I'd already complained once. But the vice-principal had been embarrassed. It didn't take me long to realise he had no power to control the football coach.

Then the coach would open the Psychology book with distaste. One day (and I swear I'm not making this up), he said, 'Right. Today we're going to find out about Freud and Jung. Only instead of saying 'Froid' and 'Young', he said, 'Frood' and 'Jung' (as in 'Jug' with an 'n' in it).

I usually let most of this class wash over me, while wishing I'd gotten stoned with Jack in the car park before school. But this, this I *had* to correct. I couldn't let my fellow classmates say Frood and Jung all their lives. They'd look like dickheads.

My hand shot up like an arrow. He nodded at me. I said, 'I think you'll find that's "Froid" and "Young," Sir.'

You had to say 'Sir' to coach. Only if you were connected to the football team could you call him 'Coach'. It was meant to be a great honour.

He looked up at me with a sneer. 'Okay, Miss Smarty-pants,'

he said. 'If you know so much about them, let's hear it.'

'Well,' I began, 'Jung was a student of Freud's, so perhaps we should start with Freud. Freud was a doctor when...'

'Nobody can hear you,' he said. 'I'd better stick with the book.'

Cue much laughter. Coach bent down his head and furrowed his brow. 'Sigmund Frood was the father of modern Psychology. He was a young doctor when...'

The school photographer was cross because I wouldn't smile in my Senior Portrait. I said, 'I don't feel like smiling.'

He said, 'Well, give me something here; you've got no expression at all.'

I said, 'I've got an idea. Why don't you just take the damn picture?'

I was wearing a light blue T-shirt and scarf. I liked the picture, but the school was outraged because my nipples were faintly visible – I still wasn't wearing a bra. The school photographer had flatly refused to have me for retakes, so the yearbook staff had to ask the photographer to crop the photo. Everyone else's had to be cropped, too, to make the photographs work in the yearbook. Once again, I was terribly popular.

I wasn't all that thrilled about being in the Pep Club for football season, but after the whole yearbook thing, I didn't think it was wise to try and slide out of it.

By now, one of my cousins was coaching Flagle, who were in our conference. Flagle was part of the City School District, and so racially they were mixed, like all the City schools. Except for ours, of course.

If you're ever in a racist institution, you'll know it, because race will never be mentioned. At an institution that isn't racist, someone can say, 'Go ask Paul over there. He's the tall black guy in the nice suit.' At a racist institution, first of all, Paul won't work there...but if he should have been hired as a token, you'll hear something like, 'Paul will know, ask him. He's the...er...tall man with the dark, curly hair.'

Race was never mentioned at Burner, except when someone was indulging in a bit of light-hearted banter with the Mexican-American kids. The same lovely people who daily asked me to speak up, or sing them a song, asked the Mexican kids if they had beans in their lunch, or if they needed a towel for their wet backs, and so on. They'd be excluded for it these days.

Since our school was so entirely white, I was dumbfounded in pep rally the week we played Flagle, when our cheerleaders debuted their new cheer.

'We've got something you ain't got and that's soul,' the blue-eyed blondes chanted. 'S-O-U-L, Soul.'

It had a good beat, and it was catchy, and nobody, and I mean *nobody*, could figure out why I went absolutely mental about it.

I remember covering my red face with my hands. Seriously, I thought? You seriously think this is a good cheer against *Flagle*? I turned to my friends, expecting to see the same horror I felt on their faces. But they were smiling and singing along to the cheer.

Oh, God. They had to be saved from themselves.

After the pep rally, I took the cheerleader's coach to one side. She was a nice, perky gym teacher. She and I weren't close, of course, because I would do absolutely anything to avoid gym, but there was mutual respect.

'You can't have the girls cheer that against Flagle,' I said. 'Or Humner. Or Garmon.'

She looked at me as if I had finally gone completely insane.

'Why?'

'Because it's all about soul,' I said. 'As in *black* soul? Like in *soul music*?'

She laughed and patted me on the shoulder. 'Oh, Coco. You're too sensitive. Nobody else will think that. And the girls have been working so hard on it.'

Nobody would listen to me. I'd done my best, I thought, lying awake and squirming with dread that night. There was nothing else I could do.

There was a custom for each cheerleading squad to go over to the other team's bleachers and do a cheer for them. During the Flagle match, I watched our girls cross the field with dread. They couldn't. They wouldn't.

They did.

I have prayed many times to disappear through the earth. That was one of them.

You could hear the laughter from where we sat. My cousin told the story at Thanksgiving dinner. He said that whenever Burner was mentioned, all the other schools in the conference said Burner had *so much soul* and laughed until they were sick.

The cheerleaders were still bewildered by their cheer's reception that night when they got to Don Chilitos. By then, I had given up trying to explain.

I wrote a poem about it in my Careening notebook when I climbed into my sleeping bag that night.

I had been sleeping out in the garden. Being outside during the summer had made me so happy that I had decided to move there. I set up my sleeping bag under the big elm tree, with a couple of pillows and a small table for my notebook, glasses, reading books, flashlight, water and alarm clock.

Sometimes Jack came by and snuggled into my sleeping bag with me. Several mornings, he woke up and found he'd stayed all night. He just used our shower and went early to school. I don't know what his parents thought. They were strict with his sister, but Jack seemed to be running totally wild.

Ed thought mom was letting me be a bit wild, too, and worried that somebody would come by and hurt me. But mom was cool with this insane thing, if my old dog was with me. It actually did a lot for my confidence. I went inside when mom got home and we'd have dinner and watch television together and everything, just like normal, but then I'd brush my teeth, wash my face, put on pyjamas and go to sleep in the garden. I'd tidy it all away the next morning under a tarp behind the elm tree and then go in for my shower. It wasn't like it was obvious – nobody could see me from the road…or even from our driveway.

If Ed and I went to a late show or something, I'd just go make my bed in the garden without going into the house at all. It drove him crazy.

I felt like I could breathe better outside, and that I was getting stronger by being in contact with the earth. Oh…I can't really explain it. I know it's a bit weird. It really got odd when it started to get cold. I had to lay down a tarp and run an extension cord out to power my electric blanket.

But it was wonderful sleeping out there, really magical. The animals got used to the dog and me and there was a robin who would peck at my glasses. Something about the reflection, I guess. Many mornings I'd wake up to his tiny 'tap, tap, tap.' When the squirrels were playing their crazy chase games they'd sometimes run right over my feet. Rabbits loped across the lawn. I think they'd dug a burrow under my neighbour's garage. Deer came and browsed, up from the cutting for 69 Highway, not far behind our house. One moonlit night, I watched a coyote hunting mice while the old dog cowered against my leg and growled.

But then it started to snow and mom made us move back indoors.

I was nominated for Homecoming Queen. It was just one brave boy and he was jeered at by my entire homeroom, but he insisted. I can't remember his name, but I still adore him for it. I can still see his dark hair and his head bent down, blushing under the insults of the other boys. Truly heroic.

I actually got more than twenty votes. I was astounded.

Of course, I didn't come close to winning.

But still.

In the New Year, there was a big meeting at the hospital. Doctor Morris and Doctor Kular, my speech therapist (we'd forgiven each other by then) and somebody from Child Psychology. They were just about done with me at the hospital and were planning the end of my care and how I should manage my health after I finally left them.

It was the same week that I went to see the Guidance Counsellor at school. It seemed like everyone was planning to get rid of me.

The Guidance Counsellor was a kindly lady I hadn't seen much of before.

I was completely freaked out when I opened her door and found my dad sitting in her office. How did *he* know my appointment was that day? *I* hadn't told him. My mother didn't speak to Dad anymore, so *she* hadn't told him.

That meant Dad was in touch, somehow, with my school. The idea made me feel sick.

I stood there for a second, gawping. Dad grunted a greeting, then immediately looked at his watch, as if to tell me I was late and wasting his time. I'd only just opened the door. I hadn't even stepped through it yet, but I had already disappointed my father.

The Guidance Counsellor started asking me questions and I tried to answer, but I found it very hard to concentrate. I felt like I'd been hit hard on top of my head.

I stumbled as I found my way to the chair.

Dad sighed and started cleaning his nails with his pocketknife.

The Guidance Counsellor had said, 'What do you want to do with your life?'

'Excuse me?' I said, around the pressure in my brain. What was Dad *doing* here? And why couldn't I bring myself ask him? 'I'm sorry,' I said to the counsellor. 'What did you say?'

'For work,' the counsellor explained kindly.

'I don't know. I thought I was going to go into the theatre, but now...I just don't know.'

My father sighed. He looked at the Guidance Counsellor as though they'd already been through all that. It made me feel sweaty.

'Well,' the Guidance Counsellor said, looking over my file. 'You're a bright girl. Perhaps you could be a secretary. Not, perhaps, a legal secretary or anything where you had to use the telephone, but perhaps for the railroad? Or the shoe factory?'

I felt like I was going to be sick. I said only one word. 'No.'

Now it was her turn. 'Excuse me?'

'No. No, I won't go be a secretary at the shoe factory. I'd rather die.' I turned to my father. 'I'm going to university. I've already been accepted onto three programs. Tell her.'

Dad shrugged. 'Well...' he said. 'So you go to university. What will you do after that? You'll have to get a job sometime.' He folded his pocketknife shut with a snap, and pointed the handle at me. 'What will you take at university, anyway? What degree are you going to do?'

'I don't know,' I said. 'I thought I'd do English Lit.'

Dad rolled his eyes. 'And just what do you think you'll do with that?'

I thought, 'I think I might become a writer.' But I didn't say it. Not there, not then, not to him. It was too tender of an idea to survive a cold blast of my father's scorn.

Here the Guidance Counsellor intervened. 'You like the theatre? What about working behind the scenes?'

I couldn't see myself in costume design or makeup or anything useful.

I said, 'What about TV? How do you become a script writer?'

They looked at each other. The Guidance Counsellor said, 'I think you have to go to university.'

My father frowned. 'Why not become an electrician, that's useful for theatres.'

Me, an electrician? I'd kill myself my first day, daydreaming and forgetting about the live wire.

The Guidance Counsellor said, 'There's an agency that gives financial help to help disabled people train for jobs. They might help you with your university tuition. Shall I give you that information, Major DuLac?'

My father looked a little happier.

I said, 'Did I really need to be here at all? Why don't you both just decide for me?'

The Guidance Counsellor said, 'I'm sorry, Coco. Would you like to discuss…'

But my father interrupted. 'She hasn't got any idea.'

Which was, of course, more or less true. But it still felt like a slap.

I got up and opened the door.

I left my Guidance Counselling Session in a daze and went past the little waiting area they'd rigged up down the hall, where I saw a boy from the football team. He was wearing a suit for his session and both parents were with him. He looked nervous, like it really meant something.

I got the feeling that I'd failed a test that I hadn't even known I was taking.


Mom and I were having dinner.

'So,' she said. 'How did your Guidance session go?'

'Dad was there. He wants me to train as an electrician.'

My mother dropped her fork onto her plate. 'What?'

I shrugged. 'He wants me to get a job.'

'Oh for Chrissakes.' Mom jumped to her feet and went to the phone.

I could tell Nina had answered by the face my mother made. She turned her back and spoke calmly and politely. For a while.

'Well, I'm eating my dinner, too,' she eventually yelled. 'Only I can't eat it, because my stomach's upset, because Eugene has interfered in my daughter's life and has seen her without giving me notice. I've just found out.'

A squawk on the other end of the line.

'Then you've got two choices, honey,' my mother said. 'You can cover your ears or you can get that asshole you stole from me off his fat butt and onto the phone.'

I had never heard my mother speak like this before. I sat there with my mouth open.

'Eugene?' My mother said. 'Don't say a word. Just listen.'

She took a deep, calming breath. 'Your daughter got thirty-eights and thirty-nines in all her ACTs except for math. Your daughter *is* going to college. She doesn't know what she's going to do for a job, but she doesn't *have* to know, because she is going to be busy for the next *four* years. At *college*.'

Silence.

'Did you hear me, Eugene?'

A small sound from the telephone.

'I'm glad we've had this chat, Eugene. Let's do it again, the next time you mess up. That shouldn't take long, the way you're going.' She slammed down the phone and came back to her chair at the table.

I closed my mouth.

We looked at our cold dinners.

'Screw it,' my mother said. 'Let's go get some tacos. I'm driving the long way. And I'm *not* turning left.'

It was strange going into a conference room with all my medical team. I saw my doctors without white coats or scrubs for the very first time since Dr Kular had called me Frankenstein. Both Morris and Kular looked tired and I realised it was after school on a Wednesday and that they'd probably been in surgery since early that morning.

We sat around the shiny table and the nice receptionist who ran the clinic came and asked if we wanted coffee.

They were there to read me a document they'd put together

earlier. Doctor Kular read it out loud and they all nodded when they got to the bits that they'd put in themselves. It was about my future health.

I've remembered the salient points, which I think I'll write as a list.

So:

1  I would be subject to frequent respiratory infections.
2  My heart would be under considerable strain, given the low oxygen levels in my blood. I should be careful not to walk uphill or use too many stairs – say more than two flights a day.
3  I would not be able to give birth.
4  Which was just as well (Kular's phrasing) because I would probably not be able to run a home. The strain of housework would exhaust me. So normal family life was beyond my capabilities. I should make this clear to any potential spouse.
5  I would probably have reoccurring psychological problems. The post-traumatic stress disorder could be triggered by all kinds of stressful situations and I would have to be aware of the fragility of my mental health and avoid any work or study, which involved high stress or pressure. I would need to be careful about my relationships as well. Frequent arguments might be a trigger. Again, it might be best for me to avoid family life.
6  I would not be able to work full-time.
7  I would not be able to work in any job that meant meeting the general public. The strain on my voice would be too great.
8  Despite these precautions, I would be unlikely to survive past my thirtieth year. I would probably die from a respiratory infection before then. This was another good reason for me not to attempt family life.

Mom and I were stunned. We sat on our chairs and gaped at each other.

Doctor Morris said, 'You need to give this document to your lawyer and sue the insurance company of the driver of the car.'

I said, 'I can't sue Kim.'

He said, 'No,' and smiled. 'You don't sue your friend. You sue her insurance company. The help you'll need could be expensive. You'll need money to pay for it. And remember, this isn't for the next year or so. This is for your whole life.'

Doctor Kular turned to my mother. 'That might not be the longest life, either. So it's a good idea to insure Coco's life, for funeral expenses.'

Typical. He still always said the exact wrong thing.

He looked young without his white coat, even though he was so tired. He only looked a little older than me. He rubbed his face. He always did that when he was tired, and I thought about how well I knew him. He had found a girlfriend, I'd heard from Cathy. They were talking about getting married. He was going to make a very strange father...

Although I knew I was leaving them, it felt like they were leaving me, that I was being abandoned all over again.

But I also had this silly sense of freedom. It sounded very final and very sobering, all the things they were telling me, as if they were passing judgement and, like Dad, finding me defective.

But I didn't believe any of it. I didn't really take much notice of that long, scary list.

They were just trying to keep me safe. It had been their job to keep me safe and alive for so long that they hated to let me go, hated for me to be in charge of that myself.

They were like a mother on her kid's first day of school. They were running behind me, reminding me about my bus number and lunch money.

And anyway, I knew they were wrong. They got a whole lot wrong.

They had told me to take small sips of water. They had told me to keep my trach tube in. They had told me that I had gone crazy, when really my throat was growing shut. My medical team did their best, but outside of an operating theatre, they didn't really know all that much.

Some of the things on the list were true, but I knew, even then, that most of them weren't.

I knew it hurt when I walked up hills or stairs. I just couldn't move air fast enough and lactic acid built up quickly in the muscles of my legs and bum. Everything burned. And I got distressingly breathless – I knew I'd never be able to go running again, or play a game of tennis. And I had always got a lot of colds, so I was certain that wasn't going to change. Too, I already knew I was on thin ice, insofar as sanity was concerned. But I was fairly certain that the rest was bullshit.

Everyone else was grim, thinking about my blighted future. But I was smiling at them, because I was so fond of them. I said goodbye to my Psych coordinator and my speech therapist, who still seemed to feel I could do better if I would only try. She offered to have me come back, whenever I wanted, to work on my 'eeeee' and my other stuff. As if that would ever happen. I shook her hand and she and the Psych coordinator went the other way down the long, puke-pink hall.

Morris and Kular walked us to the elevator.

When it came, I hugged Doctor Morris and he held me tight. And then I turned to Doctor Kular. He held out his hand, but I walked into his arms. Slowly, they tightened around me. It was surprisingly comfortable, hugging Doctor Kular.

I still wasn't happy about him saving my life. But it was just Doctor Kular, just how he was. He couldn't help rushing around and trying to fix throats.

Another doctor would have just flipped a sheet over my face and let me go, but Doctor Kular couldn't walk away from an interesting throat trauma without having a go. It wasn't in his nature.

Doctor Kular saving my life hadn't been personal, I had decided. He had just been in the wrong place at the wrong time.

The lift came and I let go of him and got inside. My mother pushed the button. My surgeons stood waving, as the door squeezed shut.

# Chapter Twenty-Nine

### Soundtrack: 'Low Rider' – War

Mom's stint in the acid baths had made her noticed at work. The company had expanded and they needed a new customer service person. It had to be somebody who could deal with both the schools' administration and the student yearbook editors. Somebody charming and bright. Mom was asked if she'd like to do the job.

It was a huge rise, I remember, nearly half again what she'd been making. She had to buy some more suits for work. She was so happy it nearly hurt to look at her. I wanted to put her in plastic and keep her like that forever. I never wanted her to be unhappy ever again.

But now a new era began for me. The time of surgery was over. The time of lawsuits had begun.

My father had heard somehow that we'd been advised to sue the insurance company. He rang to give his support to this idea. He suggested mom could use the lawyer he'd chosen for the divorce settlement. My mother laughed at this. He couldn't understand why she was laughing and this made her laugh harder. Finally, he put the phone down because mom was crying with laughter and trying, sputtering, to explain that she hadn't had a very good experience being represented by that particular lawyer and she wasn't about to hire him again.

Instead, someone on her bowling team told us about Mike.

Mike was a young lawyer who was working out of a small office in the suburbs. He looked at me and at the scary list from the hospital and heard the story. Then he said that he'd take us on for a percentage of the settlement (which means once we got the money, we'd give him a bit of it). He also had us look at how much it was going to cost for me to get my own health insurance, after I came off my dad's. It was astronomical.

Mike the lawyer took some time to think about how much to ask for in the lawsuit. He thought about it, talked it over with his wife and his colleagues and finally suggested we ask for thirty thousand dollars.

It didn't seem all that much, but on the other hand, it would certainly get me through university. Mom and I signed.

I told Kim.

We were still, technically, friends. Something had died in me that night in the camper van. I didn't adore her any more. But I still loved her.

I knew that she flinched every time the accident was mentioned. So, I tried not to mention anything about it in front of her. I tried not to talk about my surgeries at school. I tried to make it go away. But sometimes, when we were all riding around together, if I forgot and whispered along with the radio or something, Kim would get…she'd just kind of shut down. And then she wouldn't want to be around me for a few weeks.

Bobby had been right. It bothered her.

I thought when I told Kim about the lawsuit, it would set her free. I thought she'd feel like we were now even. I thought all her fear and guilt about the accident would be erased. I not only *told* Kim about the lawsuit, I *couldn't wait* to tell her.

I ran up to her at school and blurted it out like it was the best news ever. And she looked at me as though I'd said I was going to kill her family.

I hugged her, even though her body was rigid with outrage. 'I'm not suing you, silly. It's your insurance company.'

She said, 'But you said it was as much your fault as it was mine.'

I said, into her ear, still trying to cuddle her stiff body, 'I know, I know. It's nothing about that. It's just because I have to live with some problems.'

Kim bristled and pushed me away. 'We all have problems, Coco,' she said sternly.

'But we'll need the money.'

'Then you should get a job,' she said. 'You should get a job. You never work.'

This wasn't fair, but she didn't know it.

I'd applied for loads of jobs, but nobody would hire me. It was perfectly legal then to discriminate on the basis of disability. And the employers I had approached were perfectly happy to do the discriminating. It wasn't as if I'd gotten a good reference from the YCC programme…

Of course, I wasn't happy to be such a loser that I couldn't get hired at McDonalds. So I'd lied (big surprise) and acted too cool to have a job. I said I might do some modelling (I am blushing as I type these words).

I said, 'I could get really sick in the future.'

'So could I. Anybody could get sick in the future, that doesn't mean they sue people for money.' Her considerable chest heaved. 'You know what your problem is?'

I didn't. But I was sure she was going to tell me.

'You think you're special. You always have. You think everybody owes you, because you were in a car accident.' Kim tossed her hair over her shoulder and jabbed her finger at me. 'You aren't special.' She jabbed at every word. She marched away, and over her shoulder called, 'You aren't special *at all*.'

I already knew that, I thought to myself. And I already knew you thought it, too.

But still, I felt incredibly sad.

The next day, with Bobby in tow, she confronted me again, telling me to drop the suit.

I kept saying, 'I'm not suing you, Kim. It won't cost you any money.' But Kim had learned all these things to say about the consequences of the lawsuit and how it would affect her and her family. She kept talking about higher insurance premiums and the way it would look on her permanent record.

I didn't want to hurt Kim. So I didn't mention the things on my surgeons' list. She was being hideously unfair, and I could have shut her up in an instant, but I couldn't bear her to know all the stuff that had been in that long list. It might have won me the argument that day. But it would have hurt Kim forever.

So, I just stood there, my mouth moving to almost say things, but never actually saying them. And Kim shouted at me about her insurance premiums some more, and walked away.

Soon, the entire school was discussing the ethics of the case.

Most of the kids thought what I was doing was greedy. Many of them were pleased to tell me this and to take me through their reasoning.

I told my mother about it and she repeated her new mantra.

'Screw it,' she said.

I have to say, this seemed perfectly sound to me. I thought about Kim, Bobby and Mandy and everyone else. I thought about Kim's family's higher car insurance premiums. And I said, 'Yes. Screw it.'

Despite my classmates' objections, we sued and won a settlement. Very, very easily. Mike thought we should have asked for a lot more. Evidently, the insurance company's lawyer said he'd been authorised to settle for ten times the amount we were awarded. Mike kept apologising.

But we took him to the taco stand to celebrate. The staff all came out from behind the counter and hugged us. They were so happy to hear that the settlement had gone well. They kept shaking Mike's hand. And they put the tacos and cokes on the house.

When we got the settlement cheque, mom told me I could go and buy a car. Anything, she said. Buy what you want.

Dad thought this was insane and so did Mike the lawyer, who kept telling me to invest the money. And I'm sure we should have. In fact, I know we should have, because mom eventually borrowed bits here and there and let me spend it on stupid things until it had all wasted away three or four years later.

But still, it was absolutely wonderful ordering a brand new Ford Mustang Cobra. It was great going to a salon on the Country Club Plaza and getting a groovy haircut from someone who not only understood curly hair but thought it was a good thing to have. It was wonderful going on a shopping spree and buying the kind of clothes I'd only ever seen before in magazines.

During the time of lawsuits, an old family friend who lived in Lawrence, Kansas, had called mom and asked her to teach him to dance. He'd just gotten divorced and wanted to get back into the dating scene. He loved country music but didn't know how to two-step. So he rang mom.

While he was at our house for his dancing lesson, he fixed the boiler.

Then he came back and danced some more and fixed the windows.

Then he came back to take us to buy some new furniture at a place he knew, and took the old dog-pissy sofa to the dump.

Then he just kind of stayed.

His name was Wayne. He managed a body shop for a Ford dealership. He had custody of two teenaged boys. I got accepted to the University of Kansas, in Lawrence and mom got engaged to Wayne and planned to move to Lawrence herself.

Mom had the higgledy-piggledy farmhouse valued.

This made me terribly sad. I thought it would always there for me. I had planned to get married there someday, outside, when the roses were in bloom. I loved every inch of that house.

I walked around it with Ed, the afternoon after mom accepted a buyer.

He'd come by to talk to me about our grades at community college and about getting our credits from YCC. We didn't know anything about how colleges and universities worked and none of our parents did, either. But my cousins had all gone to college on sports scholarships and I kept calling them up to find out things like how you got your grades and how to get credit transferred and things like that.

Dad had found me a disability counsellor. I was going to have my university fees and my books paid for. I'd sent Ed to him, too, but Ed wasn't disabled enough for fees, now that he could bend his knee. Still, they decided they'd pay for half his books.

I was very sentimental about moving. At least I tried to be, but it didn't work.

As I walked around the house with Ed, I could really only remember horridness. Where my father had stood when he told us he was leaving. Where Kim had lain on the carpet. Where I'd sat with Jack, that horrible night when I'd cried. When I'd been so hungry and trying to cook and had found bugs in the flour. When we'd been so cold.

I said something about this as I made some iced tea and we went to sit on lawn chairs. Ed was always easy to talk to.

He said that it was our hopes and dreams that mom and I had loved, more than the house. It was the life we wanted to live there that we were losing, not the life we'd actually lived while we'd been there.

He said, 'Sometimes you've got to know when to cut your losses.'

I asked, 'Isn't that just a fancy way of saying giving up?'

He shook his head. 'No,' he said. 'Because some things don't work out. They really just don't.'

I knew he didn't just mean singing and football. I looked at him and he pushed his hair back and looked me in the eye. 'Julie and me. It's never going to happen.'

I felt a big sadness bloom in my chest. I could see, when I went to the chili party, how right they had been together. But I also saw that, for some reason, they weren't right together any more.

Ed sat down on the ground and kind of leaned onto my lap and I bent over him, giving him a huge hug.

He felt good. Solid. I liked hugging Ed. He turned around a bit and leaned back, looking at the sky with his head on my knee.

'Anyway,' he said. 'I guess things change.'

And we left it at that.


The plastic surgeon was not completely pleased, but I could live with the results of his work. By then, I had a neat train track on my neck with a single line across the base of it, where the trach tube had been. I put my scarves away.


Also after Christmas, Dad and Nina got a French foreign exchange student. His name was Thierry. He was very, very cute and sophisticated and I found him terribly attractive. But of course, I behaved like a buffoon and besides, he wouldn't have touched his host's daughter with a bargepole. Dad and Nina had me to stay with them several times around this period. I think it was because you weren't supposed to have exchange students if you didn't have a child yourself. They so clearly preferred Thierry to me that the combined rejection of Dad, Nina and Thierry himself was excruciating. After every visit I just wanted to die.

Nina helpfully pointed out everything I did wrong, so that I could try again next time. But eventually, they gave up and the visits stopped.

A few weeks after we won the settlement, my father sued me to stop my child maintenance on the basis of the insurance pay-out and the fact that I had a disability scholarship. Mike was so cross about it that he represented us for free.

I had to go in and testify at the hearing.

It's quite horrible being sued by one of your parents. And it was even worse, because I couldn't help still having moments of hope sometimes about my relationship with my father.

A visit would go particularly well, without my Dad mentioning how disgusting I was and without any shouting, and I would think that we were on our way to a real reconciliation. But then I would do something wrong and spoil it. I'd spill milk on the countertop and wipe it up with the wrong thing. I'd leave a tampon wrapper in the guest toilet trashcan where anyone could see it. I'd try to sit on Dad's lap for a cuddle.

I always ruined it.

One day, I was at the junior college, just down the road from my Dad's house. We'd run late in seminar, very late, and I was very hungry. I didn't have any money and I was so hungry that my head was whirling. I thought I'd go to Dad's and get a sandwich and have a sit down before trying to drive across town.

Nina was outraged. I should have telephoned. It wasn't convenient. They were entertaining.

I peeked around her and saw a bunch of men around the dining room table. Smoke wreathed the light fitting and the table had been covered with green felt. Heavy tumblers with inches of amber at the bottom sat by each place. Dad's poker night.

I said, 'It's only poker night. I'm sure they won't mind if I make a sandwich. They won't even notice me.'

Nina sighed and stood aside. 'I'll make it,' she said.

I'd been right. The men had barely looked up as I walked past. But one of them said, jocularly, 'Now who's this? It's never little Coco?'

Nina said, 'Stopped by for a sandwich. She spent her lunch money.' She rolled her eyes, as if to say, 'You know how kids are.'

Dad said, 'Honey, you get what you need,' to me in a sweet,

syrupy voice I hadn't heard in some time. I looked hopefully at him, thinking he might have fallen back in love with me, suddenly, right there in the middle of poker night, but his eyes were hard and calculating. He glared at me above his smile.

They were playacting for the poker players, pretending that we had this wonderful, loving relationship, the three of us. Nina made a little drama out of making the sandwich, giving me all these special ingredients and insisting I sit down at the breakfast bar and eat it. She even poured me a coke, with ice and a straw.

I wanted that so much to be true that I played along. My dad's poker buddies saw a contented teenager, thoroughly at home in her father's house and close to her supportive stepmother. And Dad looked satisfied by this.

It was so successful that I believed it myself. I stopped by again, the following week. But that time they didn't let me in.

When I walked into court for the hearing, I recognised the judge. He'd been one of the men around the poker table.

I felt sick. This was going to be another charade of justice, like my mother's divorce. My dad was probably going to take all the insurance money, drop by drop, and leave us with nothing. Poor again.

He sat at his table and didn't look at me.

Mike, a father of two, put his arm around me, as if to protect me from the sight of my father's indifference.

When things started, there was quite a lot of talking that I didn't understand. But then Mike started going through some figures and telling some stories. He told about when we'd slept on the living room floor. He told about me working at YCC when I was so sick. He told about my mother's time in the acid baths. He kept asking me to collaborate things and I kept saying, Yes, that's right. About a million times.

Finally, he asked me a question. He said, 'During your time in the hospital and your recovery at home, did your father ever buy you anything – anything extra to help you and your mother?'

I thought about it. A long time. Finally, I remembered something. The silky blue nightgown and robe and the slimy slippers with the rosettes on the toes.

'He bought me a nightgown for the hospital.' I looked at Dad. 'You remember,' I said. 'The blue one with the matching robe and slippers.'

But Dad looked away.

The judge looked at me and his face softened. He swallowed, as if he had tears running down the back of his throat. And he had to clear his throat before he spoke. 'Miss DuLac, you and your counsel can go now. I'm not going to allow this to go any further. I will award your costs.'

Dad sighed and stood up.

'You, Eugene,' the judge said, 'can sit back down. I have a few things to say to you.'

Mike and I danced down the hall. Dad was going to have to pay Mike, and Mike loved that. He said he was going to bill him ten dollars for every paper clip.

But my favourite bit was driving away in my Cobra, knowing Dad was still inside the court, getting a lecture from his poker buddy.

# Chapter Thirty

**Soundtrack: 'I've Got the Music in Me' – Kiki Dee**

After Easter, the time of lawsuits was over. Instead, it became the time of parties. Graduation was approaching and my classmates were old enough to buy beer.

Every weekend somebody had a keg party. Keg parties were held in the garden (yard, we call it) and they were fairly simple to plan. You put the word out at school. You got a keg of beer. You put it in on ice in a big plastic bin. You tapped the keg. You handed out plastic cups to arrivals.

We all got drunk and drove around. Well, some of the more seriously Christian kids didn't drink, but they were rare. Everyone else did.

There was no public transport and we all had cars. We'd get trashed, then we'd get the munchies or we'd fall out with someone at the party or we'd hear there was a better party on the other side of town and we'd all pile in a car and drive ten or twenty miles. This was perfectly normal. It wasn't legal, but, like smoking marijuana, so many of us were doing it that the police were helpless to stop it.

Since most of my complete social uselessness was a result of my crippling lack of confidence, I became a great deal more likeable once I'd had a beer or two. So I usually had three.

For once, I was on trend. All over town, teenagers were getting completely out of it on cheap beer and driving around. People died. People drove off bridges, ran over friends, bashed into strangers and killed kids. But nobody seemed to take it too seriously.

Not only was I more of a social success, but I had also landed an actual job.

I worked a few nights a week at the amusement park on the other side of town where I'd had my date with Rob Savage. Of course, I couldn't be inflicted on the general public with my scars and voice, but I was allowed to sweep up the streets and car parks and empty the trash bags. I was enjoying making money and I met new people, who hadn't been informed that I was a social outcast. I actually got along with everybody. It was a revelation.

When the people I worked with went somewhere after work, they always asked me. They thought I was funny. They thought I was good-looking. They even thought I was nice.

So, what with working, and parties, and the upcoming move to Lawrence, the end of my high school life sped by.

I went with a gay friend to prom and we looked fantastic. I talked him out of the pastel polyester, wide-lapelled tuxedos popular at Burner and into a proper black dinner jacket. A few years later, he got in touch to thank me.

We sat with Kim and the other dweebs at prom. We were all on speaking terms again by then. I don't know if Kim ever came around to understanding the lawsuit or not, but she had managed to forgive me. We still talked to each other a lot at parties. I was always drawn towards her, and she was drawn to me. But the awkward space between kept on getting bigger.

That awkward space had always been there. Once it had been empty, but now it held the whole story of the accident. I was always trying to grab her across this space, which seemed as deep and dangerous as a chasm. Now, for the first time, I felt she was trying to grab me, too.

But I stood on the other side of it, helpless. And at prom, when I learned all the dweebs had been out together and hadn't asked me to come, I just gave up. They'd gone to McDonalds in their prom outfits. They'd taken tablecloths and silver cutlery and candelabras (which they weren't allowed to light) and ordered their Big Macs and poured their Cokes into wine goblets.

It sounded silly and fun and just the kind of thing I'd really enjoy. But they hadn't asked me. And them not asking me hurt so badly, I couldn't believe it. I nearly curled up with the pain of it.

I know it was petty and small. And I know I had other plans. But there it was. I was heartbroken again. I just couldn't get over it. Every time Kim and I would start talking, I'd remember that she, Bobby, Mandy and everybody went and did that without me and…it just kind of killed me.

As graduation drew nearer, Kim started to make an effort to see me. She'd call me up or come by to see if I wanted to go for a coke. She'd talk to me in the hall, whenever I actually attended Burner.

If she'd done any of that, just a month before…if they'd asked me to come to McDonalds…if I'd remembered to call her before my second round of surgeries…if I had run after her, that day with the Mylar balloon, and made her read what was on Donald…

I don't know. I remember standing in my living room, with boxes all around me, and Kim, nervous, hitting her keys against the leg of her jeans, asking if I wanted to go get a frozen yoghurt and…it was like I was seeing her from a million miles away. I didn't feel anything but pain looking at her. I didn't go for Fro-Yo with her. If I had…

But I can't think that way. I'll go literally crazy thinking that way.


The next night, I went to a party just up my street.

I wore a light blue T-shirt with a Corvette on the front and, in a neon-inspired font, the word, *Cruisin'*. I wasn't really familiar with the term 'cruising' as in 'looking for sex'. I just spent all my time in my car, and so I'd liked the T-shirt.

When I say I spent all my time in my car, I mean I spent *almost all my free time* driving around. I *ate* in my car. Sometimes I *slept* in my car.

I totally loved my car.

On hot nights, when I couldn't sleep, I would drive hundreds of miles, just listening to the stereo or the radio. I'd drive to Wichita (200 miles away), and drive through for a coke and drive back. Perhaps in my nightie. And then I'd slip back into the house at dawn.

So, I bought the Cruisin' T-shirt and wore it to the party. With it, I wore shorts. They were tight and white and had go-faster stripes down the sides in pastel colours: pink, blue, yellow, lavender and light green. I wore a nice big pair of cotton panties underneath them and my favourite Tretorn sneakers on my feet. And I wore absolutely nothing else, except for my tan and my burgundy lip-gloss. Even I knew I looked amazing. I'd gone to the supermarket in between seeing Kim and going to the party. A man had been watching me walk and stumbled into a stack of cereal boxes, knocking them everywhere. He'd been terribly embarrassed.

I can't remember the name of the boy who had the party. I remember being shocked that we lived so close to each other and never spoke. We spoke that day, because I had a beer or two. There was a barbecue: burgers and onion dip. All the dweebs came and even the cool kids and the jocks were there.

But then I forgot about who was there and even about the onion dip, because Rob Savage had arrived at the party, alone.

His relationship with his girlfriend had survived his slight wobble of commitment. From then on, she'd gone everywhere with him. I suspected they even showered together.

But there he was, fancy free.

Without even thinking about it, I made a major play for his attention. In no time, I'd taken him around the corner, into a doorway, and was snogging him within an inch of his life. He was enthusiastically responding. I kept trying to get him to come home with me or meet me later that evening, but he kept talking about his relationship with his girlfriend. Like I cared. Like it mattered to me. I had finally decided I didn't want to graduate without losing my virginity to Rob Savage and he wasn't being cooperative.

After kissing me and groping me quite a bit, he finally tore himself away from the party. He should have received a medal for services to monogamy. I really did look seriously hot that day and was loaded for bear.

I had my third beer and walked the four minutes to home.

The next morning was my graduation and I woke up embarrassed. I'd gone way too far. In public. And I'd been really stiff and horrible with Kim and Bobby and all the other dweebs (I'd barely spoken to them) because my feelings were hurt about prom. I'd been a real jerk. Again.

I called Ed at work, told him everything and asked him for advice. He said, 'At least you know you've been kind of...'

'Nasty,' I said. 'Horrible. Hideous. Skanky.'

'I wouldn't put it that way.'

'You know what I mean,' I said. 'God.'

'Look. Just pretend none of it happened,' he said. 'It's your graduation. Just be nice to everyone and don't get all...stiff.' He paused. 'You know how you get.'

I knew. 'I'll try,' I said.

'And if it all goes wrong, call me. I get off early today.'

'Okay.'

'Just be *nice*. Pay *attention* to people.'

'I said *okay*,' I said testily.

'Yeah, and drop the attitude, too,' he said. 'Good luck, Peanut.'


Girls wore gold gowns and boys wore black. I wore one of my little white cotton button-through camisoles under my gown, and a nice black print skirt with Capezio sandals – just rings of black patent holding my foot to the thin, flexible sole. It was pretty fancy – for me. I looked in the mirror and forgave myself.

Both mom and dad attended my graduation. Sitting together. And almost speaking to each other, though dad kept looking at his watch. Dad informed us after the ceremony that he'd made reservations that evening at the best steakhouse in town. All the richest kids at Burner would be there with their parents – it was a real social big deal to be there on the night of graduation. It was just for the three of us, no Nina, no creepy grandparents. It was nice of him.

I was tempted. But then I said that I was sorry, and I had other plans. The look of relief on my mother's face was amazing. She mouthed, 'I love you *so much*,' and it made me grin. We were going to our taco stand and out to a movie that night, with Grandpa. Oh, yeah, I really knew how to party. But it was what I wanted…

After the ceremony, all the graduates went to a big alcohol-free party down the street from my house, just two blocks away from the site of Kim's and my car accident. We *had* to go.

We handed back our gowns and hats and got a little leather case with our diplomas inside. Then we were meant to eat cake and chat. The principal was coming to talk to us and we were meant to sign up for reunion information and other things.

We'd been assigned places at tables, kind of randomly. And there just happened to be a lot of people at my table that had been at the party the day before.

'I can't see Rob Savage,' one of the boys said meaningfully. 'Can *you*, Coco?'

He explained to everyone in earshot about my relentless pursuit the day before. Everyone laughed.

I remembered what Ed had told me. I laughed, too, and acted like it was no big deal. The boy went on and on about it, as if I was the first person to ever try to pick somebody up at a party. Kim was a row away, talking to someone else. She caught my eye and winked and I kind of smiled. I didn't really know why she'd winked. In solidarity? Or because she thought I was a slut, now?

Or because she thought I should have had sex with Rob Savage when I could, that night in the back of the boy's uncle's RV?

The boy who had been talking loudly about Rob Savage and me was now talking loudly about something else. I really tried to pay attention, but it was about somebody throwing up at yesterday's party and it made me feel a bit queasy. I actually spotted Rob Savage across the room, where they'd already had their cake, sitting near his girlfriend and hopefully unable to hear anything from our side of the room. We were still waiting for our cake to be delivered.

I looked back at Rob and realised that he was starting to lose his hair…just a little, at the front. And, suddenly, I was totally over Rob Savage. I could see how his eyes had dark marks underneath them and that the hand he used to hold his cup was a bit grubby. He was…just a human. No more, but importantly, no *less*, either. How much had I actually thought about him, in all my longing for him? Not much, I realised.

He glanced up, met my eye, and looked quickly away.

The punch was too sweet. I found myself wishing I had a beer and then thinking that was a bit dangerous. I didn't want to start wanting beer every single time I had to be around people.

I could see my gay prom date, sitting with Kevin G, not far from Rob and his girlfriend. Bethany was over in a corner near some other musicians – our friendship had never recovered. Bobby, Shanice and Mandy were sitting by each other, deep in conversation. I couldn't see Karla, but she had to be nearby. Jack was talking to the tough kids, some of whom I had *never* seen attend classes. I wondered what was inside their leather cases. I didn't think it was diplomas.

Kim caught my eye again, and smiled, and I got up and walked over to her. But she kept talking to the people by her chair, and didn't even look up at me, so I went back and sat down at my place again. That was humiliating, but it was so familiar, getting rejected by Kim, that it nearly felt cosy. Rejecting her had been too weird. This felt normal.

It was normal to be sitting silently on my own, waiting for something I didn't even want, because I'd been told to do it. It was normal watching everyone else having social interactions that obviously meant something to them, while I watched from the outside, as if they were in a room and I was looking in through a window.

It was normal, but it was boring. God, I was bored. I was so, so bored.

And paying attention *hadn't* worked. I'd ask Ed about it, because I was paying attention like anything and I didn't have that scowl on my face he was always complaining about. I hadn't gone all stiff, even when Kim ignored me. I'd kept smiling and kept on noticing the other people and...I'd done *everything* Ed had told me to do, but it hadn't worked.

And then I realised ...it was *too late*. This was graduation. It was the *end* of high school. It was too late to try. It was *over*.

# Chapter Thirty-One

## Soundtrack: 'Jet Airliner' – The Steve Miller Band

I could hear Ed's voice in my head. 'Some things just don't work out,' he had said. Suddenly, I realised that my high school years were one of those things.

I stood up, got my bag and went outside to the phone booth. I put a quarter in the slot and dialled Ed's work.

When he answered, I said, 'I tried. I really, really tried.'

If you listen closely, and you're on a good line, you can hear somebody smile over the telephone. He said, 'I had a funny feeling you'd be calling. Do you want me to pick you up?'

'I'll drive.'

But Ed said, 'There's no way on earth I'm letting you drive in the mood you're in. Last time I let you drive when you were mad, we were halfway to the Oklahoma border before you turned around. I have to work in the morning.'

It sounds mean, written down like that. But it wasn't mean. His voice was warm. He *liked* me. Even though I really *had* driven him nearly halfway to the Oklahoma border a few weeks before.

It made me smile. 'I'll meet you.'

Not Don Chilitos, half the school would be there. Not McDonald's, it was too close to his work and all his colleagues would think we were dating. We settled on Sonic. They had bitchin' limeades and were far enough out of town so that I could blow off some steam driving there. I'd buy. He'd been treating me for years and now I actually had some money of my own.

'Drive safe, Peanut.'

I promised I would.

I probably should have gone back in to say goodbye to everyone, but when I put my coin purse back into my bag, I noticed that I'd already taken my leather diploma case with me.

I'd known I wasn't going back.

I stood there for a moment, and looked at the door. Everyone I'd grown up with was in that room.

I felt tears come into the back of my eyes, but it was like my house. I was sorry to lose the friend I'd always wanted Kim to be, not the friend she actually was. I was sorry to leave behind the group I'd been such a part of three years ago...but really, I'd left them...or they'd left me...ages ago.

I *hadn't* grown up with those people, I realised. I hadn't grown up at Burner at all. I'd grown up in the University of Kansas Medical Centre, with Ed, and with the memory of Des, and with Doctor Kular and Doctor Morris and Nurse Starchy and Cathy and Bob and my orderly, Maybelle. All the stuff you do in high school, all that learning to be with other people, had happened to me there.

Mom and I were moving to Lawrence and I was starting at KU. I actually *wanted* to go eat tacos with her and Grandpa that night. I would tell her everything about the cake party and she would get it, she would totally understand.

And that was...I suddenly realised...because *she* was my best friend. Mom was the one I always wanted to tell stuff. Mom was the one I didn't need to talk to when I just wanted to fume. She was the one I always forgave, that I always understood, that I cut slack. I remembered the night we'd both come home early and drank tea, sitting on the sofa. We hadn't even told each other what had gone wrong. We hadn't had to. We'd just sat there and been upset together.

Nobody could ever be my best friend like my mom was my best friend. And if that was weird...well, I was used to weird. I was never going to be anything but weird. And that was okay.

I got in my car and started to drive to Sonic. And that's when I noticed the tree.

I slowed down, waited for a car to pass me, and pulled off onto the grass shoulder of the lane. It was the cottonwood tree

Kim had hit the morning of the accident. It was the place where everything had happened. I could see the barbed wire fence that had been in my memory loop and my stomach tightened, in fear that the loop would start again…but it didn't.

I opened my door and got out of the car, scrambled down the ditching, and went over to the tree.

The wound in its bark had weakened it and the leaves in the front were dry and dwarfed. I'd passed it hundreds of times since the accident, but until now I hadn't realised it was dying. I put my hand on the wounded bark and the place where it had peeled was smooth…it felt defenceless.

And something about that bothered me. My eyes filled with tears and I leaned against it, giving it a hug. I told it I was sorry.

Getting back up the banking almost started my memory loop going again, but I leaned against the car and breathed deeply, like I'd learned to do in one of my umpteen therapies, and it went away.

Back in the car, the black leather seats were warm from the sun and, when I switched over the ignition, the Beach Boys cassette started to play. The sun was bright and my windows were down.

I turned slowly and carefully and then decided I'd take Rollercoaster Road. 'Wouldn't It Be Nice' played on the stereo and my wonderful haircut flowed out behind me in the wind. The road dipped and twisted and my hands were sure on the wheel and the shifter.

Anything can happen to any of us, I thought, at any time. Anything can happen, anything at all, good or bad. We only really know about *now*.

I flew down the hill, revving up for the bump at the bottom. You could make your car fly for a few seconds, if you hit it just right.

I hit it just right. For a moment, all four wheels came off the tarmac. I laughed like a lunatic as the car crashed down onto its shock absorbers. And then I remembered I'd promised Ed to drive safe and felt warm and guilty at the same time.

The slanting afternoon sun turned the air to gold. The wind, my hair, my hands on the wheel, the music, feeling warm, feeling guilty. Knowing each moment is unutterably precious. Even the bad ones. Because now is all we've got. It's all we'll ever have.

I was, I suddenly realised, happy to be alive.

Ed was leaning against his truck. When I pulled into a slot at Sonic, he walked over and opened my passenger door. He was limping a little, because he'd been standing up all day at work. He limped a little less every time he did it, though. There was going to come a time when nobody who met him would know what he'd been through with his leg. And that would be kind of weird, because it was such a big part of him and they'd never understand him if they didn't understand that.

He slid in and shut the door and slumped down a bit and let his pain show on his face. And then he looked at me and shook his head. 'You're so *happy*, you freak,' he said. 'You just ran away from your graduation party and you are totally stoked about it.'

'I know.' We grinned at each other and then the speaker squawked, asking me to order and I braced myself because sometimes they could hear me and sometimes they couldn't.

'Could I have two large limeades,' I screamed at the box. 'And a corndog,' (that was for Ed), 'and some onion rings,' (they were for me). I waited. I hated when Ed had to lean over and order for me. But they'd heard me okay and I relaxed.

Ed relaxed, too. Not that he cared, but he knew I did.

There was something weird going on at Sonic. Usually, they had music playing. There wasn't any. I'd turned off the Beach Boys when I'd pulled in, but I could have kept the tape playing...their music must be broken.

One of the managers was walking down the row of cars, talking to everybody. Probably about the music, Ed and I decided, as we watched him walk.

I don't know what it was. I'd only ever met him once before. But I caught a glimpse of blue eyes when the manager was three cars away and I just...I just knew. Even before he got close enough to read his nametag.

It was Des.

Des had survived his bone cancer. Des was alive and wearing a dorky Sonic manager's outfit and walking right towards us. He would be here in just a few moments.

Beside me, I felt Ed stiffen and heard him swear. I glanced over at him and saw him start to smile, but then I looked back, because I didn't want to miss any of it. Des was talking to the next car over. He was smiling at them and passing them something. Then Des stood up and started to walk towards Ed and me.

I thought about it, lots of times. If I hadn't snogged Rob Savage at that kegger, if Kim had spoken to me at the cake party, if Ed had been happy to go to McDonalds and have everyone think we were dating...if the assistant manager of that Sonic hadn't called in sick, if Des hadn't agreed to go across town to work for him, if the music hadn't broken down...

But I decided not to think that way, a long, long time ago.

# Epilogue

*I must have slept. I don't know when the music ended. My phone is just a black rectangle of glass in the pale morning light. Feet pound upstairs, and I can hear Des using our shower. I uncurl from the chair to stretch my back and the dog arches and pushes out his feet to stretch his, too. There is a mirror on the wall by the door, but I don't look at the scars on my neck, or the wrinkles around my eyes, or the way my hair still curls madly. I've had enough of thinking about myself.*

*I go straight to the kitchen, fill the kettle and start slicing bread for toast. The dog scratches to go out. Someone shouts that something isn't fair and I hear shoes clattering down the stairs. 'Mum?' one voice calls and then another says, 'Don't listen to her. It's not true!' In seconds, I will be in the middle of a busy family morning, and, it seems, refereeing a teenage argument.*

*In those few seconds, I smile. I close my eyes. I whisper, 'Thank you, Doctor Kular.' And then I step away from the darkness of my past.*

# Acknowledgements

You write a book by yourself, but you need a great many people to make it possible.

I am grateful to Bath Spa University and the Royal Literary Fund, for supporting me with work that enabled my writing time. John Murray coached me through some of the difficult times of this manuscript and Professor Steve May at Bath Spa University paid for me to receive the coaching.

My agent, Sophie Gorell-Barnes of MBA, tried very hard to get this project to a more traditional publisher and gracefully let me take it when I found John Hunt Publishing through the excellent work of the Geneva Writer's Group. John, Maria Moloney and all at Lodestone/John Hunt have my utmost gratitude for taking it on and working with me in their own, rather revolutionary way.

My friends and family are amazingly understanding people. In particular, my husband Andy Wadsworth and my daughter Olivia Wadsworth do much more than most husbands and daughters, so that I have time to write, and their constant affection and support keep me going through the tough times. My mother, Katy Beard, all the Ritter clan and all my friends, especially Joan and Annemarie Strong, Sue Yates, Deirdre Hirst, Samantha Kelly and Alison Harrington-Rowsell very kindly put up with long periods of utter neglect. My colleagues at Bath Spa University and Cardiff University School of Journalism are very talented writers and kind colleagues, as are my writing group/family; Tanya Appatu, Victoria Finlay, Emma Geen, Susan Jordan, Sophie McGovern, Peter Reason and Jane Shemilt.

I have gifted professional helpers, too. My speaking agent, Karen

Cooper, is a dear friend and a constant source of support and joy. Jean Edwards, Karen Hall and Roger Taylor keep the household running and the dog entertained.

But, for this book, I am also deeply indebted to Dee Dee Dempsey Shoemaker and all the classmates who forgave decades of silence to friend me on social media, meet me when I came to town, and help me with *Hospital High*. They have included: Karen Giger Ammacher, Vendola Anderson, Geri Burke Anderson, Richard Anderson, Connie Clement Baldwin, Mary Benton, Debra Bledsoe, Sheila Moore Brown, Steve Brown, Linda Burch, Rich Carter, Becky Wakefield Cheatham, Robin Converse, Terri Christopher Corp, Pam Erie Dastmalchian, Kathy Davis, Paula DeSeure, Sheryl Routh Dollar, Donna Elsbury, Larry Flaherty, Michele Garrett, Lori Garrison, Pam Garrison, Bruce Gentry, Laura Lovell George, Kimberly Armstrong Hager, Christy Steineger Haycraft, Tammy Helm, Becki Hill, Ramona Hyde-Ammerman, Jay Johnson, Teresa Lowe Jones, Randy Keltner, Steven Koperski, Donna Lehman Krum, Lori LaFon, Patsy Leathers, Patrick Libeer, Cindy Libeer-Cygan, Jon Males, Phillip McLane, Marvin Melton, Ginger Meysenburg, Donna Montoya, Bobbie Moore, Teri L. Moore, Cynthia Grimes Norton, Tammie Peterson, Cheri Post, Fred Potter, Susan Preston, Donna Barger Pugh, Carol Robertson, David Ross, Yvonne Shatto, Eric Shoemaker, Barb Shull, Jay Shultz, Julie L Smith, Michael Spero, Karen Stack-Kennemore, Jeff Taylor, Susan Thornton, Tammy Scheel Tremblay, Stephen Wiseman, Christopher Wiss, David Wood, Cindy Rowland Yulich, Scott Zielsdorf and Dorothy Chase Zinnert.

And of course, thank you to the real Kular and Morris and all the staff at the University of Kansas Medical Center. Without them, there would have been no story and no one to tell it.

LODESTONE
BOOKS

Lodestone Books

YOUNG ADULT FICTION

Lodestone Books offers a broad spectrum of subjects in YA/NA literature. Compelling reading, the Teen/Young/New Adult reader is sure to find something edgy, enticing and innovative. From dystopian societies, through a whole range of fantasy, horror, science fiction and paranormal fiction, all the way to the other end of the sphere, historical drama, steam-punk adventure, and everything in between (including crime, coming of age and contemporary romance). Whatever your preference you will discover it here.
If you have enjoyed this book, why not tell other readers by posting a review on your preferred book site. Recent bestsellers from Lodestone Books are:


**AlphaNumeric**
Nicolas Forzy
When dyslexic teenager Stu accidentally transports himself into a world populated by living numbers and letters, his arrival triggers a prophecy that pulls two rival communities into war.
Paperback: 978-1-78279-506-3 ebook: 978-1-78279-505-6

### Shanti and the Magic Mandala
F.T. Camargo

In this award-winning YA novel, six teenagers from around the world gather for a frantic chase across Peru, in search of a sacred object that can stop The Black Magicians' final plan.
Paperback: 978-1-78279-500-1 ebook: 978-1-78279-499-8


### Time Sphere
A timepathway book
M.C. Morison

When a teenage priestess in Ancient Egypt connects with a schoolboy on a visit to the British Museum, they each come under threat as they search for Time's Key.
Paperback: 978-1-78279-330-4 ebook: 978-1-78279-329-8


### Bird Without Wings
FAEBLES
Cally Pepper

Sixteen-year-old Scarlett has had more than her fair share of problems, but nothing prepares her for the day she discovers she's growing wings...
Paperback: 978-1-78099-902-9 ebook: 978-1-78099-901-2


### Briar Blackwood's Grimmest of Fairytales
Timothy Roderick

After discovering she is the fabled Sleeping Beauty, a brooding goth-girl races against time to undo her deadly fate.
Paperback: 978-1-78279-922-1 ebook: 978-1-78279-923-8

### Escape from the Past
The Duke's Wrath
Annette Oppenlander
Trying out an experimental computer game, a fifteen-year-old
boy unwittingly time-travels to medieval Germany where he
must not only survive but figure out a way home.
Paperback: 978-1-84694-973-9 ebook: 978-1-78535-002-3

### Holding On and Letting Go
K.A. Coleman
When her little brother died, Emerson's life came crashing down
around her. Now she's back home and her friends want to help,
but can Emerson fight to re-enter the world she abandoned?
Paperback: 978-1-78279-577-3 ebook: 978-1-78279-576-6

### Midnight Meanders
Annika Jensen
As William journeys through his own mind, revelations are
made, relationships are broken and restored, and a faith that
once seemed extinct is renewed.
Paperback: 978-1-78279-412-7 ebook: 978-1-78279-411-0

### Reggie & Me
The First Book in the Dani Moore Trilogy
Marie Yates
The first book in the Dani Moore Trilogy, *Reggie & Me* explores a
teenager's search for normalcy in the aftermath of rape.
Paperback: 978-1-78279-723-4 ebook: 978-1-78279-722-7

**Unconditional**
Kelly Lawrence
She's in love with a boy from the wrong side of town...
Paperback: 978-1-78279-394-6 ebook: 978-1-78279-393-9

Readers of ebooks can buy or view any of these bestsellers by clicking on the live link in the title. Most titles are published in paperback and as an ebook. Paperbacks are available in traditional bookshops. Both print and ebook formats are available online.

Find more titles and sign up to our readers' newsletter at http://www.johnhuntpublishing.com/children-and-young-adult

Follow us on Facebook at https://www.facebook.com/JHPChildren and Twitter at https://twitter.com/JHPChildren